Praise for *The Ho...*

'A fabulous adventure, full of...'
Jo Thomas, author of *Love in Provence*

'This book gave me all the feels and then some. I read the last 25% of it through tears. Tears of sadness and joy'
Kim Nash, author of *The Bookshop at the Cornish Cove*

'From Marilyn Monroe sightings to flapper girl fashion, this adorable time-travel saga is a laugh-out-loud romp in the witty style of Nora Ephron'
Jan Moran, author of *Seabreeze Library*

'Eras change, characters change, the emotions range from euphoria to heartbreak but one thing remains consistent: you, as the reader, are gripped'
Nigel May, author of *Quilling Me Softly*

'Each era was beautifully detailed and so truly believable, I felt like I was really there'
Tishylou's World

'Written with such vividness and sincerity that [it] is thoroughly enjoyable from start to finish'
Love London Love Culture

'A heart-warming, feel good, wonderful read that left me with a proper fuzzy feeling in my heart and my stomach'
Kim The Bookworm

'The perfect escape novel. I found it a joy from start to finish'
Short Book & Scribes

'[Belinda] is a genius at bringing the settings of her book to life ... Escapism, in every sense of the word, at its best'
A Little Book Problem

After a career in journalism, **Belinda Jones** went on to become a *Sunday Times* bestselling author. She wrote twelve spectacularly escapist romcoms and two travel memoirs under her own name before branching out in a new direction. As **Molly James**, Belinda authored two further romance novels with wonderfully magical twists.

Originally self-published, *The Hotel Where We Met* is Belinda's final novel and is published posthumously by Quercus Books.

Also by Belinda Jones

Divas Las Vegas
I Love Capri
The California Club
The Paradise Room
Café Tropicana
The Love Academy
Out of the Blue
Living La Vida Loca
California Dreamers
Winter Wonderland
The Travelling Tea Shop

Writing as Molly James
Skip to the End
One Day to Fall in Love

Short Stories
'The Rum Deal', *Sunlounger*
'Capri Blue', *Sunlounger 2*

Non-Fiction
On the Road to Mr. Right
Bodie on the Road

The Hotel Where We Met

BELINDA JONES

QUERCUS

Previously self-published in 2019
This edition first published in Great Britain in 2025 by

QUERCUS

Quercus Editions Limited
Carmelite House
50 Victoria Embankment
London EC4Y 0DZ

An Hachette UK company

The authorised representative in the EEA is Hachette Ireland,
8 Castlecourt Centre, Dublin 15, D15 XTP3, Ireland (email: info@hbgi.ie)

Copyright © 2019 Belinda Jones

The moral right of Belinda Jones to be
identified as the author of this work has been
asserted in accordance with the Copyright,
Designs and Patents Act, 1988.

All rights reserved. No part of this publication
may be reproduced or transmitted in any form
or by any means, electronic or mechanical,
including photocopy, recording, or any
information storage and retrieval system,
without permission in writing from the publisher.

A CIP catalogue record for this book is available
from the British Library

PB ISBN 978 1 52943 371 5
EBOOK ISBN 978 1 52943 372 2

This book is a work of fiction. Names, characters,
businesses, organizations, places and events are
either the product of the author's imagination
or used fictitiously. Any resemblance to
actual persons, living or dead, events or
locales is entirely coincidental.

Cover design: every effort has been made to find and credit the illustrator.

1

Typeset by Jouve (UK), Milton Keynes

Printed and bound in Great Britain by Clays Ltd, Elcograf S.p.A.

MIX
Paper | Supporting
responsible forestry
FSC® C104740

Papers used by Quercus are from well-managed forests and other responsible sources.

The Hotel Where We Met

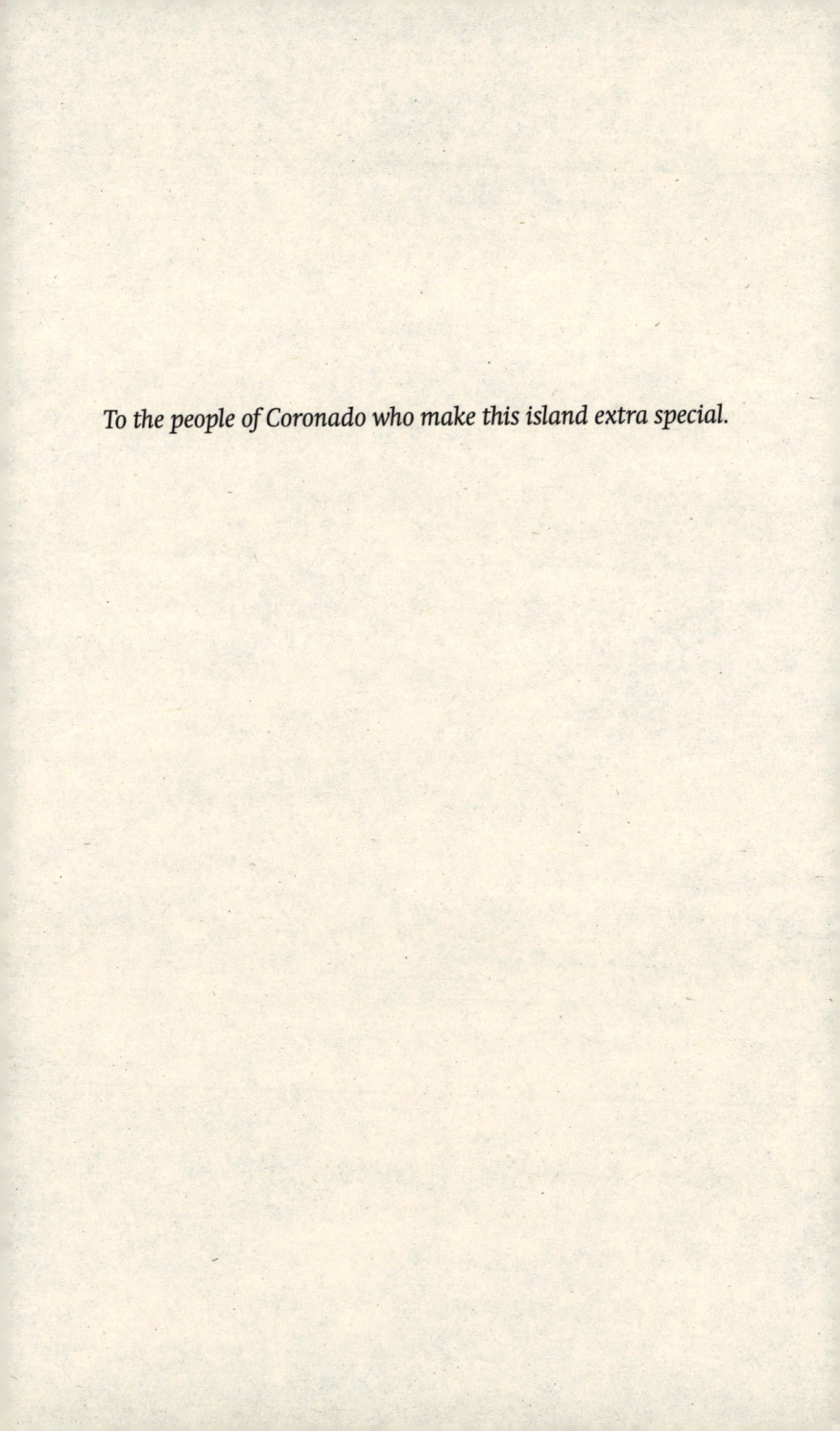

To the people of Coronado who make this island extra special.

1

I wonder what the chances are, statistically speaking, of being seated next to the future love of your life on a plane?

With all the personal data available on us now, you'd think we could get a little extra guidance in terms of seat selections, maybe have a Hollywood casting director pair up our passport photos or divide the plane according to who, at seven a.m., opted for a cocktail over a coffee in the departure lounge.

I'd probably add a 'special meal' section so those folks don't have to feel quite so self-conscious about peeling back their foil ahead of everyone else, and assign a 'quiet' row for the sleep-eager types already sporting their neck pillows at security. There's just so much scope for matchmaking.

Of course, now that we're boarding, the thing we have most in common is the mutual dread of being assigned the human germ-dispenser or armrest-hogger as our neighbour. The fact that I have the middle seat would normally make me feel all the more hemmed in and disadvantaged, but not today. Today I tell myself I now have *twice* as many chances of being seated next to someone life-changingly wonderful. Lucky me!

'Just for the duration of this trip, I want you to be open to the possibility of romance,' James implored. 'From the minute you get your itty-bitty bag of pretzels just keep telling yourself, "This is my time, my turn! The universe has a treat in store for me!"'

And James was not the sentimental or spiritual type, far from it. It's just this place I'm headed to – this island paradise lapped by the Pacific Ocean – made him believe in love because year in, year out for over a decade, his heart was transformed there.

The original plan was for us to travel to California together. I suppose in a way we are, I decide as I reach down and check my carry-on bag for the hundredth time. My stomach dips as I make contact, but I yank up my spirits and reach for my pendant, silently chanting, *This is my time, my turn!*, rubbing the gemstone like it's a mini Aladdin's lamp.

And then it happens. A handsome man appears in the aisle. As he shuffles along checking the seat numbers I take in his upsweep of dark hair, face-contouring stubble and superfine white V-neck T-shirt, tapering from broad shoulders to black jeans. When he stops beside my row and reaches up to put his case in the locker above I can't believe my luck. Not least because I just caught a glimpse of his bronzed stomach. Perhaps he's a teensy bit young and toned for me but as inflight entertainment goes . . .

'Do you mind if I . . .?' His grey eyes meet mine as he motions to the window seat.

Do I mind? 'Not at all,' I say, eagerly clambering out, if not in the most elegant way, accidentally yanking the hair of the woman in front as I grab the seat back to steady myself.

'Sorry, sorry!' I apologise to her and then fluster to him, 'It's all such a squeeze, isn't it?'

He sighs the sigh of the long-legged. I want to say that the seat dimensions must be the revenge of a man with a Napoleon complex but don't want to start babbling before he's settled. I wait patiently as he tucks his essentials into the seat pocket, pulls out the pillow from behind his back, sends a last-minute text, etc.

'So, are you heading – Oh!'

I stop short – he's already got his headphones on, serious matt black Beats ones.

'What was that?' He lifts one ear can.

'Um . . . From your accent, I was wondering if you're heading home or just visiting San Diego?'

There's a fraction of a pause before he replies but it's enough time for me to see this thought flit across his eyes: *Oh god, she thinks she's in with a chance.*

Suddenly I feel like I've sidled up to a guy in a bar, offered to buy him a drink and been turned down flat, only to find I'm stuck on the adjacent bar stool for the next *eleven hours*.

I feel my face flush and a rushing in my ears as he makes his monotone reply, something about how he'd just been in London for work.

'It's my first time going to California. Can't wait!' I say and then turn briskly away and give every ounce of my attention to the movie options – preferably ones devoid of love scenes. They really should have little blinkers on the screens so not everyone can see what you're watching. I had such a near miss with *The Shape of Water* on my last flight. Perhaps I'm better off choosing from the classics – ones I've already seen . . .

I'm so tense and self-conscious now. I want to tell him, 'If no one takes the aisle seat, I'll move along, give us a bit of space . . .' But I feel like he'd file a restraining order if I so much as touched his arm. This is why we should be pre-sorted before the plane. I'm not in the same league so I shouldn't be in the same row. I make a show of looking out towards the rest of the plane and catch the eye of the flight attendant assisting an elderly woman. He gives me a little 'lucky you' wink but I want to hiss, 'It's not what you think, Isaac. If there's an empty seat next to a giant, crying, frothing baby, I'll take it!'

Still, it is looking like I should be able to move along – we're getting close to take-off and no one has claimed seat 38C. I gently unclick my seat belt and start levitating in that direction when a flurry of last-minute, ran-all-the-way heat and blush-pink sportswear arrives.

'Oh my gosh, I didn't think I was going to make it!' She swishes her waist-length, silky blonde hair as she settles into place.

'Well, you can relax now!' I smile reassuringly as I inhale her candyfloss scent. I've been in her shoes too many times. Well, not literally – I would never wear peep-toe, dagger-heel ankle boots to fly in – but I know how awful it is to be rushed and panicked.

I watch as she glugs at her silver water bottle and then catches sight of my neighbour.

In turn, I sense his whole demeanour change. Before he was pressed so close to the window I thought he was considering wing-walking. Now he's fully in the huddle.

'Hey!' He gives one of those cool-guy head jerks.

'Hi,' she says coyly, before her mega-lashed eyes widen. 'Aren't you with Sunset Models?'

'Yeah!' he cheers. 'I thought I recognised you!'

'Summer.' She offers a bangled hand.

'Kai.' He reaches across me.

Could this get any worse?

Before they start discussing their best angles and the burden of being physically blessed, I offer to swap seats. 'So you guys can chat?'

'Sure!' Summer enthuses.

We're just unbuckling when the engines rev and a female attendant tells us, quite firmly, that we'll have to wait until the captain turns off the seat belt sign before we can switch.

'No worries,' Summer chirps, 'we can wait.'

Can we?

If I had a cloak of invisibility, I'd drape it over the pair of them so I didn't have to witness the illuminated, engaged expressions on their faces. Even looking at the seat-back screen feels like I'm interfering with their eye contact so I take out the airline magazine and keep my head down, pretending to read an article on hot air ballooning.

I wish James were here. He'd just roll his eyes at them and make everything better. I listen to them talking about how they got signed, their least favourite booker and best SoulCycle instructor, then:

DING!

I'm out of my seat quicker than if it had an ejector button.

'Do you need your bag?' Summer goes to reach under the seat.

'Oh my god – James!' I bash her leg in my eagerness to grab it and grasp it to my chest.

The pair of them eye me suspiciously.

'Precious contents!' I say, though it probably doesn't help that I take it with me every time I get up to stretch my legs.

Ultimately pheromones win out and I cease to be of concern.

Is there anything more annoying than flirtatious giggles when they are not your own? It's all so excruciatingly intimate I feel like I'm sharing a table with one of the *First Dates* couples. A few times the changing light causes me to glance towards the window and I see him looking at her the way I would have hoped – for a millisecond – he might look at me. Obviously not now that I know what he's like but just the concept of having someone's eyes rove over you in such an appreciative way . . .

'Pulled pork or pasta primavera?'

Great, now I have to act as the waitress on their dinner date as I pass along the trays of food and plastic wine glasses.

They make the same selection, watch the same movie and choose the same filter for their selfies.

Twice Summer flips her hair and flicks me in the face, the second time several strands adhering to my lip gloss. That's when I decide to take my emergency sleeping tablet, even though I was settling in for an eighties movie marathon. I so envy James graduating from teens to twenties during that decade. Give him a curly wig and a baggy sweatshirt and he could do all Jennifer Beals' moves from *Flashdance*. I feel my voluminous hair was so much better suited to that era but I was only a toddler then. All those missed opportunities for rah-rah skirts and scrunch-drying.

'Blueberry or strawberry?' Isaac the flight attendant stops by with our frozen yoghurt options.

'Do you have any gooseberry?' I ask.

He gives me a sympathetic look. 'Sorry, we're all out but I do have something for you.' He beckons me along to the galley and hands me a mini bottle of champagne. 'By way of consolation. The flight is full or I'd upgrade you in a heartbeat.'

'That's so kind of you,' I gasp, regretting having taken the tablet. I probably shouldn't mix the two. 'I might save it for a bit later?'

'Whenever you like. See if you can give him a black eye with the cork!'

I smile, feeling a little bit better. Besides, it's not Kai's fault the great matchmaker in the sky did such a sterling job. And it doesn't mean there isn't still a chance for me. Maybe when I get to my resort – I'm hardly looking my best now and really I should try and catch some zzzs prior to landing. One last circuit of the plane and I'll call it a night.

As I inch along the darkened aisle I study the movie selections of the few passengers who have yet to nod off, all the while hugging my bag to my chest, whispering to it as I go.

'The Diane Keaton collection is proving popular,' I note. 'I wouldn't mind watching the original *Book Club* again, just for Candice Bergen and her twisted Spanx – remember how we watched her scenes over and over?'

James was always my favourite person to sit on a sofa with – best commentary, best snacks. I kept threatening to pitch us to Gogglebox but he said he'd never agree because the lighting was so harsh. He had a point, it is glaringly bright. I much preferred the ambience he created with his dimmer switch and outsize candles. Come to think of it, he was exceptionally well-lit the first time we met . . .

I'd bought tickets to one of those immersive experiences, taking you back to a New York jazz club in the 1940s. I'd previously had great fun at a Gatsby flapper party with my girls but this time I'd made the mistake of going with my boyfriend. Steve refused to don the trilby and a wide, deco-print tie I'd sourced for him and remained testy and closed off even after his third Sidecar cocktail. At one point I excused myself to powder my nose and the event photographer asked me to pose with this stunning man sitting at a small table set with two champagne glasses and a Carlyle lamp. His suit was the same rich burgundy as the ruched silk lampshade and he looked so dapper with his dark, brilliantined hair.

'James.' He introduced himself as I approached, and then paid me all the compliments about my cinched-waist dress that I'd hoped to hear from Steve. My mood lifted exponentially, making the return to Steve's side all the more of a downer.

I tried to persuade him to join me on the dance floor, reasoning that it was so dark no one would see him, but he was having none of it. I was on the verge of giving in and going home when, out of the shadows, a hand extended towards me.

James!

I turned to Steve, who gave a disinterested shrug, then stepped into his arms, just as the song changed to Ella Fitzgerald's dreamy rendition of 'Time After Time'. Swaying along with the swish of the cymbal brush and tinkly piano, I felt both like I was floating and finally anchored. It's a feeling I'll never forget.

I split up with Steve that night and moved in with James a month later. I still had the occasional dud relationship over the years, which James said helped remind him why that part of his life was now over for good. Friends always said it was a waste that someone so lovely was single and they were forever trying to fix him up with gay relatives and co-workers, but in many ways we were each other's significant other. And I feel very lucky to have had that.

I roll my eyes as I return to my plane seat – the lovebirds have raised the armrest between them and are snuggled under the blankets. But they are not asleep.

I couldn't be any more uncomfortable. I consider my little champagne bottle. It's only a glass or two and it was a herbal sleeping tablet.

Pop goes the cork.

Turning away from them, I scroll through the options on my seat-back screen, looking for something short to entertain me while I sip – maybe a sitcom or even a game? Oh, here's the chat screen. I wonder whether anyone actually ever texts a stranger in another seat? I should've paid more attention to other passengers while I was walking around. Mind you, by now most of them would probably take a session with a chiropractor over an offer to join the mile high club.

Calling 38C! The dark screen springs to life.

Have I accidentally started it? I hold up my hands, afraid to touch anything else. Is that an automated message?

Please click to start conversation.

Do I dare? I hesitate but the champagne tells me it's the right thing to do.

Hello, gorgeous!

My heart immediately sinks. They must have seen Summer take this seat and not realised she's switched.

'I think you want 38B, but she's otherwise engaged,' I type.

Chloe Sinclair?

How does it know my name? I twist around to see if I can see Isaac. Is he up to mischief? Trying his best to keep me amused?

This new airline really does go above and beyond, the least I can do is enter into the spirit of things.

'Go ahead, mystery typer!'

Suddenly the screen fills with balloons and animated crystals clustering to form the word *Congratulations!*

What's he up to now? Am I going to get to visit the captain in the cockpit? Will he be Andy Garcia?

You have been chosen to have a question answered by the In-flight Oracle.

Oh. Okay. That's not bad either – I do like a bit of online tarot. What shall I ask?

You have a choice of three questions.

Well, that narrows it down. I eagerly await my options. Here we go:

1) *How can I make a million dollars?*
2) *How long will I live for?*
3) *Why have I not met my Mr Right?*

Hmm. Aside from the morbid and possibly threatening number two, I guess it's pretty obvious I don't have a million dollars from my economy status and anyone can see I'm not wearing a wedding ring.

Need help deciding? The screen prompts me.

'Just give me a minute!'

I definitely don't want to know how long I'm going to live – imagine if it said fifty-nine minutes and I'd be the only person on the plane to know it was going to go down? Of course, it could just be me expiring, but I've been thinking about death way too much of late so a firm no to that.

A million dollars would be nice but it seems as though I get this offer twelve times a day in the form of Facebook ads – *How to 10x your income while eating 5x more chocolate!*

I look accusingly at number three: *Why have I not met my Mr Right?* Have I not asked this question enough times? Not even in a particularly sulky or complaining way of late. These days I'm more curious than anything – is there a rational reason, something that would help me accept, once and for all, that I am destined to fly solo? Or maybe there's a simple tweak I could make and after a lifetime of miserable mismatches things could really turn around. I can see the Oracle's suggestion now: *Take up martial arts or home brewing and have men falling at your feet!*

'Number three!' I make my selection. 'I'm all ears.'

You have not met Mr Right because he does not exist.

My shoulders sag. All that build-up for a trite dismissal. 'Tell me something I don't know!' I type.

He doesn't exist because he was never born.

I frown at the screen. What does that mean?

He was never born because the right sequence of people did not get together throughout history.

I was already starting to feel muzzy-headed, now I'm also peeved. 'What exactly am I supposed to do with that information?'

You must go back in time and matchmake four generations of couples to ensure his birth.

Is this going to turn into some kind of game? I wait for the screen to show me a calendar with the pages flipping back to some significant date and then adjust my headphones in case there's a soundtrack. Nothing happens.

This is not something you can do online. The Oracle reads my mind.

'I thought everything could be done online these days.'

Introduction, yes, attraction, yes, but not conception.

That's true, I suppose.

Your journey will begin when you check in at the Hotel Del Coronado.

I startle when I see my accommodation named. But then I recall filling out the address on my ESTA. Like I say, our data is out there for way too many eyes to see.

'Can you give me a little bit more information? Any tips or clues about how this will happen?'

Let me start by saying this: he's worth the wait.

My stomach dips and I feel a little giddy – the mere thought that there really could be someone out there meant for me brings a tear to my eye. Imagine being with someone you don't have to convince to love you, someone who would meet you and think, *Oh, there you are!* And you'd actually feel good and buoyed up. Hope. I feel a flare of hope! I bet James had a hand in this – a persuasive word with the cosmos.

'Sorry.' Summer nudges me. 'I need to get by.'

Now? I turn to her.

'Hold on!' I type.

By the time I've let her and then Kai file by, my screen has returned to the sky map.

Nooooo! I frantically try to backtrack but to no avail.

'Isaac!' I reach for my sympathiser as he passes, now with a tray of waters. 'How do I get back to the chat screen?'

'Oh, that function is not available on this flight. Sorry, hun.'

'Well, the In-flight Oracle then – you know the one with the three questions? I was about to find out how to travel back in time.'

I didn't mean to say that last bit out loud.

He looks down at my empty champagne bottle then leans in. 'Did you mix the fizz with any meds?'

'No,' I lie.

'Because we get a lot of passengers hallucinating wildly on Zolpidem.'

'It was just Valerian,' I confess. 'It's a herb.'

'Well, I suggest you close your eyes and let it do its thing.'

'So it wasn't you, messaging me?'

He shakes his head then nods to the illuminated call button above 34A. 'I have to get that.'

I watch him head on his way. Now I'm really confused. However absurd it sounds, I know what I saw. That being said, I can feel the druggy drowsiness kicking in. Is it possible I was dreaming? Could I have dropped off without realising?

I get up again to let Kai and Summer back in, half hoping the reconfiguration of our row will bring back the Oracle. But it doesn't.

Now I just feel foolish. It seems my pledge to be open to romance has stirred up some longings in me that were best left dormant. On the upside, that is a terrific explanation for me not having met my guy – he doesn't even exist!

I drain the last drip from the champagne bottle and then try to prop the airline pillow on my shoulder but it keeps falling off. For now, I just tilt my head back, close my eyes, and the next thing I know I'm waking up to the breakfast tray.

All I can face is the diced melon and tea with extra sugar. Whereas Summer and Kai look as camera-ready as when they boarded, I take a little more effort – holing up in the toilet cubicle to revive my make-up and change from my cropped cargo pants and cardi to a red and white polka-dot sundress. I give a little snuffle at my choice of perfume – Charlotte Tilbury's Scent of a Dream. Well, it was a helluva dream and it got me through the flight.

I feel a flare of excitement as I return to my seat. California here I come! The intertwined hands of my travel companions don't trouble me now. I chew on a mint and prepare for landing. But then, as we bump down on the tarmac, my heart catapults skyward . . .

While everyone else is cooing and peering out of the window trying to catch their first glimpse of the San Diego sunshine, I am staring open-mouthed at my screen, which has jolted back to life.

Chloe, it says. *You weren't dreaming.*

2

He sees me before I see him.

'Chloe! Over here!'

'Ross!' I respond with genuine delight. He's even more attractive than in his photographs, which barely hinted at the twinkle in his chambray-blue eyes. The laughter lines, silver-flecked hair and brown flip-flopped feet only deepen his appeal. For a millisecond I want to turn back to Summer and Kai and go, 'Ha!' but then he envelops me in a hug and I cease caring what they – or anyone – think. I just feel saved.

'It's so good to finally meet you!' He pulls me closer, rocking me as I revel in his Californian physique and Tom Ford fragrance, immediately recognisable from James's aftershave collection.

'You too!' I sigh, wanting to burrow deeper and call this warm nook my home. But all too soon our charged excitement ebbs away, leaving us with a slumping sadness as we register the reason for our meeting.

When we step apart, our eyes are glassy with tears.

'We're going to do him proud,' Ross insists.

I nod, unable to speak.

'Is he with you?'

I hold up my carry-on. 'Right here – in his own inimitable way.'

Ross closes his eyes, pained.

'I'm sorry,' I grimace. 'This really is the weirdest thing.'

'You know, I've done this before, a few times, just never with such elaborate instructions. Which is quite something when you consider the company I keep.'

I raise a brow.

'Come on!' He reaches for my suitcase. 'Let's get you over to the island.'

From the way James spoke about Coronado Island, I always pictured it as a kind of Never Never Land, more of a fantasy backdrop to his romance with Ross than an actual place. Yet within minutes of leaving the airport car park, I catch my first glimpse.

'See?' Ross directs my gaze beyond the marina.

'It's so close we could swim there!' I gasp.

He gives an amused snort. 'You wouldn't want to wade up onto that shore – that half of the island is all Navy base.'

'Oh!' I gulp. 'More of a twenty-one-gun salute than a flower garland welcome?'

'Exactly.' He gives me a crinkly smile, telling me we're just going to hop on the freeway for speed.

Sounds good to me – I'm already thrilled. So many airports have a drab surrounding area; here the gratification is instant and glamorous with cloud-dusting palm trees, silver-glinting waters, even a flashy cruise ship or two. Merging onto a multi-lane highway, we get an eyeful of San Diego skyline, but nothing too intimidating, just a cluster of gleaming high-rises enjoying the bay and mountain views.

'I can see why James kept coming back.'

Ross peers over the top of his sunglasses at me.

'Of course, you were always the primary draw!'

'Well, I am right up there with TripAdvisor's must-see attractions!'

I give a little chuckle. And then I realise he might be serious. 'You have a show on now, don't you?'

'Yup, that'll have me tied up in the evenings but by day I am all yours.'

'Wonderful!' I beam.

'So tell me, how are you with heights?' he asks as we change lanes and head for an exit ramp.

'Heights?' I squint and then find myself gawping at an arc of blue steel slicing through the sky, linking a now industrial-looking downtown with a verdant island.

'Fun fact – it's only a mile from shore to shore but this bridge runs over two miles long, reaching a height of two hundred feet to allow the Navy's aircraft carriers to sail underneath it!'

'Wow!'

'They had to build it on a curve or it would be too steep for a car to climb.'

I certainly feel if we floored it now, there would be a good chance of getting airborne – all I can see is the concrete barrier running alongside the road and a vast expanse of sky, giving me a keener sense of flying than when I was on the plane. Up there I was surrounded by people and baggage and row upon row of seats. Here it's just me and Ross, soaring at the level James now inhabits.

And then we reach the crest of the curve and the island reveals itself: toasting us with its champagne sand and bevy of immaculate white sailboats. No parched castaways here – the parkland and golfing fairways are emerald bright and we have a bird's eye view of the evergreens leading all the way to the Pacific shore.

'See that red-turreted resort on the far side of the island?'

'Yes!' I squeak, straining at the seat belt.

'That's where you're staying.'

I feel a little light-headed – isn't this all a bit implausible? To wake up this morning in Turnpike Lane and now have this splendour be my life for the next few days?

My eyes feel positively aglow from the beauty surrounding us.

And then we come to a halt.

'Well, this is unusual.' Ross peers ahead, trying to assess the hold-up. 'I think there might be some kind of security check.'

I don't mind it at all – it's like the dramatic pause on a roller coaster before it goes hurtling and tilting on its way. I'm loving the sensation of being suspended between two worlds – the shiny, sun-kissed city and the sparkling, seaside fairy tale . . .

If I was impressed before, I now have a full-body understanding of why James wanted this to be his final resting place.

'It's where I felt most alive – most in love with life,' he told me, reaching for my hand. 'I want to be certain you'll go there and at least have the chance to experience that elation. And not in a "someday" or "I'll add it to my bucket list" way – sooner rather than later.' And then he opened his ear plug case, signalling that my visit was over.

I was just reaching for my brolly when he added, 'I transferred the money into your account this morning so there's really no excuse.'

'James!' I exclaimed. 'You didn't need to –'

'Yes I did. Anyway. I have to sleep now so you need to leave.' He pulled his eye mask into place and turned his back on me.

Strangely I loved him all the more for his brusqueness. We used to joke that he had an emotional short circuit – anytime feelings ran high, his famous dynamism would dissipate and he would shut down cold. Phone calls ended equally abruptly. I might have just shared a heartfelt insight or troubling dilemma and he'd say, 'Okay, bye!' and be gone. Once I got used to it, it actually left me with a fond feeling. Because he knew I got it. He didn't have to go through the motions with me and that's one of the reasons our friendship endured. Though I do remember one time giving him a taste of his own medicine and it totally backfiring – he was at a convention and came across an Elvis impersonator, persuading him to serenade me down the phone as a surprise . . . I was right in the middle of something at work and answered with a curt: 'Not now, James!' leaving him standing awkwardly with a burring phone line and a man in a bejewelled jumpsuit.

I wondered if that was what ultimately went awry with Ross – too much emotion? The most I'd get out of James is that it went the way of most long-distance relationships. I'm curious to hear Ross's take on things – we didn't go into too much detail on WhatsApp, mostly focussing on the logistics of the trip. Besides, it's not like James had even introduced us – Ross heard from me out of the blue, after James had . . . well, after he was gone. He wouldn't let me get in touch any sooner.

'He's probably married. Or hardly remembers me – it's been fifteen years,' James had reasoned. 'Once I'm gone you can contact him if you want and, if he's receptive and has a little time on his hands, maybe he could show you a few of our old haunts.'

'Haunts, James?'

'Sorry. Unintentional. I tell you what, I'm going to write you a list of the places I'd like to be distributed.'

I rolled my eyes. 'Could we please say "commemorated" or "celebrated" or something a bit more civilised?'

'Whatever you prefer.' He tutted. 'It's all so easy to offend on the topic of dying.'

'You're certainly offending me *by* dying.'

'I know, darling, it's a terrible bore but we've had some

wonderful times, haven't we? And at least we can still actually remember everything we did together. I'd hate to be thirty years down the line, thinking, *Who is this weird woman and why is she visiting me every day?*'

I loved his certainty that we'd know each other thirty years on. And that he knew I'd be there for him every day, no matter what. I just wish I had some video memories of us, something I could play for company, especially footage of him laughing – James had such a good-natured yet childish tee-hee of a laugh, completely at odds with his strapping six-foot form, especially in business attire. Those friends you can picture utterly convulsed with laughter – puce, eyes streaming – don't you just love them a little bit more? To have lost that element from my life . . .

I heave an uneven sigh. I've only really been able to keep going this past year because I knew this trip was on the horizon – the sense of unfinished business gave me a feeling of ongoing connection with James and kept drawing me forward. Originally I planned to come out last summer but Ross was away touring and I have to say, I was a little relieved to postpone it, because I didn't know how I was going to feel when James was gone-gone and I would have to board a plane back to England and leave him behind for ever.

'You okay, kid?' Ross reaches for my knee.

'Mmm.' I return to the present. 'Just got lost in my thoughts for a moment. Oh, we're moving again!'

He gives me a knowing look. 'Ready to go over the rainbow?'

*

'Welcome to Coronado Island – which technically isn't an island because it's connected to the mainland via an isthmus but we don't dwell on that!'

'Okay!' I nod. 'What's an isthmus again?'

'It's just a narrow strip of land. Ours is called Silver Strand.'

'Of course it is.'

Ross chuckles then draws my attention to the gold of the island flag. 'You'll notice a lot of crown motifs around town: that's because Coronado means the crowned one in Spanish.'

'Ohhh! Coronado, like coronation!'

'Exactly,' he confirms as he turns away from the flow of traffic. 'I'm going to sweep around so you can get a feel for the scale of the place, and show you where I'm based, in case you need me outside theatre hours.'

'Great!'

First stop, or rather pause, is Tidelands Park.

'Kids come here to play baseball, families have picnics, the Navy holds ceremonies to honour fallen service men and women . . .' He gives a little sigh. 'And it's where James and I had our first official date, watching an open-air screening of *Some Like It Hot*.' His mouth twists into a smile. 'We're all sitting out on the grass with our blankets and snacks, engrossed in the film, it gets to the bit where the cops burst in to raid the speakeasy and the sprinkler system goes off!'

'No!' I gasp.

'Everyone got soaked! It was strangely romantic . . .'

'I bet.' I sigh, picturing Ross with a shirt clinging to his chest, wet hair sending rivulets down his beautiful face. I imagine them laughing as they scrabbled away from the spray, making memories to last a lifetime. 'You know James watched that movie every birthday until the end?'

'Really?'

I nod. 'I'd watch it with him. He always cheered when the Hotel Del Coronado came into view.'

'Those classic beach scenes with Marilyn and Tony Curtis...'

'Or Norma Jeane and Bernie Schwartz as James would call them!'

Ross smiles. 'We should watch it while you're here.' He then motions ahead. 'This is my apartment building – Bayside at Coronado. It's been massively updated since James was here – we've got everything from firepits to hanging bubble chairs now!' He gives a little *Aren't I fancy?* shoulder jiggle. 'Basically I've got the bay covered, whereas you'll be holding court at the beach side of the island.'

Someone pinch me!

Next up is Ferry Landing with its mix of flip-flop-friendly shops, restaurants and bicycle rentals. I get a waft of barbecue along with the happy jangle of a steel band.

'After you!' Ross pauses to let a green trolley bus go ahead of us, waving to the sun-hatted tourists on board. 'I've hosted those hop-on, hop-off tours in leaner times,' he confides. 'You wanna hear my patter?'

'Sure!'

'By the way, that's the Navy base straight ahead but we're

going to turn onto Orange Avenue now – this is the main artery of Coronado. You can walk the length of it from bay to beach in about half an hour, which can sometimes seem quicker than sitting in traffic at the height of summer, or when the base kicks out.'

'Ooh! It that a military person there?' I motion to a strong-striding woman in blue digital camouflage, neat black bun at the nape of her neck, peaked cap snug with her eyebrows.

'What gave it away?' Ross twinkles as we proceed up the elegant avenue with a lushly manicured central reservation mixing tropical hibiscus with English roses, coconut palms with Christmassy pines.

'It used to be lined with orange trees – hence Orange Avenue – but the jackrabbits ravaged them so it had to be replanted,' he notes. 'I won't go into all the history—'

'But could you?' I cut in. 'If I needed to know something about this place during a particular era?'

He gives me a quizzical look. 'I could. Which era did you have in mind?'

'I don't know yet.'

'Right.'

'Carry on,' I bluster. As much as I'd love to pick apart my exchange with the Oracle, I don't want Ross to think I'm cray-cray. Not just yet.

'Okay, so the island has a population of around twenty thousand and yes, there's plenty of super-rich folk in mansions and dream homes but there's also a bunch of us renters and, of course, service men and women mingling with tourists from all over the world.'

He speaks fondly of the 'lovely, light-filled library' and then motions to the police station.

'Wait!' I do a double take at the cream-coloured hacienda tumbling with bougainvillea. 'That's a police station?'

Ross grins. 'We're not in Kansas any more, Dorothy!'

What really gets me swooning is the vintage cinema, complete with outside ticketing booth, just like in the movies!

'James flipped when we went to see *Ferris Bueller's Day Off* – they still show the authentic concessions ad from the fifties: *Let's all go to the lobby, to get ourselves a treat!*'

'You can sing!' I cheer as he hits the last note.

'I hope so – my current show is a musical! In fact, this is my theatre – Lamb's Players,' Ross announces as he pulls in beside the entrance. 'I've just got to drop something at the office. Won't be a sec.'

I peer at the poster for *South Pacific*, gasping in delight as I see that Ross is portraying the dashing Emile de Becque! I wish my granny was here – she used to serenade me with 'Happy Talk' when I had my 'sad pout' on. *If you don't have a dream, how are you going to have a dream come true?* Indeed.

I lower the passenger window so I can lean out and take in more of the pale grey building housing the theatre and the adjacent parade of shops. To my right I see teenage girls slurping on fuschia-pink dragon fruit smoothies and little kids emerging from Fuzziwig's Candy Factory with outsize, swirly-patterned lollipops. It's a world away from my neighbourhood kebab and vape shops.

I'm just thinking how peppy the approaching group of seniors look, especially the thoughtfully accessorised women, when they stop directly in front of me. Using terms like 'denticulated cornice' and 'Corinthian column', I'm guessing they are on an architectural tour. The tallest woman points up to the pediment and a date painted in gold leaf – 1917. Interesting – so many theatres get turned into cinemas but apparently the reverse is true here. Ross's workplace was once a cinema with a live organ. I wonder if I'll get to see that when I go time travelling? I chuckle to myself. I have to say, I think I've got more than enough to keep me occupied in the present: James's rituals with Ross by day then maybe checking out the local restaurants by night. I might even be so bold as to try Hawaiian poke for the first time.

As the stylish seniors move on, I find myself drawn out of the car – I won't stray far, just take a closer look at the iridescent butterflies prettying up the window at Seaside Papery. I have to say, the boutiques here seem surprisingly affordable – handcrafted gifts mingling with touristy trinkets, surf wear alongside floaty florals.

I'm just drawing level with the imposingly grand Pacific Western Bank, imagining Butch and Sundance bursting out the front doors, when three guys in khaki jumpsuits and cool Ray Bans round the corner. Without even thinking I turn and follow their black boots back in the direction of the theatre.

'Feeling the need for speed?' Ross steps out in front of me.

'Are they for real?' I can't seem to curb my gawping.

'You mean, are they genuine Naval aviators or leftover extras from *Top Gun*?' Ross shrugs. 'It's actually hard to say. I think a few stayed on.'

'You mean, they were actually filming here? Like, Tom Cruise was here?'

A smile spreads across Ross's face. 'For both movies. Do I have stories for you!'

I snatch a breath and then reach for his arm. 'For the record, I'm starstruck by you too.' I nod back to his poster. 'Will I get to see you perform?'

'Of course! I thought I'd give you a couple of days to recover from the jet lag – my rendition of "Some Enchanted Evening" has a lullaby quality to it and no one likes a snoring audience member.'

I chuckle as he opens the car door for me and then, as we continue on, I ask about his early acting career.

'Well, I think I always had a slightly skewed idea of the job opportunities from growing up here – three theatres and an annual film festival on an island this size? It was something of a surprise to discover that wasn't the norm.' He pulls a face. 'I do okay, though. No major breaks but it could still happen. You know Liberace was discovered here?'

'Seriously?'

'The year was 1950. He was unknown so only a handful of

people turned up to see him play at the Hotel Del. The management offered him the night off but he insisted on performing and there in the audience was a TV producer who was so impressed he offered him his own show!'

'That's incredible!'

'So many celebs have stayed there over the years – Clark Gable, Cary Grant, Joan Crawford, Doris Day . . .' He's still listing names as we come to a halt at a red light. 'Oprah Winfrey, Steven Spielberg . . .' Then he turns and gives me a smile. 'And now you!'

3

'Hotel Del Coronado.' Ross's voice drops to a reverent rumble as he points ahead. 'Established 1888.'

'Wow!' My eyes dart around, trying to take in every aspect.

I hadn't expected the main building to be crafted from wood – so many layers of weathered white: balconies and balustrades, struts and spindles, ledges and latticework. 'It's like a cross between a fairy-tale castle and a Victorian dolls' house.'

'And that's not even its best angle,' Ross notes as we sweep around to the leafy driveway, coming to a stop beneath the canopied main entrance.

'Mr Daniels!' A young valet parker bounds over.

'Hey, buddy.' Ross reaches out to shake his hand as we alight. 'I'm just giving my friend here a quick tour before she checks in. Can you keep her close?'

'Sure thing. Call me five minutes before you want to head out and I'll have her back here.'

I think he's talking about the car.

'Ready?' Ross places an arm around my waist, guiding me along the path so I can focus on gazing upwards at the striking red, white and blue colour palette: red roofing, white woodwork and the bluest of skies.

'This is the image most people have in mind when they think of the Del . . .'

There's no mistaking the signature dovecote architecture, a star-spangled banner flapping at its pointy pinnacle.

I squint up at the mysterious top turret with its wraparound balcony. 'Can you go up there?'

'Sure – if you're with the hotel's maintenance crew.' Ross smiles. 'Back in the day Victorians would use the gallery as an observatory, checking out the guests and the view, but the acoustics weren't great so they lowered the ceiling and sealed it off – along with a bunch of memories, no doubt.'

'I bet.'

There are so many secretive-looking windows embedded in the slant of the conical roof, I can almost imagine faces from different eras peering out at me, along with the snatched squeak of floorboard as they dart back out of sight.

I give a little shudder.

'You okay?'

'Yes, it's just . . .' I try to find the words. 'Doesn't it seem like every nook is holding on to decades of history?'

'Absolutely,' Ross agrees. 'Some of the old walkways, when no one else is around . . . it's like stepping back in time.'

The Oracle's words don't seem that far-fetched any more – curiosity draws you down a forgotten corridor and before you know it you've stumbled upon a portal into another era . . .

'Close your eyes,' Ross whispers.

'I don't want to miss anything!' I protest.

'Just for a minute,' he urges, taking my hands. 'Careful, we're coming to a step.'

'I smell something sweet. Is that caramel?'

Ross laughs. 'You don't miss a trick – we're just passing the ice-cream parlour. No, no!' His hand clamps across my eyes. 'You can come back here later. Keep going!'

I hear the chatter of excited holidaymakers, a couple of businessmen boorishly negotiating contract terms and a peal of kiddy squeals and splashes from a pool.

'Just a few more paces,' he encourages. 'Okay, now you can look.'

I am so dazzled it takes me a moment to adjust to the brilliant light.

Splaying out before me is an endless cashmere blanket of sand, accented with cranberry parasols and leading to a swathe of cornflower-blue sea. I watch as a wave rears up into a sheet of glassy green then curls over and bubbles into a lively, spattering froth of white – like the ocean's can-can, ruffling and whooping up onto the shore.

'Can we?' I say, eager to kick off my shoes.

'Of course!'

The sand is warm and powder soft as my toes rifle through its silky, gold-flecked ridges. We trek out to the water's edge and then I take a deep breath, inhaling the salty freshness and exhaling all the processed air from the plane. Turning back, I get to see the hotel in all its glory – three sprawling stories of pristine balconies, almost as if each room has its own white picket fence.

'You'll be up there looking out on all this within the hour!' Ross grins.

'I can't believe it!' I shake my head, then gaze heavenwards. *Do you see me, James? I'm here! I made it!* And then I look over at Ross. *We're all here, just as you wanted . . .*

'Welcome to Mexico?' I frown at my phone screen. I just wanted to capture the moment but I appear to be illicitly crossing borders.

'Happens all the time.' Ross dismisses my concern. 'Tijuana is, like, twenty minutes from here. See?' He points to the coastline to our left.

'That's Mexico?'

'*Sí*. And those islands out there,'– he directs my attention to the shadowy forms in the distance – 'Los Coronados. Quite the spot for rum-running back in the day. They even once had a casino for off-shore gambling and boozing.'

'What about over yonder?' I squint at the attractive peninsula laying a protective arm around the north side of the island.

'That's Point Loma. The Navy's submarine base is over there.'

There's just so much to take in. I shake my head in wonderment. 'Does it ever get old, all this majesty?'

Ross smiles. 'I can't say it does. Of course, I have very specific memories attached to this place and maybe I don't always want to be reminded of them or have the associated feelings . . .' He trails off. 'But do I ever take it for granted? I don't think anyone here does.'

As manly as Ross is, I find myself wanting to smooth his hair in a motherly fashion, which I don't think would go down well, so I suggest the next best thing: 'Cocktail?'

We split a Hotel Del Colado and intersperse it with sips of Strawberry Basil Lemonade so Ross won't slur his lines on stage – and I won't be time travelling tipsy.

That being said, one whiff of rum and I tempt fate, asking him to 'take me back to 1985'.

'Were you even born then?' Ross raises a brow.

'Just.'

'Ah, youth!'

'I'd trade you my youth to have lived through that music scene.'

'It was the best!' Ross concedes. 'The clothes too. I still have my *Choose Life* T-shirt. And the little bristle brush I used to get my George Michael root lift and flick, just in case that style comes round again.' He holds up a pair of crossed fingers.

I giggle my encouragement.

'Obviously you know James and I met at a karaoke night here at the hotel?'

'It doesn't seem like that kind of place!' My nose wrinkles.

'Well, it was a private party. My friend Makoto was turning

twenty-one and introduced us to the concept. James wasn't on the guest list but Makoto's sister took a shine to him by the pool earlier that day and she invited him.'

'And he was here with his aunt?'

'Yes, she was attending a friend's wedding and asked him to come along as her escort. I was the surprise extra.'

'His Del Boy!'

Ross hoots. 'He always used to call me that! Now I can do whole scenes from *Only Fools and Horses*. "Gordon Bennett, Rodney!"' He gives me his best Cockney accent.

I can't help but clap – it's too hilarious seeing a handsome West Coaster go all East End.

'And it was love at first sight?' I hang on his every word.

'For me, for sure!' he confirms. 'All my favourite pop acts were British so the minute he broke out the English accent, I was done. I mean, you've seen pictures of him from back then?'

'Oh yes. He looked good – bit of guyliner, the dark Phil Oakey hair falling mysteriously over one eye.'

'I just loved all the androgyny. Everyone was wearing make-up and no one cared if you were in men's or women's clothes – so much of it was interchangeable.'

'Annie Lennox, Boy George . . .'

'Adam Ant had the best lip gloss pout and the most macho guys on the scene were Frankie Goes to Hollywood!'

We chink to that. And then I get wistful. 'I remember the first time James played me "Someone Somewhere in Summertime" by Simple Minds – I felt sick from my heart twanging.'

Ross sits upright. 'That was our sprinkler song – the line about walking in the soft rain!'

'Oh my gosh! I never knew that!'

'I've still got the vinyl. I'll play it when you come over.'

'Any Flock of Seagulls?'

'"Space Age Love Song"?'

'Yes!' I whoop. 'Oh, those tunes just get to me in a different way – something about the synths?'

'I know exactly what you mean!' he enthuses. 'God, I wish we could just go out dancing right now!'

'Me too.'

For a moment we sit back in a daze, side by side, staring out at the sea. Then Ross sighs. 'What I wouldn't give to go back to that night.'

Is this my cue to tell him? I open my mouth to speak but he continues: 'You know when you know?'

'I've actually never had that,' I confess.

'You will,' he asserts. 'I'm a firm believer there's a Jack for every Jill. Or a Jack for every Jack and Jill for every Jill, depending . . .'

I bite my lip and venture, 'Someone recently suggested that my Jack doesn't exist – that he was never born.'

His brow furrows in outrage. 'Who would be so mean?'

'I think they were trying to be helpful.'

'How is that helpful?'

'Well, they were also suggesting how I might fix that.'

I go to reach into my bag to get the notes I jotted down while waiting at passport control but instead pull out James's letter.

'Is that his list?' Ross pales.

I hand it to him and watch his jaw clench as if he's withstanding a surge of pain.

'Are you okay?'

He takes a moment to reply. 'It's just . . . seeing his handwriting.' His finger traces the page. 'It's almost like he's here.'

I nod silently.

'I still have all his cards.' His voice is faint now.

I don't know what to say. I don't know why these two couldn't find a way to stay together. If I thought James was still carrying a torch, Ross's is burning even brighter.

I'm relieved when he smiles again.

'This one – Toto's Beach – it's not really called that.'

'Ahh.' I nod. 'I looked it up but I couldn't find any reference to it.'

'I'll take you there tomorrow. And then we could do the ferry and the bay, the Oz spot the day after that and then conclude here at the Del. Sound like a plan?'

'I only know what half of that means but I trust you, so yes.'

'Good. We'll send him off in style.' And then he looks regretful. 'I just wish I'd known sooner. I would have liked to have seen him one more time.'

'That was the very thing he wanted to avoid – not just with you, with everyone.'

'Can't you see it's better for everyone concerned?' James had reasoned. 'Imagine these two options: first you get summoned to a loved one's deathbed to see them in this awful, deteriorated state, the worst you've ever seen and, if you're unlucky with your timing, you might even get to witness their last gasp for breath.' He gave a strangled croak for dramatic effect. 'Who wants to carry that experience onward? I don't imagine that's easy to shake off.'

'Well—'

'Second option: you hear about it after the fact. "Gosh! I didn't even know he was sick. I'm sure going to miss him, whatta guy!"' He cocked his head. 'Doesn't that sound better?'

How could I argue? James had never been a fan of goodbyes – he never once announced his departure from a party or even after-work drinks, always opting to slip away and avoid drunken hugs and pleadings for him to stay longer.

The only reason I was with him at the end was because I had come across a letter from the hospital that he'd hidden. He was actually considering telling me he'd got a job abroad so he could spare me and even though I was the only one who knew the full story, he still wouldn't see me the first week he was in hospital. But when the nurses told him I was sitting in the waiting room every day regardless, he conceded. He then began a new diversion tactic, asking for increasingly out-of-the-way treats for me to bring in – a cronut from the Dominique Ansel Bakery in Belgravia, a stick of Brighton rock – intending for me to spend more time tracking them down and less time on the ward.

'With all the germs in here and your delicate constitution you'll end up going before me.'

If I protested and told him he didn't really need a signed photo of John Barrowman at this stage in the game, he said, 'Are you going to deny a dying man his last wish?' And so I indulged him.

We still had fun, as absurd as that sounds. If I could make him laugh, it gave me a high all day. Every time he told me something I had never heard before it felt like such a bonus and every time we wandered down memory lane, I would all but toast marshmallows on the warmth of the nostalgia. He worried I'd exhaust myself going between him and work but so many things that used to matter suddenly didn't any more – mooching around the shops, feeling bad about not going to the gym, social media – so that freed up a lot of time. I didn't see my other friends because there'd be time for them later. All I wanted was to make the most of being able to hear his voice and interact with him, even if it was just trading opinions on the outfits on *Project Runway*. Just one more show. One more day. One more look into his brown eyes.

Until they closed for the last time.

'Already?' Ross's phone alarm reminds him that he needs to get back to the theatre. I trust that he's a pro and can channel the surplus emotion into his songs tonight, but I do feel for him.

'Don't look so worried,' he tells me. 'You're about to check in to one of the best hotels in the world!'

We part ways at the entrance steps and I wave until his car disappears from view. Even then I hesitate, not entirely sure of what awaits me.

The first surprise is the lobby.

In contrast to the sunny, whitewashed exterior, I find myself stepping into a capacious cavern of mahogany – all dark panels, heavy beams and a gallery with such warped flooring I can almost hear the creak of a galleon. A distant grandfather clock emits a soft gong as I look up at a grandmother of a chandelier, the centrepiece of the room, draped with so many strands of vintage crystal she looks like an over-adorned party girl.

As a lift with an ornate brass grill clunks into position I half expect the accordion gate to be ratcheted back by a chap with a jaunty hat and a shiny-buttoned waistcoat. I blink in disbelief when that exact thing occurs. Is this the portal back in time? I begin trundling my case towards him but then a family emerges led by two boys in matching Spiderman T-shirts. Hmm, maybe not.

And so I turn my attention to the reception desk.

'Hi there, I have a reservation for five nights,' I say as I slide my passport across the counter.

'Welcome, Ms Sinclair. Is this your first time staying with us?'

'It is,' I beam.

'Well, we're delighted to have you here.' She clicks at her keyboard. 'You'll be in the original building, on the third floor with an ocean view.'

A squeak of excitement escapes me but she doesn't miss a beat, obviously having heard it all before.

'Here's a list of all our amenities along with a property map.'

'Thank you.'

'We also have a new security system in place so I'm going to take a moment to explain it to you. Just the one key?'

'Yes, that's fine.'

'Okay, so this looks like a normal key card but each day you will be assigned a new four-digit code. All you need to do is hold the card under the scanner by your door and the numbers will show up in red. You then tap those four numbers into the digital entry unit and the door will release.'

'Right.' I nod. I think I've got that. 'And to lock it?'

'The door will lock automatically as it closes so no concerns about leaving it open or accessible.'

'Sounds good.'

'If you have any problems at all, you can reach us here at any hour. Would you like help with your luggage?'

'No, no, I can manage.'

Why do I always say that? Now I've got to go bumbling around trying to find my room. Still, it's a scenic bumble down interior corridors painted with the same cranberry as the parasols I saw on the beach, and exterior walkways looking down on a verdant courtyard with a gazebo prepping for a wedding. What a setting! I pause and lean over the balcony. Could this be a taste of things to come for me? Instantly I cringe – that's too far-fetched even for the privacy of my own head. I'm really not the marrying kind. Of course, I've coveted the exquisite dresses with their beaded bodices and swish of skirts, and, yes, I'd love to be serenaded by Meghan and Harry's wedding choir, but there's the whole issue of someone wanting to spend the rest of their life with you ... I appreciate Ross's words of encouragement on that topic but I hope the Oracle has placed a dossier in my room explaining exactly how to do that – must remember to check thoroughly between the room service menu and the list of laundry charges.

I'm at my door now. I take out my key – the scanner is more efficient than my local self-service supermarket and immediately gives me a reading: 1888.

Well, that seems a bit easy for burglars to guess – the date the hotel opened. It's even the name of the gift shop I passed downstairs. I wonder if it's further encrypted and the numbers are just for ease of remembering? Either way, let's give it a go. Carefully and deliberately I press the four digits, and then get a curious sense of satisfaction when the lock whizz-clicks and the handle releases. My intention is to head straight for the balcony – the curtains are closed and the room seems even darker than the lobby – but one step in I trip and hit the ground hard.

As the door clicks behind me I find myself disorientated in the darkness. My breathing is suddenly restricted and there's a tightening around my torso. Am I about to have a heart attack? My hand goes to my chest but instead of finding the cotton of my sundress I feel the rigid boning of a corset. My hand lowers to find a mix of lace and heavy fabric with some kind of beading. I try to move my feet but they are tangled in what feels like a mass of stiff taffeta. What the hell is going on?

Suddenly I freeze. Oh my god – am I wearing a wedding dress?

1888

Jasper & Sadie

4

I am not wearing a wedding dress.

As I pull back the curtains and the moonlight floods in, I see that I'm swathed in burgundy taffeta. Interesting. This would not have been my first colour choice. The beading is intricate jet, the sleeves elbow-length, the frills around my neck excessively frou-frou. When I find the light beside the mirror I discover the Jennifer Lopez of all bustles – I give a little twerk and it looks like a dancing side table from *Beauty and The Beast*. I don't so much feel dressed as upholstered.

And then realisation hits – it's begun! The time travel is real, and possibly triggered by the door code. Either that or I was knocked out and then trussed up in this outfit while I was unconscious... As I feel my head for bumps I look around the room – there's no sign of my suitcase and, when I open the wardrobe doors, I am met with a rustling array of Victorian ballgowns. The peach number is divine, I just can't see how I'd get out of this one and into the next without the help of a professional dresser, not to mention a team of horses to pull the laces taut on my corset. So the burgundy it is, along with some rather fetching antique garnet rings on my fingers. Whoever is masterminding this time travel is very detail-orientated.

As for my hair – well, is it my hair? There's just so much of it, braided and piled high in a large bun with twiddly curls around my forehead. My make-up is enough to give an Instagram contour queen palpitations – it's barely there, too natural for even my tastes, and when I rifle through my vanity table drawers looking for an enlivening lippy all I find is a little beeswax balm. I certainly won't be fending off male attention looking like this. Still, it's not me that needs fixing up tonight.

I'm just wondering how I'll know who I'm matchmaking when I notice an envelope over by the door. Did someone just slide that under? I fall upon it with eager hands. There are two pictures inside – individual portraits of a man and a woman with their names inked on the back. Jasper Montague has a noble air – dark, wavy hair, gentle eyes, thick brows and one of those sculpted faces where the jaw definition begins just below the cheekbones. He looks like the kind of person who would listen when you talked, have a natural affinity with animals and be faithful till the end.

Sadie Bayliss has clear, intelligent eyes and the confident gaze of someone who knows she has more to offer than her beauty. For a moment I wonder if she's the type to marry at all. Perhaps she has other plans for her life – unbeaten tracks on camelback? In which case I wouldn't want to divert her up the aisle, however beneficial to my love life. I glance back at Jasper. Then again, perhaps it's her pioneering spirit that attracts him and they go off exploring together?

Before I get entirely carried away, I decide to search the room for any other clues or instructions. It certainly would be helpful to know who I am. Do I have a Victorian alter ego? Having checked all the cabinets and under the bed, I empty my beaded handbag but all I find is my room key, a lacy handkerchief, a pair of mini scissors and a petite bottle of perfume with an ornate crown stopper. At least there's room for the photos. I decide to pop them back in the envelope for protection and that's when I realise I missed something rather vital – an invitation to a ball, celebrating the opening of the hotel and confirming that this is indeed 1888.

Halfway down the corridor I lose my nerve.

So far it's just been about the dressing up but as soon as I hear voices – a man and a woman talking in hurried whispers – I realise I'm not ready to interact. What if they speak to me? How will I know if my words are 1888-appropriate, never mind the matter of etiquette? I think it's best for me to dip out of view and spend a little time observing before I start to mingle.

In my eagerness to hide I tuck myself behind one of the voluminous velvet curtains and pray that my heart is only as loud as a drum in my own ears.

Naturally the couple choose to dally in the alcove right beside me.

'I have but a moment!' she cautions.

'How you tantalise me and then cast me aside!' he complains.

'Never!' she protests. 'You are interwoven with my every thought and deed. To cast you aside would be to cut out my own heart.'

Wow. I suppose it would be too much to hope these two are Sadie and Jasper? As they succumb to an ardent embrace, I dare to peep out. Nope, they are both too fair – the gent has a thick blond thatch and what must be a very tickly moustache; the lady coils and curls of spun gold, far lighter than Sadie's tresses. Her dress is exquisite – the palest aquamarine taffeta with a low-cut neckline and panels of delicately embroidered trim, draped like a waterfall of finery. Her waist is so tiny his hand all but encircles it as he clasps her to him.

'I can't sustain this torture,' he husks. 'If you would just let me–'

She places a finger on his lips. 'I cannot wish for any harm to befall him, you know he has never been anything other than kind–'

'Kind?' he cuts in. 'If kind is all you want–'

'You are what I want, all I want, all I have ever wanted.' She steadies him with her gaze. 'But I need you to be patient, my love.'

'Patient? Patient?' he rails. 'What have I been month upon month, year upon year? How much longer must I survive on only a fragment of a life?'

'I believe our circumstance is about to change, imminently.'

This stops him in his tracks.

'He has been talking lately of going away. When I pressed him on the subject over dinner, he said I'll know everything by tomorrow morning.'

'Tomorrow?'

She nods. 'For now, we must remain on different sides of the ballroom,' she instructs him. 'Do not even tempt me with one glance.'

'That is like asking the moth to resist the flame.'

I roll my eyes. She seems to go for it, though – cue more kissing. With a final caution to him to stay off the gin, she promises to get word to him by morning.

'I will count the stars until daylight.'

My love life has never felt so tame. If this is a taste of the kind of affection levels I'm dealing with, I'm not sure I'm the right woman for the job.

I wait until the coast is clear, fumble out from behind the curtain then dip down the nearest staircase, emerging into the lobby – or 'rotunda' as I hear it referred to. Although the structure is the same as when I checked in, the furnishings are quite different: the floral centrepiece has been replaced by a range of seating options – wicker chairs clustered around a hand-carved Indian table, large armchairs set with even larger cushions, two rockers offering the opportunity for synchronised squeaking.

I notice there is a telephone on the reception desk. But who could I call? I've never traced my ancestral line (I doubted there would be anything sensational to discover) and, as a consequence, I couldn't even tell you the names of my great-great-grandparents. It feels a little ill-mannered to admit that right now. Absent-mindedly I pick up a newspaper, pretending to read as I monitor the comings and goings.

'Did you have a flutter on the horses?' A white-whiskered gent shuffles up beside me.

'What's that?'

'I see you're studying the racing pages.'

So I am. 'Well, I always like to keep an eye on their form,' I say. 'My grandfather was a racing man.'

This is actually true. He was a bookie his entire life. Never made enough to fulfil his dream of owning a thoroughbred horse so named all his dogs after legendary winners.

Fortunately the man's wife hurries him on before he can ask me for any tips, or a spare *Sports Almanac* . . .

Flipping through the pages, I find an obituary on *Little Women* author Louisa May Alcott, a report from England on another gruesome Jack the Ripper murder and a review of the 'Kodak Box Camera' which comes pre-loaded with a 100-exposure roll of film – what I wouldn't give for a few selfies right now. And then I spy an ad for Crown Lavender Pocket Salts – the bottle looks identical to the one in my bag. I loosen the top and give it a sniff.

'WOAH!' My head reels back as a glass-shard sharpness soars

up my nose, prompting a few choice expletives to escape my mouth. 'Holy –' I squeeze my eyes together, blinking and shaking my head, trying to shift the pain. I can certainly see how that would revive a soul. *Jeez*. Notes of lavender, yes, but perhaps they should mention the rocket blast of ammonia? I use my handkerchief to dab my eyes. The one upside to not wearing mascara is not having it streaked down my face. Oh. Everyone's looking at me. Excellent.

'Excuse me.' I cough as I hold up the bottle. 'First time.'

I hurry out of the main door to get some air.

Not so long ago I was stood on these steps waving goodbye to Ross. Now I'm disorientated by the absence of the car park and attendant tower blocks, though of course it would be weirder still to find them there. I seem to remember the ballroom being around this corner ... I'm not quite looking where I'm going and bump into another equally distracted woman.

'Oh, please forgive me, I am quite turned around!'

'I know just how you feel!' I say, studying her face but finding no trace of Sadie.

'Do you happen to know where the women's entrance is?' she asks me.

'The women's entrance?' I repeat in confusion.

'Yes, yes, madam, allow me to direct you.' A small man in an immaculate hotel uniform introduces himself as Miguel.

I watch as they head up a second set of covered steps. Is this the entrance I should be using? I shuffle further down the pathway. Is that music I hear? The chatter of party guests?

'Are you in need of guidance?' Miguel returns to his post.

'Well, yes and no.' I turn back to him. 'I'm just curious – why do women have a separate entrance?'

'It is merely an option for women travelling alone, so they might feel at ease and not under scrutiny upon arrival.'

'Oh! That's very considerate.'

'We also have a separate billiards room for women.'

'Really?' That seems excessive but then again, why not?

'You have just arrived at the hotel?' he asks me.

'Yes, just an hour or so ago – I'm still trying to get my bearings.'

'Indeed.' He beams proudly. 'There is no property quite like this. We offer every possible activity: bowling, croquet, swimming, boating, bicycling, archery, golf – anything you like to do, you only have to ask.'

'Well . . .'

'We have special rooms for reading, writing, cards, chess, music, smoking.'

'Gosh.'

'You only have to ask.'

I get the picture. If only life in general was so obliging – ask and ye shall receive. Or would that make us unspeakably spoiled and life rather dull? Perhaps unpredictability and a dash of disappointment is essential to our well-being.

Miguel is still regaling me with hotel attractions. 'Of course, you must visit our Natural History Museum.'

'You have a Natural History Museum at the hotel?'

'It's just over here.' He points to where I had seen modern towers earlier in the day. 'We have the finest collection of specimens west of Chicago. There's the dodo bird egg and an octopus with arms ten feet long. Quite soon we shall have our own woolly mammoth!'

Okay, now I know he's pulling my leg. 'Oh, Miguel! How you tease a newbie!'

'Not at all, madam. I can assure you it's quite real and on its way.'

'Well, in the meantime,' I say as I take out my invitation, 'I was wondering if you could direct me to the ballroom?'

He gives a little bow. 'It would be my pleasure.'

I am greeted by a ball in full swing and champagne in free flow. I accept a glass to calm my nerves and sip rather too quickly as I take in the circular room with its soaring, wood-panelled ceiling, two tiers of tall windows and groups of rattan chairs set around the perimeter. The music is coming from a small violin-led orchestra on the raised stage, prompting a swirl of waltzes on the dance floor. Men sport starched collars with elaborate white bow ties, pristine, low-cut waistcoats and black frock coats, perfect for peacocking, while the women bring the colour – in every hue from Wedgwood blue to powder pink, ruby red to deep amethyst.

There's a definite 'more is more' approach to ribbons and bows and several ballgowns appear to use a full roll of fabric on one slim frame, folding and flouncing until every last yard is incorporated. I wish James was here to give me his fashion commentary – I picture him pointing to the lady with the excess of ruching and suggesting that she might reveal a puppet show if she just lifted her hem.

I'll say one thing – women can't be ignored when they take up at least twice as much space as their male counterparts. Plus, there is zero possibility of a pinched bottom.

As I take in the men's wacky facial hair I wonder if I have found a purpose for the scissors in my bag. A hipster barber would have a field day here. The beards are far too wayward and springy for my liking and I'd love to wax some of those moustaches to a precision Poirot point. I'm just mentally grooming a group of men near the stage when I realise, with a flurry of excitement, that one of them is Jasper. Or at least his outer shell. Though his features are a match for the photograph his face is now gaunt, his eyes distant, seemingly immune to the gaiety of the occasion. Perhaps he's had a lovers' tiff with Sadie and doesn't know how to reconcile. I'm sure I can help mediate but would it be unseemly for a single woman to approach a man? I look around to see if Miguel might be on hand to offer some tips and that's when I spy Sadie – tucked behind a potted palm, conveniently alone – so I decide to start with her.

Her sage tulle dress isn't quite so fancy as the others and she seems happy to be more observer than chatterer. I'm just on my way to her when I realise I'm being watched. What the gentleman in question lacks in height, he makes up for in width. The hair sprouting from his face far exceeds that on his head but his outfit is expensively tailored and his cane comes with a heavy silver handle. Something about his stare makes me feel uneasy so I avert my eyes and quicken my pace but just as I am about to pass, he steps out in front of me.

'Alfred Vear,' he announces, adding, 'I don't recall the pleasure of meeting you before?'

His tone is slightly accusatory. Can he tell that I'm an imposter?

'I'm new to the era,' I breeze.

'Area?' He cups his ear. 'New to the area?'

'Yes!' I gulp.

'I like new.' His gaze slithers over me, though good luck to any man trying to undress this excess of layers with his eyes. 'Join me on the dance floor.' He extends a hand.

'No, thank you,' I decline. 'I must speak with someone.' I go to step away but he latches his cane onto my wrist like a silver claw.

'I don't like the word no,' he growls, tugging me towards him.

I feel a fluster of adrenalin as I meet his gaze. 'And yet you must hear it all the time.'

'Champagne?' The waiter makes a timely entrance, flourishing his scallop-edged tray.

'Thank you.' I shake off the shackle and take two glasses so that any further grabbing or hooking would risk spillage and/or breakage. 'If you'll excuse me.'

My heart is pounding as I weave through the guests. I daren't even look back in his direction. My insides feel on red alert and the sense of menace is still lingering as I approach Sadie.

I take a breath and adopt my friendliest smile. 'I see you don't have a drink and I have a spare . . .'

'How kind of you, Miss . . .?'

'Sinclair,' I say with a little curtsey, which may or may not be appropriate.

'I do enjoy champagne but it would not be prudent for me to be seen drinking at this time.'

'Oh,' I falter. 'Are you on duty?'

'I am hoping to find employment tonight.'

'I see,' I say. 'What nature of employment, if you don't mind me asking?'

'I am a governess.'

Interesting – she is indeed a smart one. After a little more small talk I learn that her current employers, who she has been with for the past nine years, are moving away. They graciously invited her to join them tonight, in the hope that they may be able to introduce her to a new family with children in need of an education.

'Most considerate.'

'The Westons have been wonderful. I shall miss them all terribly.'

I ask if she often gets the chance to socialise and am surprised to learn that, rather than being sequestered away in the nursery, the Westons included her in dinner parties and family holidays.

'Such privilege is not always the case,' she notes, seeming a little trepidatious as she looks around the room at her prospective employers.

'Do you know many of the people here?' I try to sound casual.

'A small number personally, a few by reputation.' She names assorted families as if identifying trees in a forest. I feel we're getting warmer as we get to a string of Merriwethers and Mitchells . . .

'What about that fellow in the group beside the piano, the one who looks so desperately serious?'

Her face changes and her voice becomes a breath filled with longing. 'Mr Montague.'

'You know him well?' My eyes stay on her.

'We visited his estate last year. He has the most beautiful library: velvet chairs with mohair blankets, whole collections of Dickens and Austen.' She looks enchanted. 'It's rare to meet a man so well-read and keen to discuss the ideas of the texts as an equal, not lecturing or imposing his beliefs.'

'I'm sure.'

'And he's not just interested in the older, established authors but newer talents like Robert Louis Stevenson. Do you know Mr Montague was in San Francisco when Mr Stevenson was preparing to set sail with his family early this year? They had the opportunity to exchange ideas on the subconscious mind set forth in *The Strange Case of Dr Jekyll and Mr Hyde*.'

From the look on her face she clearly finds this topic more swoon-inducing than any romance.

'Have you had the chance to read that yet?' she asks.

I want to tell her no, but I've seen a fair few film interpretations. Instead I say I'll add it to my list.

I have to say, their bond sounds both promising and appealing – I've personally never dated a 'reader' but I can imagine it could add another layer to a relationship, offering a whole new way for your minds to connect. It seems it's only shyness and opportunity keeping Jasper and Sadie apart so my plan is to nudge him over to her side of the room with the suggestion that she has some surprising opinions on the most romantic pairings in nineteenth-century literature . . .

'Well, I hope you find more than employment here tonight.' I go to bid her adieu.

'Excuse me?'

'Maybe a little romance!' I wink, nodding at Jasper.

'Miss Sinclair!' She sounds scandalised, ushering me deeper into the corner.

'Sorry, sorry.' I cringe. Was I too forward? 'Perhaps a dance?'

'You do realise that he's married?' she hisses.

'Who?'

'Mr Montague!'

My face falls. He can't be. 'Mr Jasper Montague?' I clarify.

'Yes!'

'Are you certain?'

'I met his wife during my stay.'

'And they're still together?'

She looks bewildered by my reaction. 'Of course – she's here with him tonight.'

'Where?' I need to see her with my own eyes.

She discreetly manoeuvres me so that she can direct my gaze. 'You see the woman in the pale blue dress with the fan, that's Amelia.'

My stomach dips. It's the same woman I saw canoodling in the corridor.

I try to replay the conversation I overheard – she was plotting something and tonight was significant in some way. But she wouldn't reveal the details to her lover. Why would that be? I can't decide whether this bodes well for a split or whether I have been sent on this day to intercept some foul play . . .

I look up as Sadie touches my arm. 'Please excuse me, the Westons are summoning me.'

'Of course.' I wish her well but she hesitates before she leaves.

'You seem especially surprised to find him married?'

'I do, don't I?' I attempt a light laugh. 'I just pictured him with someone else. I don't suppose there are any rumours of a divorce?'

She looks taken aback. 'I hope not, for the children's sake.'

They have children? I wail.

'Two girls.'

Now I know why I'm holding two glasses of champagne. I down them both.

5

I slump heavily into the nearest chair. What a complete and utter disaster.

'More champagne, madam?' A waiter dips beside me.

'Just leave the tray.'

'Madam?' He hesitates.

'I'm joking.' I smile at his worried face. 'I've had enough for now.'

Oh, what to do, what to do . . .

I look around for some kind of clue – something I'm missing . . . Why would I have been dropped in at this juncture in their lives? Why not when he was eligible? I'd demand a reset to an earlier date but the Hotel Del Coronado didn't even exist a year ago and the Oracle made it clear this location was key. I sigh. I have to talk to Jasper – see if anything he says can shine a light on where we go from here . . .

I get back to my feet and look over towards the piano but he is no longer with the group of men. I begin weaving through the crowd, nodding politely at all and sundry, giving Alfred Vear a wide berth and then slowing as I pass Amelia, so I can eavesdrop. She is merely discussing an upcoming Christmas party where the founder of the Hotel Del Coronado – Mr Elisha Babcock – will be dressed as Santa Claus and handing out presents to all the local kiddies, which her companions think is a charming idea.

Sadie is now only a few feet from Amelia, talking with the Westons and a stick-thin, sour-faced woman who I hope, for her sake, is not to be her new employer.

I'm despairing of finding Jasper in such a bustling ballroom when I catch sight of the wooden gallery running around the upper level – from there I would be able to survey the whole floor and then drop Mary Poppins-style to his side. Perfect.

Hoicking up my dress, I take the steps two at a time, then do three circuits, admiring the quadrille patterns from above but catching no glimpse of Jasper. No sign of Amelia's thatch-haired suitor either. Could he have lured Jasper off somewhere? I'm starting to get an uneasy feeling. The corset is too tight and my head too champagne-swimmy to think straight. I wonder if Miguel's eagerness to meet a guest's needs would extend to me trading outfits with one of the maids – I'd feel as deft as a cat burglar in one of their plain black dresses, though I'd keep my lace-up boots – far more comfortable than my twenty-first-century party shoes.

'Tomorrow we'll take a picnic out on the boat!'

'Oh, Virgil, that would be heavenly!'

A young couple step in from the outer balcony. That's what I need – fresh air!

The moon is full and luminous, creating a bright silver pathway on the inky black waters. I take a deep breath and then exhale. *That's it – just breathe in, breathe out, be calm.* I close my eyes for a second, half hoping that when I open them I'll be back in the present. But I'm not.

And then something catches my attention at the water's edge. Is that a bird flapping its wing? I try to decipher the white shape moving in the darkness. Oh my god, it's a man! He's removing his jacket now, showing more of his shirt. Who would go paddling at this hour?

And then my heart stops – it's Jasper, and he is wading out to sea . . .

'STOP!' I call out. 'Wait, *please*!'

He can't hear me and even if he could, would he listen? He's obviously not in a rational frame of mind. I have to get down there. I turn and scurry to the steps but halfway down my passage is blocked.

'We meet again.'

I flinch at the sight of Alfred Vear.

'You have to let me pass!' I blurt. 'It's a matter of life and death!'

'Go ahead,' he says, conceding a sliver of space.

I charge at it and he jams me against the wall with his protruding stomach and then presses closer.

'Let me pass!' I howl, writhing away from his face.

'Say you'll meet me here at midnight.'

'Anything!'

'Anything?' he leers.

'Let me go!' My frantic surge of repulsion and fear is enough to dislodge me but the minute I reach the beach the sand feels like a series of traps gripping my ankles and slowing my gait. These stupid skirts!

I call out to Jasper but he seems lost to his thoughts, standing still now, the water moving around his thighs. Is he trying to get up the courage to go further? Having second thoughts?

'Jasper!' I cry again and again.

Finally he turns around.

'Please,' I pant. 'Come back in.'

He looks startled and takes another step.

'No!' I blunder forward. The salty water grabs hold of layer upon layer of fabric, tugging and dragging me down. The deeper I go, the heavier it gets and then a wave causes me to lose my footing. I gasp as the water slaps my face and then swirls over my head, burbling in my ears, stinging my eyes. I try to reach upwards but there is nothing to grab on to – my struggling and twisting just seems to further anchor me to the seabed. I don't even know which way is up now.

Suddenly I feel a pressure under my arms and I'm hoisted, spluttering and gasping, to the surface. I try to find my feet as I'm dragged like a sack of laundry back to the shore.

'What are you doing?' He sounds almost angry as he props me lopsidedly against a rock.

'What am I doing?' I spit. 'Trying to stop you from drowning!'

'By drowning yourself?'

'That wasn't part of the plan.' I swipe the loose strands of hair from my eyes.

He shakes his head. On the plus side the unreachable, veiled look in his eyes has been replaced by something decidedly more present. But it's not enough to deter him from his seafaring. 'Do you promise to stay here now, and let me go?'

'Obviously not!' I protest.

'You wouldn't . . .'

I heave myself up, stagger forward only to fall back down, sloshing this way and that in the shallows.

Once again he hauls me out.

'You don't understand.' He's getting vexed now. 'This is the best thing for everyone.'

'Really? Including you?'

'You don't know my situation.'

'I know a little.'

His eyes narrow in a mixture of curiosity and suspicion. I decide to go for it.

'I know you're with the wrong woman and, yes, I'm sure divorce is highly frowned upon–'

'An impossibility,' he asserts.

'Okay, even if that actually is the case and not just some nonsense about reputation and fortunes, is this really the best alternative? What about your children?'

'My children?' He scoffs. 'What makes you think they are mine?'

Oh. Oh dear.

'But you care for them?' I venture.

'Of course! Of course I do. But the older they get, the more apparent it is . . .' He wavers. 'It's not just that.'

'What then?'

His face crumples. 'Do you know what it's like to wake up every morning and see disappointment in the eyes of your spouse?'

'Well, not my spouse, but I've had a few guys look less than thrilled.'

He looks a bit taken aback.

'Let's not dwell on that.'

He's pacing now. 'Every day I know she wishes I was someone else or somewhere else. She's always waiting – waiting for me to leave, waiting to be with him.' His voice cracks. 'She only stays for the money and the children.'

'So this other guy doesn't have any money?'

He shakes his head. 'This way,' – he motions to the sea – 'she inherits everything and the children get their natural father.'

'And you, a watery grave.'

He gives an involuntary shudder.

'I know you don't want to go through with this.'

Weakened now, he takes a step and then slumps down on the sand beside me. 'It seemed like the right thing to do.'

I feel a stab of pity – how demeaned and defeated he must be to even come to that conclusion. The way he sees it, he's nothing but a thorn in her side and an outsider in his own home. He no longer feels he has a part to play in his own life.

I swish the sand between us. I have nothing to lose now so play the only card I've been given.

'What if you had someone of your own, someone's whose eyes brightened at the sight of you, someone who couldn't wait to spend time with you . . .?' He looks unconvinced until I add, 'Someone you could huddle up with by the fireside, discussing the latest Robert Louis Stevenson novella . . .'

I see a glimmer.

'Just think of the worlds you could explore together, page after page, taking turns to read and share your thoughts . . .'

He looks searchingly up at me, his breathing accelerated.

'Can you imagine that?'

His eyes are glassy as he nods.

'Say her name.' I whisper encouragement.

He looks away, as if ashamed, caught out, afraid to reveal a secret wish . . .

'It's okay,' I soothe. 'She feels the same way.'

'Sadie?' he gasps.

I smile.

His hand covers his mouth. And then he scrutinises me. 'How do you know this? And who *are* you?'

I scratch my head, inadvertently unravelling the last of my up-do, draping kinked, damp hair all the way down to my waist. 'There are some things I simply can't explain,' I shrug. 'I'm just happy that you like her too.'

'Of course, she's –' He cuts off.

'Yes?' I wait patiently for him to continue.

His voice is quiet now, rapt . . . 'She's everything I would have wished for, if I had been choosing for myself. If I had met her first . . .'

There it is. Absolute confirmation that the attraction is mutual.

'Come on then.' I hold out my hand, needing him to get me back upright. 'Let's see if we can get your new life underway.'

'Looking like this?' He motions to our sodden clothes, muttering something about *The Wreck of the Hesperus* as he contemplates my dishevelled form.

'I may be beyond repair but all you need is a quick change of suit and then you can set things in motion.'

'You do realise your suggestion is unconventional, to say the least?'

'And yet it still has the edge over your solution.'

For the first time he smiles.

I take his arm to jolly him along as we head back to the hotel. 'If we just slip around – Oh!'

I stop in my tracks as I see not only his wife but Sadie, standing on the terrace steps.

'Jasper! Whatever has happened?' Amelia rushes towards him.

'Forgive me!' I lunge forward. 'I drank too much champagne and, in a moment of utter utter madness, decided to end it all!'

'End it all?' She looks directly at her husband, stricken. She knows it was him in the grips of desperation.

'All is well now,' I assure her. 'I've entirely come to my senses. Cold water and the counsel of this man.'

Jasper opens his mouth to speak but nothing comes out, which is probably for the best.

'Do you have someone here with you, someone who can help you?' Amelia looks me over with a mixture of concern and disdain.

'Um . . .' I look beyond them for someone to point to but see only my barrel-bodied nemesis. 'I'm sure –'

'I can,' Sadie volunteers.

I heave a sigh of relief.

'Well, do come back to us after,' Amelia urges Sadie before placing a hand on her husband's arm. 'I think we've found our new governess.'

His jaw drops and he looks at me in amazement.

I can't help but beam back. 'That's wonderful news – what a splendid choice!'

'I hope you don't mind me going forth with this decision, Jasper. The Westons were fielding offers and I felt quite certain she was the perfect addition to our household – remember how the girls loved her *Treasure Island* games?'

Silence.

I give him a little nudge.

'Yes, yes, I do.' He comes back round. 'And I quite agree. As long as this pleases you?' He looks so vulnerable as he addresses Sadie.

She looks back at him with dreamy assurance. 'There's nowhere I'd be happier.'

As his eyes flood with hope it's all I can do not to punch the air.

And then I hear a slight cough to my right. 'Excuse me, madam?'

'Miguel!' I cheer.

'Is there perhaps something I may assist you with?'

'As a matter of fact there is!' I reach for his arm. 'There, Sadie, you're free to make your arrangements.'

'If you're certain?' she peps.

'Absolutely. I'm in good hands now.' I turn to the group. 'I wish you all the very best in love and life.'

Amelia steps back to clear my path, not wanting to get drips on her silk, but Jasper hurries after me, taking me aside for a private word.

'What can I say but thank you, *for ever*,' he gushes. 'To think, if you hadn't been there . . .'

We both shudder at the mere thought of the awful alternative.

'I can't bear to think of all the good things you would have missed out on!'

'For that reason, I want you to have this . . .' And then he reaches for his pocket watch, unhooking the chain.

'What? No, no. No need.'

'It's all I have of value on me.' He presses it into my palm. 'You gave me more time, it seems apt.'

My finger traces the fine engravings and flourishes on the surface of the gold casing.

'It is beautiful,' I concede. And it would be staying in the family if my missions prove successful. I could keep hold of it for his great-great-grandson. 'If you're sure?'

'I am.' He gives a little bow. 'Until we meet again . . .'

As I watch him walk in the direction of his new future I feel a mixture of 'job well done' contentment and – what is this? *Longing?*

'This way . . .' Miguel helps me drag my sopping form away from the ballroom, adding, 'You know, madam, if you needed a swimsuit, you only had to ask.'

Present Day

6

A ringing phone.

I open one eye and gingerly ease myself to a sitting position – I don't want to move too fast for fear of activating my hangover. For me, three glasses of champagne is the equivalent of three magnums and yet my skull doesn't throb, the room doesn't spin, there's no dry mouth or nausea. My hand goes to my head – my hair is back to normal.

'Well, whaddayaknow?' I cheer as I realise the booze has had 130 years to wear off. This time travelling lark could be fun!

I throw back the covers and jump out of bed. I'm in my white poplin pyjamas, though I have no recollection of putting them on, let alone unpacking my case. The last thing I remember was Miguel summoning two female members of staff to escort me back to my room. I asked for them to wait outside for a moment, unsure of what might happen to anyone crossing the threshold, and the next thing I knew – well, this is the next thing I know: a ringing phone.

I feel suddenly nervous. Maybe it's the verdict: a deep and mysterious voice telling me whether my matchmaking mission was a success.

'Hello?' I whisper tentatively as I pick up.

'Don't sound so worried, it's just me – Ross!'

'Ross!' I sit down. Not entirely disappointed.

'How was your night?'

'Um . . .'

He waits in vain for me to summarise my experience.

'Okay, let's start with a more primal question: what level of hunger are we looking at for breakfast?'

I consult with my stomach. 'Surprisingly minimal.'

'Well, that rules out the hotel buffet, you'll need to be ravenous for that. How about a revitalising smoothie?'

'Perfect!'

'Meet me in the lobby in twenty?'

'Twenty!' I scoff. 'You know I'm a girl? Not even James could get ready in twenty.'

The guy had even more potions and pomades than me. Even though his hair was short he'd still snap at every tuft with his ghds of a morning. And that was after a full bubble bath. I kid you not, he'd start each day with a tub of frothy ylang ylang and a chirpy sing-song – anyone would think he worked at Disney, not a combative ad agency.

'You don't need to be ready-ready,' Ross insists. 'Just a quick shower, hair in a top knot, pair of sunglasses. Today is beach casual.'

'Is it?' I head over to swish open the curtains, only to reel back with scorched retinas. 'Oh my gosh, it's so bright!' And then it hits me: *I'm in California!*

'Well?' Ross is still in suspense.

I peer at my reflection. I suppose I wasn't that far off an au naturel look last night, and that was for a ball.

As for the rest of me, I've been working on being beach-ready for the last few months – more so on my mental attitude than any physical shortcomings: I switched all my Instagram follows to body-positive accounts and reminded myself that nothing feels as good as sunshine and warm water on bare skin. Of course, it's one thing communing with your muffin top in the comfort of your own home and another parading around a world-class resort in the most body-conscious state in the US but that's how it works: once you say you're making a stand for something, you will be tested.

'Make it twenty-five minutes and I'll do it.'

'Attagirl!' Ross cheers.

I pull off my pjs en route to the bathroom then duck under the raincloud shower, quite a step up from my Victorian washstand. No time for bathrobes, it's straight into my peasant dress, which feels epically wafty after my recent corsetry. I don't suppose I'm going to have a chance to process all that happened last night until Ross goes to work so I guess I'll just press pause on those thoughts. For now, I have to focus on my face: BB cream, waterproof mascara, big ole flourish of bronzer, slick of coral lip gloss . . . Mwah! I locate my bag. I'll keep my passport zipped in the pocket, just in case. Sunglasses, swimsuit, beach towel, money, phone – what else? Ooh. James! As I reach for him, I feel a terrible stab of grief and my knees buckle.

I'm not sure how long I remain in that agonised daze, but the ringing phone stirs me. Ross is waiting in the lobby . . .

So this is what it's like to start the day with someone looking pleased to see you . . .

'Good morning, beautiful!' Ross picks me up and twirls me around like I'm the light of his life. Due to the centrifugal force I press my cheek a little too close to his and transfer a significant amount of my bronzer onto him. I go to brush the flecks of gold from his face but instead he suggests I even it up.

'Really?' I say, taking him at his word and reaching for my palette.

'Just none of that silver highlighter,' he cautions. 'I don't want to look like the Tin Man.'

I chuckle, recalling how James used to call two of his work colleagues 'Pearl and Sheen'.

'But then he could talk. Whenever we went past a beauty counter he would dip his finger into every glittery product and use my face as a canvas. I'd end up looking like a child's Christmas painting.'

'And how do I look?' Ross asks as I finish whisking his brow.

I tilt his face to the light. 'Like a Greek god.'

He smiles, content with my reply, and then steers me around a swarm of conventioneers.

'So, where to for the smoothie?' I ask.

'Tent City.'

'Tent City?' I frown.

'It's the name of the café.'

'Why on earth would they call it that?'

'The term has very different connotations on Coronado – I'll explain more when we come back to the bike rental place.'

'Bike rental?'

'What are you, a parrot?' Ross laughs. 'And don't worry about your dress, Nicole from the library goes flying down Orange Avenue with yards of fabric floating behind her – it's actually a really cool look.'

'Until it tangles in the spokes.'

'We can hook it up. Nancy will have a brooch or something.'

I go to say, 'Nancy?' but realise I'm at it again so simply follow his lead as he sidesteps into a gift shop lovingly named Adorn.

The dark-haired woman at the counter is busy with some customers so they mime a few things back and forth and he tells me to pick out whatever I need.

'I have a trade tab here – show tickets for trinkets. Look what she got me last week . . .' He reaches into his rucksack and pulls out a yellow canvas pouch stamped with the words *Maybe she's born with it, maybe it's an Instagram filter!*

'Love it!' I giggle.

'How about this one?' Ross points to a simple pin with crown motif. 'As a Coronado memento. You can just hook up the side of your dress like you are mid-flamenco move.'

'All right!' I swat his hands away. 'No need to hitch it up until it's absolutely necessary.'

He laughs and then holds up the pin to Nancy and says he'll see her at the show on Thursday. This is the first time I've coveted the idea of community. I always thought the anonymity of London suited me well, no one knowing my business, no knocks on my door at inconvenient times. I'd see my friends and then go home and put the key in the door of my flat, happily oblivious to what was going on with the humans on the other side of the walls. I do have a little chat with the guy on the late-night till at Sainsbury's Local from time to time, but that doesn't really compare to the easy warmth of Ross's experience.

'So here's Tent City.' Ross guides me across the street to a corner café with a black and white striped awning and massive grey columns looming either side of the entrance.

'Coronado Historical Association.' I read the plaque upon high.

'This is their building; the museum is right next door. It's free so you can pop in anytime you want.'

'Really?' That could be very handy.

'The main room has a pocket history of the island, then there's a more in-depth, side exhibit. I'm not sure what's on at the moment, the theme changes all the time.' He hands me the smoothie menu. 'What's it going to be?'

My eyes skim over organic offerings. While Ross goes for a tropical option with spinach, I settle on a banana base with added matcha. Because I'm a matcha-maker.

'I'll wait here while they do the blending if you want to take a peek in the gift shop?' Ross offers.

When I turn back and see he's on the phone I stray a few paces further, into the museum . . .

The room labelled 'Hotel Del Coronado Revisited' takes a look at all the guests who stayed at the hotel in its opening year and then returned time after time, generation after generation. I'm drawn to an outsize photo album which has images of the guests with a small paragraph on their visits and the family members that subsequently joined them. I flip through the pages, desperately hoping to see Jasper and Sadie beaming back at me. Did they ever come back? It seems as if so many of their contemporaries did. Wait! Was that Amelia? I turn back to the blonde beauty. It's unmistakably her. With Jasper. My heart sinks a little as I look at the date. 1894. Six years on from the ball and they were still together, now with three children. The two fair-haired girls are teenagers in this photograph, their little brother considerably younger with a ruffle of dark hair. I peer closer and then gasp in delight – I can clearly see Sadie in his features and Jasper in his colouring. So they found a way to make a family within a family. I wonder if Amelia's lover moved into the home on some pretext and they had one wing, with Jasper and Sadie in the other. I lean closer, squinting at the small print with the children's names: Rose, Ruby and Jesse.

'Jesse,' I find myself saying out loud. That's who I should be meeting next. But who knows when? It could be when he's any age from twenty-something to fifty-something. I count on my fingers, estimating that I should be re-emerging anywhere between 1910 and 1940. Perhaps I could do a quick bit of reading up?

'There you are!' Ross surprises me with a nudge and hands me my smoothie. 'It's easy to get lost in all the history, isn't it?'

His words jar a little – lost in history?

What if I were to get lost on one of my travels, unable to find my way back? I've spent so much time wishing I could turn back the clock but for the first time in a long time I find myself both present *and* looking forward to the future. Or at least looking forward to the rest of this week. It's quite something when you start to find your life interesting again . . .

Speaking of renewed fascinations – I can't help but wonder if my history grades would have been much improved if I had had a teacher like Ross. He's so good at sparking your imagination. Like now. We're over at the marina (opposite the hotel) and he's asking me to try and picture the stretch of land ahead without its modern-day condo towers and apartment blocks. Of course, I do have quite the advantage in this case, having seen it in its bare, pre-construction state last night.

'So, the Hotel Del had been up and running for over a decade when, in 1900, they launched Tent City – literally a city of tents for holidaymakers to enjoy all the benefits of the beach, without the cost of a resort room.'

'And how much were they paying?'

'Well, I saw a tariff from 1919 and eight dollars a week would rent a two-person tent with wooden floors, electric light and hand-me-down furniture from the hotel. You paid an extra couple of dollars if you wanted to add a kitchen tent.'

'I can see why it was such a hit.'

Ross tells me the whole thing looked like a cross between a circus encampment and a pyjama party. 'There were all these red and white stripy tents grouped together and then rows of huts with Polynesian-style raffia roofs, but categorically no coconut bras – the women were in their full-length Victorian dresses with their lacy parasols, parading with their families.'

'They must have been so hot!'

'Well, they did get to cool off in the bathing pool – you can see some of the later swimsuit shots here . . .' We cross over to Glorietta Bay and study an al fresco exhibit featuring photo-printed tiles.

'The whole place is rammed!' I gasp at an image of a watermelon feast on the beach. 'It's like a festival!'

'Well, they did have concerts at the pavilion and water sports and all manner of entertainment – there was even a weekly newspaper detailing the programme.'

I wonder if my pal Miguel ever got involved? He was such a good ambassador for the hotel's attractions.

'There was even a kind of 'Who is Where' listing,' Ross continues, 'like "Mrs G. M. Simpson and family are spending the week in palm tent 2304!"'

'Handy!' I nod. 'So it was quite the social scene?'

'Absolutely. And such a success. It thrived for forty years.'

I find myself excitedly biting my lip – if things worked out for Jasper and Sadie, there's a good chance I'll get to experience Tent City first hand on my next time travel trip, and all I'd need to do to locate my couple is look up their names in the paper. Nifty!

It feels good to have a heads-up – helps me with the nerves. Not that they are that bad, all things considered. I feel like James helped psych me up with his pep talk about being open to possibilities. Besides, when dealing with something this bonkers I feel like gung-ho is the only way to go. Gung-ho with a side of preparation . . .

I try and log as much information from the display, taking in everything from a food tent offering a 'good square meal for twenty-five cents' to a woman seemingly waterskiing on a wooden door held up by two thick ropes. I'd like to try the first of those.

When I look up, I see Ross has drifted over to the edge of the marina. I join him beside the shiny white yachts, surprised how instantly tranquil I feel, watching the sun bouncing brightly off the water.

'This place . . .' I sigh.

'I know.' Ross smiles. 'James loved this spot – said we should get a boat and name it *Hello, Sailor*!'

We chuckle as we read out some of the more pun-tastic names – from *Knot Shore* to *Dock Holiday* and my personal favourite, *Marlin Monroe*. And then our thoughts turn from sailing to cycling . . .

7

I hadn't bargained on a tandem bike. And we're only astride that because I managed to talk Ross down from the four-seater 'surrey with the fringe on top'.

'Right, it's a straight shot along Ocean Boulevard to the dog beach,' Ross informs me as we join the main road. 'I'll do all the heavy pedalling, you just play "Which mansion would I choose to live in?"'

I'm enjoying the breeze and casually comparing old-school Colonial with angular modern, both jutting balconies at every level, when suddenly we're swerving wildly to avoid clashing with one of those monster pick-up trucks with elevated tyres.

'Watch where you're going, buddy!' Ross slams the side panel then yells at me to take my feet off the pedals, grabs the back corner of the truck and freewheels us at a terrifying pace until the driver slams on the brakes, nearly sending us flying.

'You okay?' He turns back to me as he tilts the bike so I reconnect with solid ground.

'I will be,' I say, waiting for my heart to stop yammering as I stumble over to the stack of giant rocks lining the pavement. 'I've got to tell you, Ross, I'm not really the adrenalin-junkie type – you might have to take it down a notch.'

'Not a problem,' he assures me. 'Let me just sort out this mother–'

'You looking for a fight?'

The truck driver is out of the vehicle and in Ross's face. I'm in shock – am I about to witness a bludgeoning, right before my eyes? But before I can react, their confrontational chest bump morphs into a locked-body hug.

Are they wrestling?

'Good to see you, bro!'

Bro?

'Meet my meathead sibling Robbie.' Ross gives a little flourish.

Robbie is basically Ross but with dark hair, double the muscles and a rugged, stubbly edge.

'Hi!' he says, reaching for and then crushing my hand. 'I'm the younger, straighter one.'

Ross leans in. 'Note how he says straighter, not straight.'

'Funny.' Robbie rolls his eyes. 'Where are you guys headed?'

'Dog beach.'

'You got Toto in that basket?' He points to the bike.

'No, our dearly departed friend James.'

'Ross!' I tut.

'Actually . . .' He turns back to his brother. 'Do you have time for a tour?'

Robbie looks me over. 'Sure. You got any photo ID on you?'

'My passport,' I offer.

'That'll work. Sling the tandem in the back of the truck,' he directs Ross. 'Best place for it since you can barely ride it.'

'I can ride it better than you can drive your macho-mobile,' Ross taunts.

'Is that right? You wanna take over the controls on the chinook today, seeing as you're so fly?'

And to think I could be quietly reading the displays at the Coronado Historical Association.

'Where exactly are we going?' I ask as Ross opens the passenger door and invites me to climb on up.

'I thought you might like a quick tour of the base.'

'So your brother's a sailor?'

'Little bit more than that,' Ross shrugs. 'He's a Navy SEAL.'

If I was starstruck at Ross's theatre poster, I feel like I'm in the presence of a unicorn with Robbie – albeit a highly trained, combat-ready unicorn. I am way too intimidated to speak and terrified of accidentally touching him in case he springs into action like a human Swiss army knife, though he probably wouldn't care for me mixing militaries.

I hold my breath as we draw level with a gate guard sporting a bulky machine gun. He salutes Robbie then falls silent as he inspects my passport and Ross's driving licence. I don't know that I've ever felt more nervous – I'm convinced he's about to discover some lie I told my parents aged twelve and then haul me out of the vehicle for my punishment. But instead the barrier lifts and we are told to have a good a day.

'And breathe,' Ross prompts me.

I take a grateful gulp of air and then frown. 'Is that a golf course?'

'Sure is,' Robbie confirms. 'And I've got a three p.m. tee time.'

'Really?' This is not what I was expecting.

'Wouldn't it be great if that was the new battlefield?' Ross muses. 'All world conflict gets resolved on the course, and bunkers are nothing more than sand pits to chip from.'

'Woah!' We duck as a plane comes in, seemingly grazing the roof of the truck and landing on the airstrip ahead of us.

'That was close!'

Robbie gives me a little smirk. I'm guessing he's seen closer. Maybe even observed Tom Cruise in action? Is he the reason Ross has inside info? I don't want to nose for fear of violating some security code so I make some innocuous comment about how big the base is, complete with its own stretch of beach. They even have a utilitarian version of the Hotel Del – all cream arches and terracotta roof tiles.

'There's a bowling alley, movie theatre, department store, supermarket, Starbucks . . .'

'And the cheapest gas on the island by a mile,' Robbie adds.

'Amen to that!' The guys high-five each other.

I'm starting to think of this place as a regular town with a military membership when we turn onto the waterfront and find the entire San Diego skyline obscured by a vast hulk of grey metal – a real live warship.

I gawp up at it, feeling like I'm seeing something I shouldn't. It's certainly a big wake-up call as to the purpose of this place.

'This one just got back from a six-month deployment this morning,' Robbie notes.

I shiver at the thought of spending half a year in what looks like a hulking prison cell.

'What's it like inside?'

'Have you ever been on a cruise ship?' Ross asks. 'All the chandelier bling, the crazy carpets, multiple restaurants?'

'Yes?' I nod.

'It's the opposite of that. Pared back to absolute basics – instead of sweeping staircases there are tight-squeeze ladders between the floors, barely any daylight or air, totally claustrophobic. Buddy of mine slept in a bed that was basically a big drawer; he couldn't even sit up in it.'

'And yet you'd happily lie out on a tanning bed with the lid three inches from your face,' Robbie snorts.

'Why would I pay to get a tan when I can just let nature take its course?' He points to the sun.

'Says the dude wearing gold face paint.'

As the two brothers banter on I get an ever-clearer understanding of the extremes of their genes: macho versus showbiz; covert versus spotlight; one is out to save the world, for the other the whole world is a stage. I half expect them to break into 'Anything You Can Do I Can Do Better' and frankly I'd pay money to see that routine.

'I was just headed to the food court.' Robbie cruises onward. 'You guys want to grab a snack?'

'Are we allowed in?' I ask as he pulls into the car park.

'You are if you're with me.'

While Robbie orders two bacon cheeseburgers and a lifetime's supply of cajun fries, Ross and I pore over the Mexican menu.

'I can't decide between lobster and mahi mahi tacos.'

'I always get the cilantro lime quinoa bowl,' Ross tells me.

'Of course you do.' Robbie rolls his eyes as he refills his already drained Coke, adding an avalanche of ice.

While we wait with our order tickets, I furtively look around at the other diners. They seem surprisingly normal and, weirder still, cheerful. I can only imagine my disposition if I had to wear that great bulk of uniform on such a hot day. Of course, that would be the least of my problems.

'What do you reckon?' Ross frowns at the tables overlooking the car park. 'Shall we head back to the beach for a better view?'

Robbie responds by holding up his overstacked burger, dripping with barbecue sauce and sighing. 'Is there really any better view than this?'

'Do you mind if I ask one thing?' I turn to Robbie as we sit on the sand, bellies full and in a more relaxed state now.

'Shoot.'

'Why did you sign up? I mean, aside from wanting to serve your country and your natural Action Man inclinations – why pick the most extreme of all the forces?'

He looks at me as if the answer is too obvious to warrant a reply. 'Wouldn't you want to find out how far you could go? To test yourself, and push yourself to the max?'

'No,' I confess. 'Quite the opposite, really. Although, when you put it like that, I suppose I might be a tiny bit curious to know what I'm capable of.'

'Well, I was one hundred per cent curious. To me, it's no good half-assing your life – I mean, who's the loser in that scenario?'

I'm at a loss for a response so turn to Ross for his take.

'I have to say, I feel the same way.' He shrugs. 'Why not go all out?'

Why not, indeed.

I wonder why my default attitude is so often, 'I can't really be bothered.' Is it an English thing, not wanting to be seen to be trying too hard? I have to say that one of the great liberators of this time travel quest is that no one knows what I'm up to – no one knows the lengths I am going to trying to conjure the man of my dreams. I don't have to be embarrassed or worry about being judged. The burden of being responsible for the birth of another human being seems oddly light compared to my fear of reaching for something that I'm not sure I deserve.

Ross nudges me as a group of shirtless Hemsworth clones jog

past in formation, looking like their bodies are hewn from granite rather than flesh and bone. My eyes flit between them and Robbie.

'Do you feel you could pretty much take on anyone?'

He smiles. 'Of course I have to say yes.'

I nod and then confide: 'I've always had this fantasy of looking as I do now but being a secret black belt – so this gang goes to mug me in some alleyway and I leap into action, shocking them all. I mean, can you imagine being utterly fearless in that situation?'

'Yes,' Robbie says simply.

I give him an envious look.

He looks back at me. 'So how many classes did you take?'

'Classes?' I repeat.

'Martial arts, Krav Maga . . .?'

'Oh. None.'

'And yet you say this is a fantasy of yours?'

'Well, yes, I just think it would be amazing to have those skills.'

'Just not amazing enough to do something about it.'

Ross holds up his hands. 'I'm staying out of this because I know you can handle yourself.'

Robbie is up on his haunches now, facing me. 'Tell me this, have you ever felt intimidated by a man?'

'Yes, of course, many times.' Now for one. Last night with Alfred Vear to name another. I could go on.

'Have you ever felt that you had to play nice so as not to incur their wrath?'

'Yes.' A few too many times with ex-boyfriends. I'd get an uneasy feeling and back down.

'Now imagine if you could take that imbalance out of the equation – if you could speak your mind and answer back, without fearing the consequences.'

'I'd feel like a superhero,' I tell him. 'To have that kind of confidence – it would change everything.'

'You know what step one is?'

I shake my head.

'You have to be okay with not being liked.'

I blink back at him.

'Girls are trained to be polite and pleasing, not to offend, not to make the other person uncomfortable. My belief is that you can have impeccable manners but the second someone crosses the line, you respect yourself, not them. Blast them back. Set them straight.'

'I just think it's easier sometimes to let it slide.'

'Is it, though? Is it easy to live with a mindset that accommodates their dominance? It doesn't have to be a given. We have short guys, skinny guys that are SEALS. They didn't buy into the beefcake bullshit that I happen to be a natural fit for.'

He's starting to surprise me now.

'The trouble with letting things slide is that it becomes a habit – and you know what Lao Tzu says about that . . .?' He flips some sand at Ross to get him to deliver the quote, which he does with full gravitas.

'Watch your thoughts; they become words. Watch your

words; they become actions. Watch your actions; they become habits.' Ross holds up a finger to make sure I pay special attention. 'Watch your habits; they become your character. Watch your character; it becomes your destiny.'

I get chills.

'If you get in the habit of indulging the bully, biting your tongue, then what happens in a relationship when your boyfriend gets a bit heavy-handed or controlling? What's going to be easier: stepping up and setting a boundary or letting it slide?'

'I see your point.' All too well.

Ross gives me an encouraging smile. 'You can do this – you've got a bit of sass.'

'I have a trace,' I concede.

'So work that muscle.'

'You guys are slightly blowing my mind right now.'

'Good.' Robbie takes my hands and pulls me to my feet. 'Let's see if we can get your body involved.'

'Wait! What's going on?'

'I'm going to teach you some basic self-defence moves.'

'What, now?' I panic. 'Oh no! I couldn't—'

'What are you waiting for?' He stops dead, looking me directly in the eye.

I open my mouth to speak but daren't form an excuse – and why would I want to? Opportunity is knocking.

'Okay.' I swallow hard, feeling a surge of adrenalin.

'Excellent!' Ross cheers, pulling his cap over his eyes. 'I need a little nap.'

'A nap?' I look down at him, incredulous.

'He won't stop until you get it.'

'Oh my god!' I wail as Robbie rolls up his sleeves and comes at me.

I have to admit he's a good teacher, ultra precise and methodical, making sure I understand every aspect of the technique – how it's about balance and leveraging their weight against them, teamed with swift, simple actions. He tells me that if someone were to grab my arm or handbag, not to pull back but follow the direction of their energy with a kick or shove so they will fall back.

'It's counterintuitive but way more effective.'

As we work on the open-hand strike, targeting the neck of the attacker, he challenges me to channel all my frustration and battle against the voices in my head telling me I'm getting it wrong or this is not me.

'Don't pull your arm back before the strike,' he corrects me. 'You don't want to alert them to the move. Keep your elbow in front of your ribs.'

Again and again we go through the motions until I start to get some form.

'Now we're talking.' Robbie cheers. 'Again!'

'But I got it right!' I protest. Surely we can stop now?

'It needs to be second nature. And right every time.'

'Oh, good grief.'

Grab-grapple-bam!

'Again!'

Grab-grapple-bam!

'Again!'

Suddenly Robbie's phone bleeps a very particular sound and his face changes.

'Now?' Ross asks.

Robbie is already heading to the truck, leaving me staggering slightly.

What's going on?

'Just throw the bike out on the sidewalk,' Ross calls after him.

Robbie raises his arm in acknowledgement and then turns back to lock eyes with Ross. Even from a distance it's such a charged look, as strong as a tug of wire rope between them. So much seems to be said in that fraction of a moment – this clearly isn't the first time they've had to part so suddenly and with such significance.

I stand by, feeling stunned. Eventually I hear myself ask, 'Has he gone on a mission?'

Before Ross can reply the sky screeches and roars above us and I look up and see a series of dart-like planes flying over our heads. Surely he can't be out of here that fast? I mean, I know the airstrip is right there but . . .

'We should go.' Ross starts walking towards the discarded tandem.

I scuttle after him, not knowing what to say. He looks so lost to concern I hardly recognise him.

We are so blasé about seeing our friends and relations, never expecting them to suddenly vanish from our lives. At least with James I had a kind of countdown. This must be so strange, watching someone leave and knowing that the odds of them returning are well below average. And even if they do come home, what might they have endured or executed in the name of patriotism?

'It never gets any easier,' Ross admits. 'I just have to tell myself that he chose this life, and he loves this life – so much so that he would be willing to die for it.' He blinks at me. 'How many of us can say that?'

8

We pedal to the dog beach in silence and then trek across the sand in the direction of a baby blue lifeguard tower. I can still feel Robbie's hands on me, the sensation of him guiding me and resisting me. It felt good to engage with a human being, especially such a powerful one. I feel like I want to hold on to that connection, even beyond my new Wonder Woman skills.

Finally Ross speaks: 'You know it's funny, I always come here when Robbie goes away. It helps get my mind in a lighter state – watching the dogs playing, not a care in the world.'

They are all around us now – frisbees and Frenchies, Chuck-its and Chihuahuas – leaping in the air and reflected in the mirror-wet sand of the shoreline. Owners stand in rolled-up trousers or sunbathe in bikinis, trusting their dog will eventually return to their side, once they are done sniffing around someone else's towel and snacks.

'I'm coming back in my next life as a dog for sure,' Ross notes.

'A Coronado dog,' I specify. 'Maybe with a guy like that as the owner.' I point to a blond surfer dude carousing in the waves with his adoring, grinning yellow Lab.

Ross raises a wry brow.

'So, why was this place so special to you and James?'

I am pleased to see Ross's expression lift as we take a seat. 'It was the first place we'd come when he stepped off the plane. I always wanted to get him to the freshest of air, somewhere he could stretch out and relax. And if he didn't feel like talking straight away, we had all this entertainment laid on . . .' He highlights a motley gang trotting along the beach recruiting new members for their canine *Ocean's 11* as they go.

I smile delightedly, both at his observation and the fact that Ross understood James so well – many times he didn't want to talk but he did still want to be in the same room as you, chiming occasional comments. That's tougher to accept in a romantic relationship when you want your partner to be in a constant state of enchantment with you, but Ross doesn't seem overly needy. I wish I could say the same about me.

'Sometimes we'd pretend we'd come here to shop for a dog,' Ross continues, 'trying to decide which one would be the best match for our lifestyle – if we could just decide what that lifestyle was going to be: city life or beach life, touring actor or stable sitcom sets. We were never convinced about having a dog in London unless we lived right by a park.'

I reach for my water. 'So that was actually on the table – relocating and moving in together?' I didn't know this.

'That's part of where we fell down, the logistics.' Ross shrugs. 'Back then same-sex marriage wasn't an option in the States and I'd just signed for a TV series filming in Los Angeles. Every time we tried to suss something out we hit a road block so ultimately we decided an ongoing holiday romance was our best option – no issues with visas or domestic bickering, always something to look forward to . . .'

'I can see the appeal,' I say, taking a moment to think whether that could suit me – if I did indeed meet my guy here. Presumably he must be American? That hadn't really occurred to me until now. 'You know one of the things I envy most about couples? The joint planning. I mean, I can sit here and tell you all my hopes and dreams but it's just talk. There's something about setting targets with another person that makes it more real.'

'The power of two,' Ross confirms. 'James and I certainly did more in our few weeks together than I did the whole of the rest of the year. It's just such fun – thinking of things your loved one would get a kick out of.'

'I always wondered what that would be like – to have your partner surprise you with something, simply to delight you.'

Ross looks me over. 'You've never been married?'

'Not even close.'

'So what *is* your romantic story?' He turns over to lie on his stomach as if settling in for an entertaining tale.

I look away. Nothing makes me feel worse about myself than

trying to explain my poor choices and emotional shortcomings. I find it best to just not go there.

'Story implies content.' I smile. 'I'm just a string of mismatches that have led me to believe that I'm not really destined for a big relationship. Although I promised James I would try to keep my heart open on this trip.' I dig my toes in the sand. 'In fact . . .' I flirt with the idea of bringing up the Oracle's prediction.

'In fact . . .?' Ross looks expectant.

'Well, I did get a kind of fortune told that suggested there could be someone meant for me here.'

'I told you – a Jack for every Jill!' He looks smug.

'Well, I have to jump through a few hoops to get to him.'

'Is he a Cirque du Soleil performer?'

'No,' I snuffle. 'At least, I don't think so. I don't have too many details at this point. But even the notion that there might actually be –' I stop short.

'Go on.'

'You see, I can't even say it. It seems too unlikely that I would actually get a match.'

'Is this a self-esteem thing?' he asks, looking for clues.

'It's more my track record. You wouldn't look at my dating history and say, "Boy, she's on course to meet the love of her life!"'

Ross gives a sympathetic smile. 'Luckily I don't think it operates that way – it's not like working your way up the career ladder. It's a little more spontaneous than that.'

'Anyway.' I shrug. 'I don't even know what I'd do with him if I found him. I'm pretty set in my ways.'

'And you enjoy the ways you are set in?' he challenges. Like his brother, he has a way of cutting through the baloney.

I think for a moment and then confess that, 'Most of the time I'm just going through the motions.'

'So there's room for improvement?'

'Yes,' I concede.

'And you've probably got some extra space in your life since James passed away?'

I turn to face him. 'But how could anyone possibly replace him?'

Ross holds my gaze. 'Now there you've got me.'

For a while we just stare out to sea, watching a dog who can't stop barking out of sheer glee, his little paws all but levitating off the sand. Despite this, I can see the sadness returning to Ross's face. Perhaps it's too much – all this talk of James on top of Robbie's departure. I don't want him hanging on here just for me.

'Shall we do our little ceremony for James and then call it a day?' I suggest as I do some faux arm stretching. 'I think I might need a soak in the tub after all that wrestling . . .'

'Absolutely.' He gives me a grateful nod.

I move into a kneeling position. 'So, as you know, he requested to have his ashes made into little pebbles – I ordered two for each location on his list, one for each of us, and then one each to keep.'

'That's very thoughtful.' Ross nods. 'Although it still seems surreal.'

'I know,' I say. 'Mind you, my friend Amy got her dad's ashes made into a vinyl record.'

Ross looks a little thrown. 'Does it play?'

'Yes, she chose his favourite songs but you have the option of including a recording of the person talking.'

'Wow.'

'You can even get ashes intermingled with a firework display – I loved that idea: going out with a bang and lighting up the sky before you become one with the universe!' I beam. 'James thought it was a bit OTT and, of course, now I'm glad we get to hold on to a little piece of him.' I reach into my bag. 'Here's your one to keep and your one for today.'

Ross handles the pebbles tentatively. 'Isn't it funny, this is supposedly all we have left of him and yet he's everywhere?' Just as I think a tear is going to slip from his eye he jumps up and pulls me to his side. 'Come on! In we go.'

We shuffle barefoot to the shoreline and then wade in up to our knees. I go to tell Ross how much easier it is to paddle in shorts than a bulk of Victorian skirts but decide this isn't the time.

'Ready?' he asks.

'Are we just throwing them?' I check.

'As far as we can.'

'Okay.' I take a breath. 'Three, two, one!'

We propel them in unison, Ross's soaring and mine plopping

rather closer than I hoped, both pieces sending a pair of Spaniels in pursuit.

'Noooo!' I squeal as they knock us together and then bound and splash after the pebbles. 'Oh god, you don't think they'll eat them?'

'I'm sure they've already sunk,' Ross assures me. 'And even if they did get them, it'll just add to James's afterlife adventures.'

I pull a face and then laugh. 'He'd probably quite enjoy this, wouldn't he?'

'He'd love it,' he confirms before taking a hearty breath. 'Right! Let's get you back to the hotel – you can ride on the handlebars this time.'

'What?' I jump around.

'Kidding! I'm just kidding.'

This is one of my favourite holiday sensations – feeling salty, sandy and lightly ravished by the sun. I would ordinarily head for the shower and try to re-condition my straggled locks but will I even get the chance? If it's anything like yesterday, I'll get zapped straight back in time as I enter my room. I'm going to try not to fall down today. Just step into the blackness, take a moment to find my feet and then slowly feel my way towards the curtains.

I take out my room key and then pause – is there anything I could do to be more prepared? I guess I could scan the card, see the year and then quickly google the goings-on of that time . . . Though I'm not sure how that would help, and what if I missed my slot to press in the code and it switched to a less ideal date?

'Everything all right, miss?' a passing maid enquires.

'Yes, yes,' I assure her. 'Just had a bit too much sun!'

I fan myself and then step towards the card reader. Wait! I press my ear to the door – is that music I can hear?

1929

Jesse & Lilia

9

I can just make out Cole Porter's 'Let's Do It (Let's Fall in Love)'. How apt.

Suddenly I can't wait to get inside.

I fumble with the card. Up flash the red digits: 1-9-2-9.

1929! The Roaring Twenties! I don't know what that means exactly, but no doubt I'll find out. Buttons dutifully pressed, the door releases and I move through the darkness – towards the music. Oops! Too close – I jolt the gramophone, sending the needle skidding across the vinyl. I have got to memorise where the light switch is for next time.

I take a cautious step to the left and then feel my way forward until I reach the curtains. Hello, sunshine – a daytime mission this time. I scuttle my satin shoes over to the mirror. *Yes!* I have a full-on Louise Brooks bob, super shiny with a blunt fringe and the front pieces curving around my cheekbones. I'm thrilled to see I've been granted lipstick for this era – a plummy shade I have never worn before but instantly love. I feel so perky and jaunty and that's before I take in my outfit. Why did drop-waists ever go out of fashion? They are so forgiving – so much swishy fabric above the hips and a nice flounce below, stopping just past the knee. The sleeves are short and airy, the fabric a summery champagne hue. Such an improvement on the dark corsetry – I can move freely now, maybe even dance a little.

'Puttin' on the Ritz', 'Ain't Misbehavin'' . . . I flip through the record sleeves, settling on 'Makin' Whoopee' as my next track. I always thought of this as a cutesy, flirtatious little number but now I'm really paying attention to the lyrics I realise they follow a couple from their honeymoon to having a baby, then his affair and subsequent divorce. Jeez. I need a better template for my matchmaking.

'Singin' in the Rain?'

Not the most obvious choice for this blue-sky day but I'm curious to hear how B. A. Rolfe & His Lucky Strike Orchestra compare to Gene Kelly – especially since their version preceded his movie classic by a good twenty years. I gently lower the silver arm until the needle makes contact. Oh, this is fun, almost like a cartoon soundtrack. I giggle at the tinkly xylophone and warbly voice of a man I imagine to be wearing a straw boater and a preppy bow tie. Before I know it the clarinets and slide whistles have me tapping and twirling around the room – yup, that sun is in my heart and I'm almost ready for love!

All I need now is a cocktail to go with my high spirits. How about I grab a copy of *Coronado Tent City News* and peruse the guest listings while perched up at the hotel bar? Wait! My matchmaking photos! No envelope under the door this time. Unless . . . I lift up the edge of the Persian rug.

'There you are!' I cheer.

As I predicted, Jesse Montague is the man in question – and a fine-looking fellow he has grown into. His dark hair is parted on the side and swept back, his eyebrows are strong, his dimples on loan from Clark Gable. He looks as loyal and true as his father, but a little livelier. Lilia Rodriguez, his beloved-to-be, is a straight knockout à la Salma Hayek, with wavy raven hair framing her portrait-worthy features. Her heavy-lidded, long-lashed eyes have an entrancing 'old soul' intensity while her cupid's bow lips look ready to whisper enticements . . . I hold the photographs side by side. An attractive couple for sure, though no doubt she could have her pick of men. I feel inside the envelope to see if I have an invitation to a particular event but instead find five hundred dollars in cash. Gosh. That's an awful lot of twenty-five-cent good square meals . . . In fact, I could buy up a whole row of tents with that, play my own little game of seaside Monopoly . . .

Is that everything? I scan the room one more time. And that's when I see a hat on the corner of the bed – a finely woven straw cloche that slides snugly over my bob. I adjust the jewelled brooch pinning back the brim. Well, I can't possibly walk like a normal person now, I have to tootle and say things like 'Cooeee!' and blow kisses to the bellboys.

*

The time has come to party like it's 1929.

I'm greeted by a fifty-foot-long mahogany bar, polished to a gleam, crying out for either a fast-sliding drink or sidestepping Zac Efron. As I hoist myself up onto a leather-topped stool, I'm surprised at how sparsely populated the mirrored shelf units are. I'm used to beholding thirty types of gin with ever-quirkier label designs. Here there's just a mix of cut glassware and silver water jugs, dewy with condensation. The barman stops slicing fruit, wipes his hands on his apron and approaches with a smile. 'What can I get you?'

'I know it's still early but I'd love a cocktail.'

'Wouldn't we all,' he smirks. 'So, what'll it be?'

'Umm . . .' I try to place myself in a black and white movie. 'An Old Fashioned?' I venture. 'Or maybe a Sidecar?'

He squints at me. 'You're English, right? I guess you cats don't have Prohibition over there.'

'What?'

'Prohibition,' he repeats. 'You know, we haven't been able to serve alcohol here since 1920.'

'You're kidding!' I blanche. 'No one's had a drink for nearly ten years?'

No wonder the romances are stalling.

'Well, I wouldn't say that exactly – where there's a thirst, there's a way.' The barman leans in. 'If you've really got a hankering, that guy over there might be able to help you out.'

He nods to a man hunched over a small table by the window. He appears to be absorbed with some paperwork, scribbling on the page with one hand, dragging on a cigarette with the other. His dark hair is combed back but a few strands have fallen forward at the front, possibly loosened by rubbing his brow in vexation.

'He looks pretty busy.'

'He won't mind you interrupting.'

'Are you sure?'

'Nicest fella in the world. He may not have the best luck but he's the best guy.'

I sneak a discreet peek at my assignment photo. It could be him but I can't be certain from this angle. Edging over, I pretend to be looking beyond him, out towards the sea, but I can't help noticing his page is filled with numbers and dollar signs rather than words.

'May I help you?' He catches me looking.

'I'm so sorry, I don't mean to –' I fluster all the more because it is indeed Jesse Montague looking up at me, lightly tanned and sporting a short-sleeve ivory shirt with a burgundy cravat. 'Um, I'll come back later.'

'It can wait.' He closes his notebook and puts out his cigarette. 'How can I be of assistance?'

'Well . . .' I look furtively around. 'I don't know if I'm supposed to be a little more discreet or use a code word, but the barman said you might be able to help me find some booze.'

Did people back then say booze? He doesn't seem thrown by it, just looks down at his watch.

'You can make the last jitney, there should be space – I heard a few of the regulars are holding off till New Year's Eve. Tell them Jesse sent you.' He begins scribbling a note. 'Hand this to the driver out front.'

I'm sure Ross referenced a tram trundling along Tent City, not a bus.

'Where would I get off?' I ask.

'It's the first stop after the border. You won't miss it.'

'The border to . . .'

'Mexico,' he replies.

'*Mexico!*' I exclaim. 'Oh no, no. That's okay.' I hand his slip of paper back. 'I don't have my passport on me.'

He leans back in his chair. 'You're not from round here, are you? You won't need a passport. Just some money for the races and the bar.'

'Races? Do you mean horse races?'

Is this why I've been given the five hundred dollars? Instinctively I clutch my purse to me.

Jesse narrows his eyes. 'Are you travelling alone?'

'Well . . .' I really should have thought through my back story. 'I'm seeing a relative tomorrow but for today, yes. What about you?'

'What about me?' He looks bemused.

'You're not going to the races?'

'Not today.'

I feel awkward now. I can't be jaunting off to Mexico when my prospect is here.

'Jesse!' a voice booms behind us. 'Come on, buddy! The bus is revving!'

I look back and my eyes widen. There is no mistaking the Tweedledum physique of my wobbly jowled Victorian nemesis, Alfred Vear, though his facial hair has been cleanly bladed away and he's dressed like he's just stepped off a golf course. Afraid he'll recognise me, I turn sharply away.

'You're going to have to manage without your court jester today, Freddy,' Jesse sighs.

'No can do.' He lays a heavy hand on Jesse's shoulder. 'It's not a party without you. Here . . .' he says as he reaches into his wallet, pulling out a hundred-dollar bill and setting it on the table. 'See if you can't make it right. She's already on the bus.'

'With him?'

He shrugs. 'What can I say? Life's not perfect. Doesn't mean we can't have some fun.'

And then I feel his eyes upon me.

'Mmm, fresh flesh!' He smacks his mouth. 'You coming too, Babygirl? The bus is filling up but you can always sit on my knee!'

'Freddy!' Jesse scolds. 'She's English. A little decorum, please.'

He carries on oblivious. 'I'll tell the driver to hold for two more.'

As we watch his white shoes click across the floor, Jesse sighs and then slides the money over to me. 'Here. I'm taking a break from gambling. You see what you can do with it.'

I want to ask him how much he owes and what it would take to smooth that brow and get the girl – I have to assume that the woman on the bus is Lilia. Which means I need him on that bus too, even if it feels like I'm luring us both into the lion's den.

'You know my granddad was a bookie . . .'

'Is that so?' he replies.

I nod. 'He always loved telling me how Seabiscuit lost his first seventeen races and most of those were back of the field.'

'Seabiscuit?' he repeats. 'I don't know that one.'

Oh gosh. Was that the thirties? I'm getting ahead of myself. 'Actually, that was just a little local race.' I wave my hand dismissively. 'I get a bit muddled with all the funny names.'

'Tell me about it. I just lost my life savings on a horse named Sucker Punch.'

'Seriously?'

'I tried this interesting technique of choosing the horse based purely on its ability to make the amount of money I needed – all the other odds were too low.'

'I see your logic.' *And your desperation*, I think to myself. 'Maybe neither of us should go. I'd probably convince myself Grandpa was guiding me to the big win.'

I notice a glimmer in his eyes. 'Do you believe in that kind of thing?'

I feel bad giving him false hope like this but I have to keep my eye on the prize. I must have been sent on this particular day for a reason. And I can't get him and Lilia together if they are in different countries. I have to take a gamble, even if he won't.

'You know lately I'm believing a whole lot more is possible than I first thought. I mean, what if today's the day your luck changes? Not necessarily with the gambling but, you know, in love.'

He looks a little awkward. 'Well . . .'

'I don't mean with me,' I reassure him. 'What I'm saying is, just like you can't predict the outcome to a race, you can't predict how life is going to go. Every day there's a chance things could skew in your favour.'

He holds my gaze for a minute then looks down at his notebook, tapping his lip with his thumb. 'I guess nothing will really change if I sit here. And you might need a chaperone, Freddy's kinda handsy with the ladies.'

'I know!' I roll my eyes as he gets to his feet.

'You know him?' He frowns.

'Know his type,' I assert. 'Certain characteristics seem to endure through the years.'

He pulls a face as he grabs his jacket from the back of the chair. 'Yeah, I should probably apologise in advance for half the guys on the bus.'

I muster my brightest smile. 'We English are a little tougher than you might think.'

'Well, in that case,' he says as he offers me his arm, 'we're off to the races!'

10

We're stepping at quite a clip but as we round the corner to the front entrance I come to a sudden halt. There it is: Tent City, just as it appeared in the images Ross showed me, but now bustling and thriving with life – children giddily at play, women twirling parasols, men in strongman-style swimsuits. A tram clanks and dings down the middle passage between the tents, with holidaymakers hopping on and off. I wish we were boarding that rather than bussing off property.

'Perfect timing!' Freddy cheers at the sight of Jesse. 'The driver says if we leave right now, we can swing by the D & D and grab a bite.'

'Got to keep your strength up.' Jesse gives Freddy's beach ball belly a fond pat.

'You know I can't eat that spicy Mexican food.' He looks rueful.

'And yet you always do!'

The two chuckle together as we board.

I see Lilia straight away. There's no mistaking her – a rich purple orchid amid a flutter of blossom petals, fanning themselves and chattering excitedly. Her dress is African violet silk, beaded with Aztec-inspired patterning. Its lines may be straight but her curves are accentuated by a hand clamped proprietorially at her waist – a large, overly manicured male hand with a gaudy signet ring.

As I pass her I realise that what I first took to be poise is actually resignation – she barely registers the man nuzzling at her fragrant neck. But then she sees Jesse – her lips part and I see her take an impassioned breath before quickly resuming her mannequin stance.

'Well, look who's bringing up the rear!' Her man sneers at the sight of Jesse. I feel him eyeing me up and down as I pass and catch him snarking, 'I see you're finally punching more your own weight.'

I come to an abrupt halt. I think he may have just called me plain, which I may well be, but to use me to put Jesse down? I don't think so.

'Excuse me.' I turn back to have my say but Jesse hustles me on and into an empty seat by the window.

'Best not to engage,' he advises as he slides alongside me.

'Is it?' I question. 'I'm beginning to realise how important it is to get into the habit of speaking up, otherwise all we hear are the words of the bullies and the buffoons.'

'Easier said than done when those bullies and buffoons have all the power.'

'And when you say power . . .?'

He rubs the tips of his fingers together in the international symbol for money.

I shake my head. 'Oprah says money just makes you more of who you are.'

'Opera?' he frowns.

'Oprah, it's a person's name. She's super-rich herself but in her case the money just amplifies her kindness and ability to do good deeds.'

'I hear that happens from time to time.' He smiles wistfully and then adds, 'They also have guns.'

'*What?*' I squeak. 'Who?'

'Mac and his henchmen. You see the heavyset guy with the thick lip and the skinny one with the slick hair, looks kind of like a weasel?'

'I do.'

'You want to steer clear of those two.'

I tell him I definitely will, but for now I can't take my eyes off them. With those looks how could they be anything but mobsters, typecast by their own facial features?

'You want fries with that?' Freddy, meanwhile, is now filing along the aisle taking orders for the café pit stop.

'Don't be surprised if he's eaten your order before he even gets back on the bus,' Mac taunts. 'When he says he's getting a

Reuben from the deli I'm never sure if he means the sandwich or he's gonna chow down on one of his Jewish cousins.'

His abrasive tone is quite different to Jesse's fond teasing and Freddy seems especially keen to get off the bus the second we get to the D & D.

'Does it bother him?' I whisper to Jesse. 'All these gibes?'

Jesse shrugs. 'He's well-compensated for it. Or should I say, he compensates himself well . . .'

My brow furrows.

'He's Mac's accountant,' he whispers. 'And Mac has no patience for paperwork.'

Now I'm smiling. If Freddy is diverting funds, that means, in a way, the hundred dollars he gave Jesse is actually Mac's money. And it's now in my purse.

'Excuse me a moment.' Jesse responds to a beckoning pal.

They seem to have private business to discuss so I focus on looking out the window.

The D & D is a small, narrow unit with a single sit-up counter. Through the glass I can see Freddy chatting with the cook as he sizzles onions and flips burger patties on a big cast-iron plate. I can't get over how much Freddy looks like my nemesis from last night at the ball, though his personality has more of an Oliver Hardy quality in this incarnation. I mean, look at him now, trying to scoop up all the food parcels and balance them under his chin. He trips on the doorstep as he exits and half his bounty is now hanging on by a papery thread. I tell myself to mind my own business but he's clearly struggling, not knowing what to grab at and now afraid to move. I can only imagine Mac's ridiculing if he drops the lot.

'Where are you going?'

Mac's arm comes down like a barrier in front of me.

'Just thought I'd give Freddy a hand,' I sing-song.

'Is that right?' He gives me a sly look as he lets me pass and then crows, 'Would you look at that, Jesse – you've lost another one of your women!'

His laugh is stomach-churning. How I wish Robbie was here to teach him some manners. I can't see my novice moves having much impact with his armed guards in attendance.

'Here, let me help!' I call to Freddy.

He looks like he might cry with gratitude as I reach to save the packages that are breaking away from the lower section of his bundle, giving them a little wiggle to let him know which ones he can release to me.

'Ready, Freddy?'

'Careful of my hot dog!' he exclaims.

I really hope he's talking about food.

We make it back onto the bus without losing so much as a lettuce leaf and I know Freddy is grateful because he offers me one of his fries. All I need now is a bit of burger bun to block my ears from Mac's endless, attention-seeking commentary. I would say I find it hard to believe that anyone so insecure could be the head honcho but, well, you know . . .

I'm relieved when Jesse rejoins me.

'Please talk to me to help drown Mac out,' I implore as the bus starts to pick up speed.

Jesse chuckles. 'Sure. What do you want to talk about?'

I look around as if searching for a topic. 'How do you know Lilia?'

His smile fades.

'Unless you'd rather not—'

'No, it's okay.' He smiles. 'I like to remember our early days.'

There's enough general hubbub for us to talk discreetly, though he does periodically check that nearby ears are still friendly, as there's a fair bit of seat-switching going on.

The pair met two years ago at a Day of the Dead celebration at the Hotel Del. Though I give an involuntary shudder at the name, he explains that *Día de los Muertos* is actually a joyful Mexican tradition, all about demonstrating love and respect for those who have passed.

'The belief is that, once a year, the souls of the dead return to the living world to commune with loved ones.'

I feel a loop of excitement imagining having an annual reunion with James.

'You prepare their favourite food and drink to feast on. There's dancing and music and so much love.'

I'm even more sold when Jesse describes how it feels to remember loved ones collectively, as opposed to being alone in your grief. I wish the UK could adopt this tradition. It would be so lovely to sit down and bring family and friends back to life by talking about them and thinking of them, knowing everyone else was doing the same, reminding us how death is very much a part of life. I duly log the date in my mental calendar and then prompt, 'And Lilia?'

'I'd never seen anyone so beautiful or so sad.' He sighs. 'I just wanted to make her smile.' He looks at me. 'You know when you find your purpose in life? Suddenly I had mine.'

My heart sighs at the mere thought.

'She had recently lost her mother, her father was drinking too much, disappearing for days on end. I was more fortunate with my parents but there were a lot of secrets in our home . . .' He trails off, having no idea just how well I understand his upbringing. 'We found that, as different as our upbringings were, we had similar values – we wanted to create a safe place for our own family, live a simple life. But that is not what happened.'

Suddenly a great cheer goes up.

'What's going on?' I ask at the bus doors open, with no racetrack in sight.

'We've just crossed the border into Tijuana,' Jesse explains. 'Which means . . .'

'*Tequila!*' Freddy holds two huge bottles aloft.

They obviously have quite a system here, getting everyone booze the second it's legal. I was hoping to find out about the hold Mac has over Lilia but after a couple of swigs, everyone is baying for Jesse to entertain them.

'What *is* your party trick?' I ask, intrigued. I can't see him breaking into song.

'Sleight of hand magic – it works even better when their

vision is blurry.' He winks as he gets to his feet. 'Okay, okay, settle down, everyone. I've got a new one for you . . .'

'Pah! Just another lousy card trick.' Mac turns away.

'What can I say?' Jesse shrugs. 'I'm still working on how to make people disappear.'

For a millisecond he catches Lilia's eye and it becomes crystal clear: these two people need to be together.

11

Agua Caliente Racecourse is abuzz with life – we're met with a fanfare of sprightly mariachi music, women in bright flouncy dresses flirting with men in Panama hats, and a multitude of raised hands fluttering betting slips. A race is in progress and as the noise and agitation builds, I remember just how thrilling and unpredictable it all can be.

As we move through the grandstand building I notice that whereas Mac prompts much elbowing, whispering and ingratiating, the response to Jesse is of genuine affection.

Already there's an arm around him and an insistence he comes for a drink. 'My uncle will be so happy to see you – it's been too long.'

'Would you like me to show you the bar?' Jesse turns to me.

'Actually I'm going to have a little look around first, get a feel for the place.'

'If you need anything, Missy may be the youngest of the

jitney crowd but she's also the most savvy.' He points to the petite blonde currently rolling her eyes at the girlish chatter.

'Great, thank you!'

From my race book I see that the sixth race is the biggest, so that's the one I plan to bet on, but first I need some information on exactly what size win I'm going for, and why . . .

As I sidle up to Missy's group, the gossip is beginning to swirl around an upcoming proposal . . . I get a bad feeling before I even ask, 'Who's the lucky girl?'

'Well, I don't know if lucky is the right word.' Missy sniffs.

'It is if you have a taste for the finer things in life,' a redhead counters.

'But if you know those dollar bills are stained with blood . . .'

'Oh Missy, you're such a prude!'

She turns to me. 'What do you think?'

'I'm not sure I know enough to comment. Who are we talking about?'

'Mac and Lilia.' She confirms the worst.

I shake my head. 'I don't get it.' I lower my voice. 'She looks so miserable. I can't imagine what hold he has over her.'

'You don't know?' Missy hustles me off to the side. 'Everyone knows but they don't reference it. She's the payment for her dad's gambling debt. He got in over his head, couldn't pay the money back to Mac and it was either his life or her happiness.'

I'm aghast. 'Her own father traded her in?'

'It's very sad,' she concedes. 'She couldn't bear to lose him as well as her mother, so she agreed to the terms.'

'Wow.'

'I know. The girls think she has it made because of her fancy lifestyle but can you imagine being beholden to a man like that?' She shudders.

'Not to mention losing Jesse.'

'Oh, don't! He's the best. And now he's no use to any woman because all he does is pine for her.'

'Do you know how much the debt is?' I say in my best 'asking for a friend' voice.

When she tells me the amount I understand why Jesse keeps going for high odds. Casting an eye over today's numbers, I too am limited in terms of which horses could actually make a dent in the repayment, even with Freddy's extra hundred dollars.

As Missy chatters on, I look over at Lilia – so stoic in the face of it all. And then I realise she is edging sideways, away from Mac – every time he lunges towards the track or bludgeons one of his posse with some terrible joke, she steals another step. Where is she headed? Is she going to make a run for it? At one point he reaches back for her and she fans herself, saying she needs some shade. He gives her an impatient look but his cronies pull him back into their throng as the horses make their thundering approach.

She's looking around now as if searching for someone. Jesse is out of sight at the bar so she'll have no luck there. But then our eyes meet and I notice her pace quicken. I excuse myself from Missy and head towards her.

'I need you to pass this to Jesse for me.' She presses a folded note into my palm as we meet.

'Of course,' I say, swiftly tucking it down my top. 'Is there anything else I can do?' She looks so much more fragile up close. 'Anything at all?'

'What's going on here?'

I jump back as Mac barges into view with full accusatory force.

'I was just getting the name of Lilia's dress designer.' I flush. 'It's utterly exquisite!'

He snorts in derision. 'I hardly think you could carry off this look.'

I attempt a casual shrug. 'And I hardly care what you think.'

Lilia's eyes widen. She is understandably terrified but my protective instinct has fully engaged. I can almost hear Robbie cheering me on.

'Hand it over.' Mac's fingers ripple expectantly. 'The note.'

I give a snigger. 'What are you, the new headmistress? We're not at school now.'

'How dare you speak to me like that?' His shock is genuine.

'Outrageous, isn't it?' I hold my nerve. 'A plain girl like me.'

His disbelief is enough to knock him back a step and then his gambling buddies rally around him, demanding he joins them to celebrate the win he just missed.

'I'm watching you.' He points threateningly at me but says nothing more, just pulls Lilia roughly on her way.

I stand there shaken but defiant – more determined than ever to liberate her.

First things first: get the note to Jesse.

Second: pick a winning horse.

How hard can that be?

12

I scan through page after page of the race book on the way to the bar, but there's not a single horse that shares a name with one of my grandfather's dogs. I even check the columns listing the jockeys, trainers and owners, hoping for some clue, but the only name that jumps out is 'Spreckels' and that's only because there's a candy store with the same name at the Del.

Suddenly I feel taunted by the conversations around me – people talking about how a certain horse performed on its last race, the great run a jockey is having, complex wagers with names like 'quinella' and 'trifecta'. I'm way out of my depth here.

Jesse, meanwhile, is confidently showcasing another card trick. Seeing the mesmerised faces around him, I decide I'd have better odds of clearing Lilia's debt by pickpocketing these distracted, tipsy folk – between their wins, losses and bar bills, they've probably already lost track of how much cash they came with. I mean, would they even miss a wad or two? I'm eyeing my first mark when I come to my senses – what good am I to anyone if I'm being marched off to the local jail?

'Chloe!' Jesse waves me over as he concludes his trick. 'What can I get you?'

'Actually I have something for you.' I usher him to a quiet corner and slip him the note.

As he unfolds it I'm encouraged to see two large bills, but he looks dismayed by her words.

'Everything okay?' I ask, knowing full well that it's not.

He sighs heavily. 'Have you got a good feeling about any of the ponies?'

I tell him I'm about to head to the paddock, so I can look over the horses before I make my final selection.

'Really?' He looks impressed. 'Can you add this to your wager?' He hands me the money Lilia enclosed. 'I know I said I was taking a break from betting but you can't look a gift horse in the mouth.'

I smile at his pun. This addition certainly increases the scope of horses that could clear the debt by a decent nose, if they have the legs . . .

'I'm going all in on the last race,' I say. 'See you at the track?'

'I'll save you a space by the finishing line.'

*

I cross off a few overly jittery prospects straight away, another for its sweaty coat, indicating nerves. I remember my grandfather telling me that if I could see sweat spots by their kidneys, the horse may not be feeling well. Funny how these things stay with you. While some might favour a feisty, rearing steed, seemingly raring to go, he preferred a combination of calm and alert – best to conserve one's energy for the track. I'm down to five options as the jockeys approach the paddock – small, sinewy and sporting brightly coloured silks tucked into pristine white jodhpurs. I don't fancy the acid lemon or the apple green pattern. Maybe the flamingo pink? And then I see one with white and red diamonds, putting me in mind of the Del turrets. The wearer looks a little tense, eyes darting around, chin low to his chest. When his glove drops to the ground he doesn't even notice it's gone.

'Excuse me!' I call, scrabbling to pick it up, but he doesn't respond. 'Excuse me!' I call again, hurrying after him. I see him look back at me but he doesn't stop. I have to break into a run to catch up with him and when I do he turns abruptly, hissing at me, *'Please don't say anything, please!'*

I look back, confounded. And then I look closer and closer still.

It's a girl. She can't be more than nineteen.

'I just want one shot,' she pleads. 'One time to know how it feels.'

'O – of course.' I nod vigorously, still in shock. 'I didn't mean, I was just . . . your glove.' I hand it over.

'Oh.' She exhales. 'Thank you.'

'Are you not allowed to ride?' I whisper.

She motions for me to walk with her as we talk.

'It's allowed, just not exactly welcomed by all,' she says. 'Azucar's owner doesn't want the controversy, not yet . . .'

'I see.' We're nearly at the paddock gate. I have to cut to the chase. 'I know this is a crazy thing to ask but I'm looking for a long shot. Are you in with a chance?'

She stares into my eyes, perhaps seeing how much this means to me, and then tells me in a hushed tone, 'Azucar is lightning under a woman's touch. She's raced before but no one's seen what she's really capable of.'

I get chills. 'You could win?'

She shakes her head. 'I can't risk that. Too much attention.'

My shoulders slump in disappointment. Of course she's right – I know from the Grand National that the winning jockey is the only one to get interviewed and fussed over. She'd be splashed all over tomorrow's papers.

But only if she comes first . . .

'How about second?' I venture as she adjusts her chin strap, getting ready for the parade.

She looks back at me with a flash of mischief. 'Now that could work.'

As the tannoy announcement drowns out my call of 'good luck', I realise I have a race of my own – getting my bet placed before the cut-off.

*

And she's off! Hurtling through the crowds, dodging drunks and hurdling henchmen. "Scuse me, sorry, 'scuse me!'

I'm within sight of the betting booth when the wall of flesh that is Freddy steps in front of me.

'Not now,' I wail. 'I have to place a bet.'

'Bet on me,' he leers. 'I'm a sure thing.'

I try my school netball skills of darting and double-bluffing but he's too quick, locking his arms around me and pulling me close so I get an eye-watering waft of onions and alcohol.

'Come on, one little drink,' he breathes. 'You can play the gee-gees some other time.'

'Are you going to do this every time?' I despair as I struggle to free myself.

'I know you like me, why else would you come to my aid at the D & D?'

'Let me go!'

Suddenly Robbie's combat training kicks in and with some deft footwork, a belly-of-the-beast roar and one almighty, unbalancing heave-ho, I flip Freddy's bulk onto the dirt.

Oh my god! For a millisecond I feel terrible, he landed pretty heavily – I fear I've knocked him unconscious. But the second I see him catch his breath, I leap over him and throw myself at the counter.

'Race six, eight hundred dollars to place on number four,' I pant, adding, 'Azucar!' for good measure.

'You just made it,' she says as she hands me my ticket.

'Yes!' I throw my arms in the air.

'You might want to save your cheering for the race . . .'

Oh. That. I fan myself with the race book. I'm really not sure I can take much more excitement.

I find Jesse over by the barrier, as promised, with the perfect vantage point for the finishing line.

'Well?' He looks expectant.

'I put the whole lot on Azucar!'

He looks at me in disbelief. 'That's an unknown jockey on a second-rate mare.'

'Don't worry, you'll see a premium side to her today.'

He draws little consolation from my confidence, instead looking worriedly around us. 'Have you seen Freddy? He's usually here for the last race.'

'Um, I think he's having a little lie-down,' I tell him.

He rolls his eyes. 'He ate another tamale, didn't he? He knows they upset him.'

There's no time for further speculation. The horses are already lined up at the starting position and now burst forth, moving as a pack, jostling to secure a position, the favourite taking an early lead. I strain to find Azucar and the red and white silks in the mass – she must have nerves of steel, that jockey. Just watching I'm a wreck. Every time they look like they're going to clash or collide I tense up, desperate to turn away so I can catch my breath, but I'm riveted, as is Jesse.

'Come on, Azucar!' he cheers as she moves steadily forward, into the front five now.

As they pass I marvel at how the jockeys can sit so high and steady while the horses' legs canter and thrum at the ground. The favourite is being challenged by a grey horse and the commentators are focussing on that but I'm watching Azucar – she's just hit her Pegasus stride, so elegant now, prompting gasps and nudges from the spectators around us.

I glance back at Mac, high up in the stadium, face obscured by his binoculars, a definite improvement. I swear I can hear his angry yells from here, even though the noise surrounding me is reaching fever pitch.

Jesse's hand finds mine, squeezing tight. 'She's doing it, Azucar is *flying*!'

My limbs don't feel like they belong to me any more, I'm floating in space, while on the track the ferocious determination from the jockeys is palpable. The horses are now fully extended, whips smacking at their hindquarters, the jockey's arms thrown forward, moving the reins like oarsmen might row a boat, but at double speed. I realise I'm gnawing madly at my thumbnail as I watch.

'Come on, Azucar! Come on, girl!'

As they approach the finishing line, the grey loses its momentum, the favourite pounds to an assured first but Azucar is the shock second.

I stand in stunned wonder, imagining the rush my jockey girl must be experiencing. *What a ride!*

Meanwhile Jesse's head is hung so low it's almost touching the wooden barrier. 'We were so close,' he groans, taking a moment to compose himself before politely acknowledging, 'You were right about Azucar – she almost had it.'

'Come with me,' I say as I slide my arm under his.

'Where to?' He looks confused.

'Just come with me.' I lead him away from the track, giving the illusion of consoling him for the benefit of any onlookers. When we are safely in the main building I stand in front of him so I can have his full attention.

'Jesse?'

'Yes?' he mumbles distractedly.

'I bet for Azucar to place.'

His head jolts up, his eyes search mine. 'Say that again.'

'I bet for Azucar to come in first *or* second.'

'No!' he gasps. 'No . . .' His eyes glisten, his hands begin to shake. 'Are you serious?'

The best way to convince him seems to be collecting our winnings.

As the clerk counts out the cash and places it in an envelope, he remains incredulous. 'It's been so long since I had any good fortune.'

He is even more overwhelmed when I tell him that the money is all his. 'So you can clear the debt that's holding Lilia.'

'How do you know . . .? Why would you . . .?'

'I want to be one of those people who do good things with their money,' I tell him.

'Like Oprah?'

'Like Oprah.' I chuckle, tickled to hear him say her name.

But then I get serious: 'My concern is that Mac won't let her go without a fight.'

'You're right about that.' Jesse nods before confiding, 'Lilia and I were planning an escape on New Year's Eve. Her note today was telling me about some hitches, but there's still a possible out – we'd just have to hide out with her relatives for a while . . .'

'Yes?' I encourage.

'She would need to go on ahead.'

'Is there some kind of signal I could give her, to let her know?'

He takes out his money clip. 'Show her this – she had it engraved for me, she'll recognise it straight away.'

'And the debt itself?'

'Just get the money to Freddy, he'll clear the ledger.'

Oh jeez. Freddy.

'I can keep the henchmen busy with a trick,' Jesse continues, 'if you could somehow distract Mac, just for a few minutes?'

'He does seem to find me quite compelling,' I assert.

'Good, but first things first, we need to find you a ride back to the hotel.'

'Don't worry about me, I'll figure something out.'

'I couldn't possibly leave without knowing you'll be safe.' His gaze suddenly skews to the right. 'Charlie!' he calls over to a dapper chap in a cream three-piece suit. 'Do you have your car with you?'

'Just got a new one, Jesse, absolute beauty. Fancy a run?'

I've never been happier to hear an English accent.

Jesse leans in. 'I'm staying, but I need you to take this young lady back to the Del.'

Charlie's expression changes. 'It's on?'

Jesse nods.

'Best of luck,' he says, reaching for Jesse's hand.

'And to you.' Jesse pats his arm and then turns to me, softening. 'Chloe, how can I ever thank you?'

'Honestly, just knowing you'll get to conjure up a new life with Lilia, that's enough for me.'

My nerves are jangled to the max as I approach Mac's pack. I just need to brazen this out, one more time, in the name of love.

'Does anyone have any change for a twenty?' I say, holding up Jesse's money clip.

Lilia's eyes widen. '*Ahora?*' she breathes. 'Now?'

I nod confirmation.

She feigns rummaging in her beaded bag but Mac clamps his hand across hers. 'Stop! You'll have nothing more to do with this harpy.'

'All right, buddy, keep your spats on.'

'Who *are* you?' He lurches at me. 'Who sent you?'

I think for a moment and then suggest, 'Karma?'

'Carmen? Carmen Garcia?' He spits his words in my face. 'I don't owe that broad nothing. She can't prove the kid is mine!'

He gets lovelier by the second.

'Are you sure about that?' I continue to taunt him. 'I hear he has your bald spot.'

'Why, you . . .'

By the time his cronies have restrained him and his henchmen have torn themselves away from Jesse's card trick, Lilia has gone.

'She took Angelique to the powder room,' Missy says, covering for her. 'She wasn't feeling well.'

Mac turns back to me, roaring, 'I want you out of my sight!'

I check around for Jesse – apparently he's finally nailed that disappearing act.

'Okay,' I tell Mac. 'You win. Consider me gone.'

'I've just got one more quick stop before we go,' I tell Charlie as he hustles me towards the exit.

'Freddy? I know just where to find him.' Charlie guides me towards the bar, telling me he'll stand watch by the door while I take care of business.

'Another whiskey!' Freddy raises his glass to get the barman's attention, oblivious to the fact that I'm now stood directly behind him.

'This one's on me,' I whisper, leaning forward and placing the envelope on the counter.

He flinches at the sight of me. 'What's this?'

I discreetly lift the flap so he can see the contents. 'Lilia's father's debt. Paid in full.'

His pudgy jaw drops.

'Can I trust you to handle this matter?' I ask. 'For Jesse.'

For once there is no bluster or tomfoolery. 'With the greatest of pleasure,' he demurs.

'Good.' I nod and then step to his side. 'There's one more thing . . .'

His eyes dart nervously around. I'm guessing he's still sore.

'No more manhandling women,' I begin. 'No more press-ganging them or dismissing their protests. You'll endear yourself far more if you show some respect.'

He blinks up at me.

'I know you're not a bad guy deep down, Freddy. You can do better.'

He nods vigorously. 'I can, I will.'

'Good,' I say, straightening up. 'See you next time.'

'Next time?' he squeaks.

I just keep walking, giving him a little wave as I head on my way.

Charlie's getaway car is indeed a beauty – a long and low Studebaker Roadster with a monogrammed bonnet, leather seats and glossy buttercream paintwork. But of all its features, I most appreciate the driver's lead foot as we speed on our way.

'So, what do you think will happen now?' I call over the rushing wind and purr of the engine.

'Well, let me see,' he says as he changes gear. 'Mac will rage like a fury and make a million threats but if they can lie low for a few months, he'll move on to some other woman – after all, one of the major draws with Lilia was breaking Jesse's heart.'

'And he would have married her, just to twist the knife?'

He shrugs. 'It's all about competition with Mac. It made him so mad that everyone loved Jesse – he never amounted to much in business so how come he was the one to win the most desired woman in town?' He takes out a pack of cigarettes and offers me one.

'No thanks.'

'I wish I could say he'd get over you so quick.'

'What do you mean?'

He draws on his lighter. 'Pretty girls are a dime a dozen in this part of the world. But I don't suppose Mac's ever had a woman speak to him the way you did, especially with an audience to spread the word.'

'Oh, I'll be gone before he can catch up with me.'

'I hope so,' he replies.

I look at him, a little nervously. 'How far is it now?'

He nods ahead and there, like a beautiful mirage, are the tents leading to the hotel.

When we pull up outside the main entrance I thank him sincerely for his help and then hand him Jesse's money clip. 'Maybe you can get this back to him at some point?'

'I think you should keep it,' he decides. 'To mark the significant change you made to his fortunes.'

'Really?' I hesitate, knowing it will disappear the second I'm back in the room.

'He'd want you to have it.'

As I pad along the corridor, my fingers linger over the grooves in the silver. I expect to find Jesse and Lilia's initials engraved but instead there's a quote, attributed to Ralph Waldo Emerson.

Money often costs too much.

I tuck it into my purse then round the corner to find two guns aimed at me.

It's Mac's henchmen – the fat lip and the weasel.

Those vital minutes I spent with Freddy gave them the head start. Now they are standing between me and the portal that would transport me safely back to the present.

I raise my hands and try for an easy-breezy, 'Hello, boys, what are you doing here?'

'The boss wants to see you.'

'Great! I want to see him too. Let me just grab my bag.' I point to my door.

They block my path. 'No bag, we leave right now.'

'Without the bag of money?' I bluff. 'Oh no, no. I don't think Mac would be pleased if I turned up empty-handed.'

Their brows ruck. 'He didn't say nothing about no bag.'

'Maybe he didn't want you taking a piece of the pie – not that you would!' I hastily add. 'It's just inside the door – it'll take two seconds.'

They exchange a look. My heart is rattling nineteen to the dozen. *Just let me go in!*

'What am I going to do?' I reason. 'Slam the door in your face? You'd just shoot the lock off.'

'Okay, you can get it,' the weasel decides.

Oh, thank god.

'But we're coming in with you.'

Noooo!

'Okay, let me just find my key . . .' I stall for time. 'And I'll give you fifty bucks a piece if you let me change my shoes.' I reach down to remove my heels. 'My feet are killing me.'

'Get a move on.' The fat lip nudges me with the tip of his gun.

'Okay, okay!' I slot the key in the lock and slowly lower the handle.

'Oh my god, get down!' I exclaim, hurling my shoes backwards so they clatter against the opposite wall.

They turn away long enough for me to leap inside, but already I can hear the *rat-a-tat-tat* of bullets.

Present day

13

When I come to, I'm still on the floor.

As blackouts and mobster encounters go, I suppose it could be worse. I am alive, just a little stiff with a weird pain in my shoulder but I think that's the way I've been lying – like I'm ready to have a chalk outline drawn around me.

I haul myself up and stagger over to the bathroom, twisting and turning to assess my reflection for bullet wounds or bleeding. Nothing, though facially I do look like death warmed up.

I lean on the sink. Could they have killed me? If I had been shot in 1929, would I even be waking up now? Would I still have been born? So many questions and so few answers.

All I know for sure is that I'm back in the present, it's a new day and Ross is expecting me for day two of our pebble ceremony.

As I reach to turn on the shower I realise my hands are still shaking. For a moment I wonder if I'm doing the right thing. I don't have to keep doing this. If I've reached a point where I'm putting my life at risk, I could make a different choice: I could check out this morning and relocate to the Glorietta Bay across the way and, more than likely, everything would go back to normal. I might never get to meet my Mr Right but I've lived this long without him, wouldn't it be better to stick with the devil I know? The independence I know?

I take a moment to imagine how I would feel, walking away from the Hotel Del and never knowing what the future could have held for me. As shaken as I am, I know there's no way I'm giving up now. It's true that I've become set in my ways. This may be the only chance I get to experience something truly extraordinary, even if I can never tell anyone about it. Or, more to the point, have anyone believe me.

I stay a while in the shower, letting the hot steam vaporise the tension. Gradually I start to feel better. So that trip back to 1929 got a little intense, I still did what I set out to do – get Jesse and Lilia together. Why spoil today worrying about what might happen next?

My hand is nearly steady as I give myself an enlivening coral lip and add a jaunty nautical top to my white trousers, even if Ross and I are just going on a ferry ride.

He did offer to pick me up but as we're leaving from his side of the island I said I'd walk and grab a breakfast bite en route. I'm curious to see whether the D & D café is still filling bellies ninety years on. The closest joint I can find is the Night & Day Café a couple of doors down. It's a similar set-up and I take a seat at the counter, accepting a pour of coffee as I peruse the menu.

There's a Mexican flair with bumper burritos listed alongside the 'breakfast burgers' and though it feels a bit early for carne asada, fried ice cream is an intriguing proposition. Ultimately I copy my neighbour and order a pancake the size of a hubcap. As I watch the ladle of batter sizzle from creamy gloop to a buttery bronze, I ask the cook how long this place has been here.

'This incarnation, since 1954,' he replies, reaching for a plate. 'Before that we were the D & D two doors down.'

'Really?' I gasp.

'Yeah, we just shuffled along, took this big ole flat-top grill with us. This thing' – he dings the iron hood above it with the base of his spatula – 'this is a hundred and twenty-five years old, salvaged from a ship.'

'Well, what do you know?' I brighten and then decide that so many places we visit are really a patchwork of different moments in history – the building has a different year to the fixtures and fittings, the ages of the people that work there vary, as do their individual memories. The customer who broke the glass and ended up marrying the waitress who came out with the dustpan and brush, he'll think of that day every time he passes. Just as I will always think of Freddy laden with burgers, whether I like it or not.

Despite carrying extra pancake weight, I'm still a little early when I reach the bay side of the island, giving me the chance to sit on a park bench and marvel at the extraordinary view of the San Diego skyline – artfully arranged on the other side of a gleaming band of periwinkle-blue water.

You wouldn't typically describe skyscrapers as picturesque – magnificent, soaring, dramatic maybe – but this line-up, bordered with trees and yacht masts, looks as if I've turned the pages on a pop-up book. Even the hues of the buildings seem harmonious – mother-of-pearl, metallic blue, sea green . . .

Ahead of me the pathway lies flush with the water, giving the impression that you could wade right across to the mainland. I watch a catamaran glide seamlessly by, reminding me of the pens I had as a child: the ones with liquid in the barrel – tilt them and a figure moves along the backdrop. I follow the boat's gentle passage until it draws my eye to a red-shorted man over on the jetty . . .

'Ahoy there, Ross!'

He waves back, flapping along the wooden boards in his Nike sliders, once again lifting me clean off the ground with his hug. 'And how are you this merry morn?'

'All the better for seeing you!' I say, feeling exceptionally lucky that I don't have to go through these pebble ceremonies solo – I would have spent the whole time in agony at how acutely I was missing James. Instead, I get an infusion of energy and all manner of insider info. Like now, we've wandered over to the barrier to watch a couple of guys nonchalantly dangling fishing lines and I ask what they might be hoping to catch here in the bay . . .

'Could be anything from halibut to shovelnose guitarfish,' Ross asserts.

I give a scoffing snort. 'You're making that up!'

'I'm not, I swear!' Ross laughs. 'It's actually part of the ray family so they're not really aiming to hook one of those.'

'But they really resemble a guitar?' I picture them jamming on the seafloor, trying to recruit a bass on bass and maybe a leopard shark as the sexy lead singer.

'In a kind of angular, futuristic way,' Ross decides. 'Oh, here's our ride!'

I look up to see a navy and white striped ferry pulling into position, US flag flapping at the back. There's quite a crowd of us waiting to board now.

'Anyone going to Broadway Pier?' the captain calls.

The majority of us raise our hands.

'Me too!' he cheers.

As we clatter down the ramp, Ross hustles me towards the stairs, telling me to make a beeline for the back seats of the top deck, but we're beaten to it by a giggle of teenage girls, who instantly set about swishing and pouting for a multitude of selfies.

'Maybe on the way back.' Ross shrugs as we slide along the bench in the next row.

He tells me the ferry is actually free for commuters travelling to work before nine am. I tell him he must pop over to the UK and enjoy an overpriced, under-ventilated ride on the number 43 bus with me some morning, especially on the rainy day when everyone is crammed in with dripping brollies and straggly hair, wanting the day to be over before it's even fully begun.

I push my sunglasses up onto my head so I can take in the scene unfiltered. What must it be like to start your day surrounded by silky, glinting waters and have a bay breeze ruffle your hair as you tilt your face towards the sun?

There's all manner of life around us – cormorants, pelicans and the occasional military helicopter juddering above us. At water level I spy a giant Dole container ship over by the bridge, a millionaire's gin palace to our right and the USS *Midway* aircraft carrier ahead.

Ross points to the convention centre with its white circus tent-like peaks. 'That'll be teeming with superheroes by the end of the week.'

I nod, unphased.

'For Comicon,' he clarifies.

'Oh, I see.' Apparently nothing seems too improbable any more.

'It's a shame you'll be gone by then. There's a few guys I would have liked to introduce you to.'

I'm picturing myself torn between Wolverine and T'Challa when Ross reminds me that the whole ferry ride is just fifteen minutes long, so we should probably get going with our little ceremony.

As we stand with our pebbles in hand at the edge of the boat, I ask Ross if he and James shared a particular memory on these waters. 'If that's not being too nosy?'

'Not at all. It was really all about the sunsets; he used to give them names: the Disney Princess, the Wishy-Washy Watercolour, the Streaky Nectarine!' Ross smiles. 'I can picture him now the day of the Midas Touch – bathed in this golden light, he looked like he was glowing.'

I'm glad Ross has that memory of James, not his pale, pained face as he neared the end. I feel my eyes needling as I think of him in that state. And every other person who has suffered. It's just seems so cruel to drag out the final act, like a kind of torture.

'You okay?'

I can't seem to speak.

Ross tries to rally the mood. 'We could aim for the back of that speedboat, give him a thrill ride around the bay?'

I shake my head.

'It's okay,' Ross says gently. 'We'll just let go.'

A voice in me protests, *I don't want to let go!*

But I do.

The second the pebbles hit the water Ross gasps and lunges over the edge. 'Oh no!'

'What?'

'I think I hit a shovelnose guitarfish!'

'You did not!' I bump him with my hip.

Ross pulls me into a hug. I think he even kisses the top of my head, which just makes it worse – I can feel the hot tears streaming down my face. There's just no stopping the flow. As I give an involuntary sniff, he holds me tighter, enveloping me in calm. I'm in no hurry to move but people are already gathering up their bags and heading towards the staircase, eager to disembark and explore a new territory.

'So . . .' Ross steps back and puts on his guide hat. 'I have a range of choices for you: we could head to Seaport Village for the biggest selection of novelty socks in town or maybe call by the old jail, mostly as an excuse to get a police line-up photo and have lunch at the Cheesecake Factory . . .'

As he rattles off more and more options I feel a strange sense of discomfort, a resistance . . .

'Chloe?' Ross tilts his head.

'Um . . .'

As I glance back towards Coronado, his face changes. 'You miss it already, don't you?'

'What?' I blink at him.

'The island.'

My heart dips and I sigh. 'It's so silly – we're only a matter of minutes away but I feel this pull that's making me want to go back!'

I must confess I'm also concerned about somehow breaking the Del spell – stepping onto different soil and finding that my ruby slippers no longer click together. I am certain now that I want to see this mission through. I want someone of my own to hold me the way Ross does. But of course, I can't tell him that. Instead, I simply give him a pleading look.

He responds with an easy shrug. 'Okay, let's grab those flagside seats and head on back – you're still adjusting to the time difference, after all.'

'That I am,' I concede with a snuffle. But then I hesitate. 'Are you sure you don't mind? I feel like you're a bit like a puppy who needs to have his energy expended each day or he'll start chewing the furniture.'

Ross hoots. 'I'm actually more like a Greyhound – full tilt on the race track but a total couch potato in the home.'

'Really?' My eyes narrow.

'Absolutely!' he insists. 'I can movie-marathon longer than anyone I know.'

I smile. 'Always the competitive edge with you, huh?'

'It helps that I call it "research for my art".'

'Oh, I see – so you can feel like a workaholic even when you're relaxing?'

'Exactly! It's a brilliant plan.' He grins, resting his arm along the back of the bench as the ferry begins churning the water for our return journey. 'You know, today is the farmers' market; we could get some cheese and fresh berries and huddle up and watch classic movies. What do you think?'

I gaze into his eyes. 'I think I love you almost as much as James did.'

Instead of laughing he looks away, then down at his hands, suddenly inspecting his nails, trying to mask his discomfort.

Did that come out wrong? He must know I'm joking. Sort of. Before I can speak he says, 'You know, he never told me he loved me. Not once.'

The ache in his voice causes me to feel it too. 'Really? After all those summers together?'

He shakes his head. 'It's pretty much what drove us apart – my need to hear it and his inability to say it.'

Now I come to think of it, it's not that surprising. It's always been part of James's schtick – swatting away sentimentality. I would find it oddly charming, especially since his devotion would sneak out in unexpected ways – like when I found out his Netflix password was Chloe0209, that was as good as him dedicating a book to me.

'But you *felt* loved, didn't you?' I venture.

'That's the ridiculous thing – yes, of course! But I got hung up on the words – why wouldn't he say it? Why wouldn't he *want* to?'

I shake my head. 'I don't think it was about want with James – it was such a loaded phrase for him. To say it out loud would make you a kind of target.'

'A target?' Ross looks shocked.

'You know, considering what happened with his dads and mum.'

Ross frowns. 'Dads? What do you mean?'

'I'm sure he told you . . .'

'No. He always changed the subject when I mentioned his family.'

'Oh.' I feel awkward now, torn between comforting Ross and feeling disloyal to James. Was it too much of an emotional minefield for him to broach that topic? I know the hurt was still very much with him when we met.

Ross studies me for a moment. 'So now I just feel worse – the fact that maybe there was some reason for it?'

'I think it probably would have helped, if you had known.'

I look around and he seems to understand that we need a more private setting for me to continue.

'I was fine most of the time because he'd just flown thousands of miles to be with me but every now and again I'd make such a big deal.' He grimaces. 'Usually as he was about to leave. I guess you want something definite to cling to . . . But what did it really matter – three words that a bajillion other couples say to each other? What about all our unique conversations? Everything that made us special?' He shakes his head. 'My friends – well, one in particular – would tell me I deserved to be with someone who wanted to shout our love from the rooftops and every now and again I'd get all riled up and agree with him.'

'Is that how it came to an end?'

He nods, looking full of remorse.

'Coronado Ferry Landing!'

As we approach the dock I feel so sad thinking about all the extra time James and Ross could have had together. Fifteen years! What a waste. Other exes might reconvene after a break – it happens all the time – but for them it's too late.

'After you.' Ross motions for me to step ashore.

'No, after you!' I insist. And then I get chills.

What if Ross stepped through the hotel room door instead of me? What if he went back in time and found James and made it right between them? Would I do it, would I let him take my spot?

Even though mere minutes ago I was thinking how amazing

it would be to have someone of my own, the answer comes back a resounding yes. Because I know for sure their love is real. Mine is just speculation. I mean, what if it turns out I'm really not a relationship girl, no matter who I'm playing opposite?

Of course, I don't even know if this is something I could offer Ross. And before I can even consider it further I would have to successfully complete my next matchmaking mission.

Ross suddenly stops short. 'What I wouldn't give to know what you are thinking about right now!'

'What do you mean?' I blink back at him.

'Your face has just run the gamut of emotions – excitement, questioning, steely determination – I think I actually saw a lightbulb appear over your head at one point!'

'Really?' I play innocent. 'I can't think why.'

14

Freshly pressed watermelon juice, dusty indigo blueberries, yellow bauble tomatoes . . .

Ross carefully arranges our market bag, adding a selection of cheeses. 'I've got stacks of crackers at home. And chocolate galore.'

'You know that's one of the things that set James apart for me – the fact that he had bowls of sweets dotted around the flat, like a reception desk at a fancy hotel.'

Ross laughs. 'You know one of the English candy bars he introduced me to plays a part in our picnic tomorrow, but I won't say which, you'll have to wait and see!'

I'm happy to see him looking carefree again, chatting easily as he gives me a tour of the more unusual features of his apartment building.

'These are the firepits; they get lit at night and you can sit out with a glass of wine and gaze across the bay. One time The

Rolling Stones were playing Petco Park and we could even hear Mick Jagger talking between the songs!'

'Seriously?'

'It all depends on the way the wind is blowing, though – I didn't hear a note when Burt Bacharach was in town.'

He points out a workout room with a boxing ring, an outdoor cinema, even an al fresco dog wash. But I only have eyes for the expansive pool with its adjacent cabanas. How can this ever fall into the category of everyday life?

'It's what is known in the biz as resort living,' Ross explains. 'You're welcome anytime, though of course you have your own pools at the hotel. I was thinking maybe we'd do the Mermaid Fitness on your last morning – you'd look great in the rainbow tail!'

Just when I thought my life couldn't get any more absurd.

'Stairs or elevator?'

Ross's apartment is a spacious unit on the third floor with a broad balcony overlooking the tennis courts. I wasn't quite sure what his decor style would be, but it's fittingly relaxed and beachy: raffia matting, an L-shaped sofa that could seat ten, a coffee table made from a surfboard and wall-to-wall DVDs framing a giant TV.

Just as I'm settling in, ready to enjoy our snacks, he turns to me.

'I have to know. Whatever you can tell me.'

Of course, James's childhood is still on his mind.

I set down my pink juice and take a breath. What can it hurt now, for me to tell him? It's nothing that would embarrass James. Nothing that would lessen Ross's opinion of him. Quite the opposite. And so I begin.

'Did you at least know James's birth father died when he was ten?'

'I did not.' He gulps.

'Okay. Well, he did. And his mother completely fell apart. And there was no one else around to offer support or hold things together, it all got heaped onto him.'

'Age ten.'

'Age ten,' I confirm. 'She was sobbing round the clock – there was never a long enough pause in her tears for him to take his turn. Someone had to take the phone calls and heat the canned soup and keep track of her pills.'

'Oh James.'

'Within the year, she married again. He was a good stepfather. But then a few years later he died.'

'No!' Ross blanches.

'And James had to go through it all again – the wailing mother, the funeral arrangements, feeling as if everything was on his shoulders. Was this going to be the pattern for his life? These two men who he was closest to, the two men who had cared most for him, both dead.'

Ross's eyes dart around. 'So if he says I love you out loud . . .'

'Look what happens: he loses you. Worse than loses you.'

'Oh god!' Ross rubs his face.

'I don't know why he didn't tell you. Maybe he felt that even referencing it was putting you at risk.'

Ross leans back in his chair, staring up at the ceiling for a while. Eventually he asks if his mother married again.

'Well, that's the kicker: after his stepfather died she went to a psychic and she told her, "You have one more chance at love, and one only. You will go to a party, you will meet a man and you will recognise him because he'll have dark hair and a slight scar on his cheek." And what do you know? The next party she goes to there he is – her last chance at love.'

'And they got together?'

I nod. 'But he was just visiting, he lived in Spain. He wanted her to move there with him. But there was a catch: "I want you but not the kid."'

'Please tell me she didn't . . .'

'She packed her bags and left James with his older cousins, two hundred miles away.' I expel a long sigh. 'You can see why he didn't' like to get too attached or feel any kind of dependence on a person.'

'I can.'

I let Ross sit with this for a while and then add, 'You want to hear something awful?'

'There's more?' Ross despairs.

'This is more of a personal thing for me. One day I got in from work and the answer machine was flashing. I thought it might have been him calling for me so I checked it. It was a message from his mother. After all these years she'd tracked him down, she wanted to meet up and she'd left her number.'

'Oh wow.'

'I was so shocked – this was such a massive deal – that in my stunned state I accidentally pressed three for delete instead of two for save.'

'You did not!' he gurgles.

'I was mortified,' I say, reliving the blood draining from my face. 'I don't think I moved from that position, just froze there wishing I could turn back the clock. He came in from work and I was still stood by the phone, horrified at what I'd done.'

'What did he say when you told him?' Ross husks.

'He just shrugged and said he wouldn't have called her anyway.'

'What? Really?'

'Of course, you can't blame him – why would he want to speak to her? I can't tell you how many nightmares he had about her – calling out in the night.'

Ross's face changes. 'He used to do that with me.'

'But he never said what he was dreaming about?'

'He just used to say it was a monster. Always the same monster...'

'His mother.' I grimace. 'He told me that the only news he wanted to hear about her was that she had died, so that part of his life would be over for ever. I guess now there's a chance he beat her to it.'

Ross looks wrung out.

'I think we need a cup of tea,' I say, getting to my feet. 'With sugar.'

Ross points to the mugs and teabags and then sighs. 'That little kid – having to battle through life with so little support.'

'He was a fighter, though, wasn't he?' I counter as I fill the kettle. 'Have you ever known anyone more capable? More in charge of a situation?'

'Born leader.'

'I'm just going to nip to the loo while this boils.'

'Of course – down the corridor.'

Ross calls after me, adding extra directions which I don't quite catch and consequently I find myself walking into the wrong room.

I'm not sure how long I stand there in the doorway before I remember to breathe.

Rail after rail, rack upon rack of period costumes, everything from *Downton Abbey* to *Mad Men*.

I might be able to dismiss this as Ross's personal Mr Ben world (with a drag flair) were it not for the extreme range in sizes.

The clothes are neatly grouped by decade and my heart feels agitated and potentially in peril as I step towards the twenties collection.

Dare I even look? My eyes flick to the door as I hurriedly slide the hangers along the rail, searching for my dress. I see a flash of purple towards the back – the same purple as Lilia's showstopper . . . I bunch the garments together, trying to create enough of a gap to get to it, when I hear a voice behind me.

'I see you found my secret stash.'

It's Ross, standing all too close to me.

'S – sorry, I didn't mean to snoop, I . . .'

'Help yourself. These aren't museum pieces, just the result of thirty years in the theatre and a costume fetish.'

'I can't believe you have so many – you could dress a whole village,' I say, though what I really mean is 'a whole hotel'.

He shrugs. 'I had this notion of starting my own theatre company so every time there was a sale or a clear-out I'd get another trunk full, but I've mostly ended up hiring them out online – it's always good to have a side hustle as an actor.'

His explanation sounds perfectly plausible and ordinarily I might believe him but given what has been happening these past few days, not to mention his connection with James and his in-depth knowledge of Coronado history . . .

As he talks me through his favourites, my mind races around, trying to figure out whether I've just peeked behind the wizard's curtain. Or am I being ridiculous? Even if he could outfit a slew of actors, how can I possibly account for the changes in the hotel interiors and surrounding landscape? Unless it's some kind of optical illusion? But how would you fake a racing stadium? There's no mistaking that smell, those sounds. Unless I've been drugged – I did leave him alone with the smoothies and he poured my watermelon juice today. But we shared that cocktail on the patio on the first day . . .

'You seem troubled?' Ross notes.

'I – I was just thinking of all the things you could do with a collection like this, what with all your connections on the island . . .'

'How do you mean?'

'Well, for example, you could have some kind of interactive attraction like a murder mystery or an escape room but instead of solving a crime you would give the guests a task to complete . . .' This is my way of broaching the topic, without a direct accusation.

'Now you mention it, one of the cast wanted to do some kind of Kate Morgan experience for Halloween . . .'

'Kate Morgan?' I frown.

'She's the hotel's resident ghost. There have been a crazy number of paranormal activities recorded in her old room.'

'Really?' I shudder.

'I'm telling you, that place has layers and layers of history.'

'And you practically have a costume for every year of it.'

My words hang in the air as he runs his hands along the 1940s rail.

'You're really getting me thinking . . .' he speaks eventually. 'Maybe I could team up with the hotel in some way, offer themed evenings?'

'Of course, you'd have to check to see if they're already

hosting this kind of thing – instead of wine and dine, wine and time travel.'

As he laughs there's no trace of guile in his eyes, though I have to remind myself, he is a professional actor.

'Do you want to try something on?' He turns to me.

'Oh no,' I deflect, but I give myself away as I glance towards the early sixties section – possibly where I'm headed next.

'Good call! I have some great vintage pieces. Have you seen *Come September*?' he asks as he begins burrowing amid the shoeboxes. 'I found these blue satin stilettos that are exactly like the ones Gina Lollobrigida wears to play footsie with Rock Hudson in front of the nuns . . .'

I can't help but smile. There's no way this man would have had me threatened by mobsters. *Surely?*

We spend the rest of our time dipping in and out of Ross's DVD collection, which does include *Back to the Future*, but it's such a classic I don't think it counts as incriminating evidence. When we come to *Some Like It Hot*, he clutches the disc to his heart.

'What I wouldn't give to have had the Tony Curtis role in this,' he sighs. 'Do you know they brought in this legendary drag artist called Barbette to coach the guys on walking like a lady in heels? Curtis was a natural but Jack Lemmon opted out, saying he didn't want to get too skilled because the comedy gold was in them *not* being feminine.'

We decide to save watching that most Coronado of movies

until my last day, which is already too close. When I booked this trip I thought four nights would be plenty for such a little island, now it doesn't seem nearly enough.

Come late afternoon, Ross offers to drop me back at the hotel but when I learn there's a complimentary summer bus I insist on taking that so he can have a bit of downtime before his show. I also want to feel I'm really taking in my surroundings as I head back, not being distracted by any chatter or misdirection.

I briefly think about getting out at the museum to see if I can do a bit more research but then I decide it's more important for me to take a closer look at the hotel, specifically the lobby because that's where the biggest decor changes have been taking place. I see now there are two rooms off the main space and take a quick nose behind their doors. The first is currently housing a convention exhibit so I quickly dip back out of that. The second – the Crown Room – is prepping for some kind of gala dinner. It's a magnificent space with a ceiling like the hull of a ship and crown-shaped light fixtures. I doubt any changes would be made here, other than perhaps the carpet. When I ask the concierge about any structural alterations he tells me the area beside his desk was once a library and, beyond that, the lounge where they would serve Victorian afternoon tea.

'As in, to Victorians?' I ask, not recalling seeing teacups on my 1888 jaunt.

'Oh no, I mean Victorian-style tea. I'm talking as recent as twenty years ago. We've undergone quite a few changes since then. The gift shops you see now were given a facelift just this year.'

'Really?' I say and then walk through the 'signature' shop, pretending to be checking out the Hotel Del logo sweatshirts and beach towels, but actually I'm running my hands along the walls and displays, trying to memorise the sections and get a sense of how sturdy the dividers are.

Not that anyone would go to all the trouble of reconfiguring a room just to fool me – I mean, why would they go to all that effort? I still can't really understand why this is happening to me. If indeed it is.

To think I was actually considering sending Ross into the room instead of me. I wonder what he would have made of me suggesting that?

Well, I'm going to keep my wits about me this time – not rush so much, give myself a chance to take in the whole scene.

I take out my key card as I head up to my room. I should probably be a tad more trepidatious – the last time I crossed over I narrowly escaped a barrage of mobster bullets, the time before that I nearly drowned. Yet the strongest feeling I identify is anticipation. Perhaps I've been a secret adrenalin junkie all these years, it just took time travel to bring it out in me . . .

I take a breath. Oh, please let it be the fifties! *Please!*

1-9-5-8.

Yes! Definitely a more carefree time – more Capri pants than Al Capone.

My hands are trembling as I press the digits. The lock whirrs open. I step inside, feeling a super-surge jarring every cell in my body, but this time I don't black out. Quite the opposite – I'm entirely enveloped in squint-inducing sunlight. No need to fumble for the curtains, I simply stand and wait for the picture to develop before my eyes . . .

1958

Jack & Jennifer

15

The room decor has changed again. My California king bed has been replaced by two neat, chaste single beds, the kind you see in fifties sitcoms with the married couple bickering from their respective units, him in his ironed pyjamas, her in her chiffon nightie, busily applying hand cream. The cushions on the bed have the same retro print as the ones on the low chaise, but most notable to me is the fact that both the dressing table and the coffee table are set with glass ashtrays and a book of matches. I pop one matchbook in my pocket, even though the keepsake won't survive the journey back to the present, and then turn my attention to my personal decor...

My softly waved bob and sun-kissed face are a little more natural than I expected – I had thought this might be my chance to have perfectly applied flicks of black eyeliner – but then again I am in beachwear as opposed to a cocktail dress and I do have a great pair of cat's-eye sunglasses in my pocket. I turn so

I can take in my high-waisted white shorts and matching halter-neck top. It is a flattering cut and comfortable on what feels like an especially hot day, so at least that's something.

Right. Let's get a look at Jesse and Lilia's son . . . As I slide the photos from the envelope my heart dips at the sight of Jack Montague. He has all of his father's handsomeness but with an added mischievous, matinee idol flair. My finger traces his browline. There's something so intimate about the expression in his eyes. I feel like he's looking directly at me, preparing to clasp me to him in one of those screen kisses that buckles a girl's knees. For a moment I wish it was me in the other photograph, that this was my turn. I brace myself for some doe-eyed Natalie Wood but instead find a freckle-nosed strawberry blonde named Jennifer Wilson. Hmmm. She looks like a straight-shooter, no coy posing or pouting for the camera. I imagine she'd be someone you could rely on – practical, hardworking . . . Visually they may not be such an obvious pairing as Jesse and Lilia, but then again, a photo doesn't account for chemistry.

'What's your special sauce?' I ask her photo.

And then I look back at Jack with a smidgeon more respect – he could so easily have gone for his female mirror. The corresponding pin-up girl to his matinee idol. Perhaps when you're spoiled for choice you start to notice qualities beyond the particular arrangement of features on a face. Or maybe that's the problem – maybe he did opt for the starlet and he's overlooked this honest-to-goodness girl next door.

Of course, it's possible she turned him down. Maybe he can't be trusted, maybe she doesn't like that he's always surrounded by female admirers. There's definitely a price to be paid for having a conspicuously attractive partner. Look at all Lilia went through on account of her beauty. On the upside, Jack does have Jesse's good-guy genes and what I imagine to be a loving upbringing. This is going to be an interesting one.

I return my attention to the envelope – it feels more weighty than normal and as I tip it up, out slides a handful of dimes, and then four tickets to *South Pacific* at the Village Movie Theatre. Okay. I'm guessing I'm going on a double date with Jack and Jennifer. I wonder who the other fella is? Not that it really matters – anyone to make up the numbers.

I grab my straw handbag with the cherry brooch and swing open the door only to screech, *'Don't shoot, don't shoot!'* as I am confronted with two pinstriped mobsters wielding Tommy guns.

My hands are in the air, my eyes scrunched shut, my mind racing. Is that the fat lip and the weasel? How did this happen? Somehow my room is in the fifties but the hotel is still in the twenties ... Is this some kind of unfinished business? Is this how I'm supposed to go? I don't understand!

I wait for the threats, the gibes, the slugs to the chest. None are forthcoming. Is that laughter?

'We was wondrin' how long yer gonna stay like that!'

Out of one eye I see the gangsters are giggling at me.

'You doin' that method acting thing?' the heavier-set one titters.

'Harry! Mikey!'

Before I can speak an agitated man rounds the corner and beckons impatiently to them. 'What's the hold-up? We needed you on set five minutes ago!'

On set? I frown. Does he mean like a movie set?

As they scuttle off, I peer down into the courtyard and there again it seems as if the two eras are colliding. The cast appear to be in 1920s garb while the crew are wearing 1950s fashions. At least I think that's what is going on. I need to get a closer look.

As I step away from the window I find myself doing a dance with a large man in a sunhat.

'Sorry, if I can just get by.' I point towards the staircase I'm aiming for.

Every way I move, he's there's first. Wait. This feels all too familiar. It can't be. I look up and find a man with Alfie embroidered on his bowling shirt.

'Oh my god!' I cry, beyond exasperated. 'Is there nothing in your DNA that gets a *no* when you meet me?'

'I – I –' he falters.

'Come on then, let's hear it!'

'I was just trying to get to my door.'

'What?'

He points behind me and I see that I am indeed blocking the entrance to his hotel room.

'Oh!' I flush.

He holds up his key.

'I'm so sorry,' I begin. 'I've had an unusual couple of days, it's made me a little highly strung.'

He mumbles something I don't catch.

'What was that?'

He leans closer. 'I said, "If you wanted to come in and tell me all about it . . ."' and then jiggles his eyebrows in a suggestive manner.

'Oh, good lord!' I throw up my hands. 'And there was I thinking you'd evolved.'

Once I enter the courtyard I decide it's best not to linger too long in one spot in case I draw attention to my imposter status. I'm weaving around big black boxes of equipment and cables and people busily consulting scripts and call sheets when I see a group of beachwear-clad extras heading to the oceanfront and decide to tag along with them.

The beach itself is buzzing with activity, with a substantial crowd of onlookers gathered the other side of a low rope barrier, all eagerly standing on tiptoe trying to catch a glimpse – but of what or who? I scan for famous faces but all I see is a cluster of empty chairs beside the cameras and classic Hollywood lights on stands. The sand is dotted with stripy parasols casting shade over low-to-the-ground deckchairs. I watch as a number of extras don long towelling robes and start pacing towards them, passing a man in a unitard bathing suit teamed with socks and sandals. Interesting look. There's definitely something familiar about that wicker chair set at the centre of it all . . .

'Are you lost?'

I turn and see a little boy sitting on a tan canvas chair. He can't be more than five or six.

'Hi, buddy! What's your name?'

'Chris.'

'Hi, Chris, I'm Chloe.' We shake hands. 'Are you in the movie?'

'No, but Pop is.'

'Your father? And what part does he play?'

'Well, it's complicated.' His little nose crinkles up. 'Sometimes he's playing a man. Sometimes he's playing a woman.'

My eyebrows rise.

'Sometimes he's Jerry. Sometimes he's Daphne. Sometimes he's Pop. Sometimes he's Jack.' He gives a little shrug. 'It all depends who he's talking to.'

My heart is rushing in my ears. Surely not? Surely this can't be?

'So your father's actual name is . . .?'

He points to the back of the canvas chair and there, literally in black and white, are the words JACK LEMMON.

Which means somewhere around here is a man with jet-black hair and sparkling sapphire eyes going by the name Tony Curtis.

And if that is the case, it means that . . . I can't! I can't even dare think it! I mean, if I saw Marilyn Monroe with my actual eyes . . .

'Everyone, positions, please!'

A man with a loud hailer is facing my way.

I try to move out of his line of vision but it only makes him more agitated.

'*In position, now!*' he bellows, motioning for me to step away from Chris.

'What position?' I whimper. And then I feel a hand tug me down onto the sand.

'Just lie down beside me.'

I try to arrange my body in a more ladylike position while also checking out the man I've inadvertently paired up with: honey blond hair, strong tan, square jaw, cool tortoiseshell sunglasses. I'm glad to be wearing mine so my eyes can rove around his open shirt undetected.

'You're a long way from home, aren't you?'

For a second I think he has me sussed, but then I realise he's referring to my English accent.

I'm about to come up with some bogus explanation for my presence when I see a woman in a cropped white towelling robe being led onto set escorted by a pair of uniformed guards.

A huge cheer goes up. 'We love you, Marilyn!'

As she waves to the onlookers the whooping increases tenfold.

It's a good thing I'm lying down or I would simply faint.

Marilyn Monroe is even more luminous in real life – like a moonbeam in human form, moving amid us mere mortals and brightening every face she encounters.

'How are they going to film with all this shouting?' I ask.

'Watch this . . .' He nods over as she pads barefoot towards the crowd.

Suddenly you could hear a pin drop – no one wants to miss a syllable of her speaking.

'She's asking them to be quiet for her,' he explains.

'That's amazing!' I whisper, equally spellbound.

Marilyn then joins a group of girls passing a beach ball around in a circle. I remember this scene and, on closer inspection, I see one of the 'girls' is, in fact, Jack Lemmon.

'You need to look at me, not them,' my acting partner reminds me.

'Right, right.'

'And, *action!*'

There are quite a few rogue factors at play here – mis-catches, sea breezes and, seemingly most vexing to the director, military jets vrooming noisily overhead, just as they do in the present day.

Time and again they reset and go back to the same sequence of throwing the ball. In between each take, my parasol partner and I exchange a few more words.

'There seems to be a lot of talk about Marilyn needing an unusual number of takes.' I approach the subject as daintily as I can. 'Is it true?'

'There's too much focus on that if you ask me. Sure, it's tough on Jack and Tony, they've got to hit it every time – the director made it clear that if she gets it right, he's yelling, "Print!"'

I give a little chuckle.

'But the way I look at it, she's just a perfectionist when it comes to her craft. I certainly envy her studying with Lee Strasberg – that's my dream: to master method acting.'

'Really?'

He nods. 'I keep hoping I'll get the chance to talk to his wife Paula – you see the woman dressed in black, the one with an umbrella?'

She's hard to miss, looking like a stray mourner amid the sun-worshippers.

'She's here coaching Marilyn.'

'So she really does take it seriously . . .'

'Oh yes. She's a smart one too – one of the hotel maids was telling us her room is filled with these highbrow books with passages she's marked up. Plus, not a lot of people know that she has her own production company.'

'*Quiet on set!*'

I gulp back my questions. It's a disjointed way to have a conversation but, on the upside, I get a chance to ruminate on each thing he tells me before we move on to the next topic. Plus, it's nice to be able hang out without feeling the need to speak. He's certainly easy company – like now, we're both discreetly chuckling as Jack Lemmon adjusts his padded bra.

'Would you do it?' I ask at the next break. 'Dress as a woman?'

'They seem to be having an absolute blast so I'd have to say yes.' He then narrows his eyes. 'Or are you asking because you want to switch outfits?'

I give him a playful swat, then decide to come clean. 'You know, I'm not really an extra.'

'No kidding.' He smiles benevolently. 'So what are you doing here?'

'I'm actually looking for a friend of mine, I wonder if you know her – Jennifer Wilson?'

He looks blank.

'Similar hair colour to you. Freckles . . .' I'd show him her photo but I don't want to come off like a private investigator.

'Doesn't ring a bell.'

'What about Jack Montague?'

'Jack Montague?' he scoffs, looking more than a little perplexed. 'What would you want with him?'

'I just have some movie tickets to pass to him.'

'From who?'

'Cupid,' I say, trying to be cute.

'Cupid?' he repeats, ever more intrigued.

'As a matter of fact . . .' I can't believe I'm going to do this. 'I need a second guy to come with us to the movie, if you were free tonight? It's a double-date situation.'

'It certainly would be if I came along.'

'What do you mean?' I frown.

'I'm Jack Montague.'

My heart stops. 'No you're not.'

'I'm not?'

'No,' I insist. 'Jack Montague has black hair for starters.'

'Like this?' he says, lifting up the corner of his wig.

Oh no. No, no, no.

Gingerly I reach out and slide his sunglasses down his nose. There's no mistaking those green eyes. I feel a little light-headed.

'*Action!*'

I quickly lie back down. I can't believe this. What am I going to do now? I rack my brain for someway to make this right, desperate for a retake myself.

When the next break comes, Jack is the first to speak.

'So let me get this straight: you and me are going on a date tonight?'

'Well, the date would technically be between you and Jennifer,' I say, fearing I'm giving too much away but I don't know how else to get around this.

'Why can't it be between you and me?'

'Because . . .' Oh, so many reasons. 'Because I'll be gone by daybreak. Whereas Jennifer . . .'

'Yes?'

His eyes . . . How is anyone supposed to think straight looking into those eyes?

'Jennifer is a much better bet.'

'Is that so?'

'Yes, definitely.' I stand strong.

'So who's the guy you're getting fixed up with?'

Is that a smidge of jealousy?

'Oh, I'm not, I'm just there like a chaperone. I'll probably just ask Jennifer to bring along a friend of hers, for moral support.'

'Hmm. And does this Jennifer know she's going on a date with me or will it be news to her too?'

My shoulders slump. I don't feel like I'm making a convincing case. 'She doesn't know yet,' I admit.

'So there's still a chance it could just be you and me?' He tilts his head, looking even more appealing.

This is not going according to plan. Hugely, hugely flattering but not the plan.

Suddenly there's some commotion behind us. Tony Curtis has just walked on set in his captain's outfit. As he stops to sign some autographs Jack lifts up the corner of the towel and flips through the pages of a sand-dusted script.

'Looks like they are moving on to the next scene.' Then he gives a little grunt. 'Better get comfortable – there's three pages of dialogue for him and Marilyn.'

I go to get to my feet. I need to find Jennifer before night falls.

'What are you doing?'

'I should probably be going . . .'

'And ruin the continuity?' He tuts. 'That's seriously bad movie mojo.'

I hesitate. Am I really going to risk messing up what is widely regarded as the greatest comedy of all time?

I lie back down, feeling a little more self-conscious but not entirely hating the fact I get more time with Jack. He now has his back to the action but I can see both him and Marilyn, which, I have to say, is a pretty sweet deal.

As they begin shooting we all but hold our breath. Jack has

his sunglasses in his hand now and mine are pushed back onto my head so we're fully eye-to-eye. I can't seem to look away, even though the break seems an unusually long time coming.

Suddenly there's some kind of shout but it's immediately drowned out by rapturous cheers and whistles, followed by murmurs of disbelief all around us.

'What is it, Cory?' Jack calls to the next beach couple along.

'She nailed it.'

'What?'

'Word perfect – first take.'

I'm thrilled for Marilyn, just a little sorry that my sandy play date is over.

'So.' Jack leans up on his elbow. 'See you in the lobby at seven p.m.?'

'Really?' I smile. He must think I'm a total nut. And still he's saying yes.

'Sure,' he shrugs. 'It sounds like fun.'

I walk away with an unusual amount of spring in my step.

If I'm not careful, I'm going to end the night prancing around rattling a pair of maracas.

16

I need to find somewhere cool to collect my thoughts. My other trips back in time were mind-blowing enough but this is taking things to a whole new level. It's then I spy a table laid out with cups of chilled lemonade. It looks so refreshing, do you suppose anyone can help themselves?

I sidle up, pretending to be arranging the cups into neater rows.

'*You!*'

'Me?' I startle. Of course it wasn't complimentary, what was I thinking?

'You're with catering.'

I nod back because it seems this guy will be even angrier if I say I'm not.

'Tell the kitchen we need to bring the afternoon tea service forward by an hour. He looks at his watch. 'Basically we need it now.'

'Got it!'

I go to dash off but he redirects me. 'The kitchens are this way...'

'Of course!' I tut myself and then ask every other person I pass, 'Do you know the way to the kitchens?' 'The kitchens?' 'Just along here for the kitchens?' Until I find them. And it's definitely 'them' plural. There's an area for every category of cuisine, but my nose is instinctively drawn to the warm, buttery scent of baking.

The team of white jackets are moving so deftly I feel like I'm waiting for the right moment to jump into a set of Double Dutch skipping ropes.

'Excuse me.' I reach to touch the arm of the woman nearest me. 'Oh, it's you!' I gasp as Jennifer turns to face me.

She gives a little frown. 'I hope so. What do you need?'

'I have a message from, um, the set people to say they want to pull the afternoon tea service forward.'

'To when?'

'Now.' I grimace.

She pauses, recalibrates and then issues a series of clear, succinct orders to her team.

As they speed up and start exiting laden with goodies, she turns back to me.

'I'm going to need you to help me carry out the pies. They need five more minutes in the oven. You can wash your hands over there.'

I nod. She is only young but seems a natural leader, now

tapping her fingers on the immaculate countertop as she watches the timer.

'Do you mind if I help myself to a glass of water?' I call over from the sink.

'Of course. The glasses are in the cabinet.'

As I sip I make the smallest of small talk, asking if she's worked here long.

She tells me that she's just filling in for the week. The lead baker fell sick, one of the producers ordered the spicy peach pie at Clayton's and, bam, he hired her on the spot.

'Wow!' I gasp. 'And now you're baking for Marilyn Monroe!'

'Actually she prefers the chilled vanilla soufflé.' She smiles modestly.

'I don't know how anyone could resist this smell!' I take a deep breath as she opens the oven and fills the room with a fruity perfume.

'You can have a taste of it if you like? I always like to check one slice before I serve up.'

She hands me a fork and plates up a piece of piping hot yumminess. I blow impatiently and then take a bite. It takes me a few moments before I'm able to speak.

'You could make anyone fall in love with you with this. Literally anyone.'

She gives a little snort. 'If only.'

'Is there someone you have your eye on?' I try to sound casual as I take a second bite.

She gives me an assessing look as she adds the lightest dusting of sugar. 'There might be.'

'Who?' I ask.

'I'd rather not say.' She turns away, reaching for a pair of large wooden trays.

'Cast or crew?' I persist. 'You can at least tell me that!'

'Cast.' She shrugs. 'But it's not like I'm aiming for Tony Curtis, this guy is just an extra.'

'You know, an old friend of mine is an extra here – we're going to the movies tonight. I was looking for another girl to come along . . .'

'I don't think so,' she says, checking she has everything in order.

'That's a shame. I think you'd like Jack.'

'*Jack?*' She looks up with a start.

'Jack Montague. He's probably not your type . . . I'll ask one of the make-up girls.' I pick up the tray and prepare to start walking.

'Wait!' she flusters. 'What film is it?'

'*South Pacific.*'

'Oh, well, I'd go just for that.' She tries to act cool.

'Really?'

'Yeah, anything by Rodgers and Hammerstein.'

'Is that right?' I smile. 'Shall we walk and talk?'

'Yes, yes.' She picks up her tray and leads the way.

I suggest we meet in the lobby but she says she'd rather go

home and change, so she can dispense with the kitchen smells, though personally I think they would be a plus in this case. We settle on 7.30 p.m. outside the ticket booth.

'And then maybe we could go to the diner after?' she suggests.

'For pie?' I cheer. 'Brilliant idea!'

With the table now set, I go to move on. 'There's just one more thing...'

'Yes?' She looks wary.

'Do you have a guy you could bring for me? He doesn't have to be a match romantically because I'm leaving town later tonight, just someone fun to make up the foursome?'

She thinks for a moment. 'My best friend is a big fan of musicals...'

'If he's free, that would be great!'

'Okay, I'll find someone to bring for sure.'

'Thank you.'

'No, thank you.' She looks a little giddy. 'Here, why don't you take this...' She offers me a pie, along with a handful of paper plates and plastic forks. 'For your team.'

Team Tummy is delighted.

'See you later!' I say, scurrying off towards the ballroom, just to give the impression that I know where I'm going.

Once I'm out of sight I pause and look down at my outfit. Not exactly diner-and-a-movie attire. I daren't go back to the room in case I get zapped back to the present. I wonder if I could pass off a beach towel as a kind of wrap?

And then I get an idea . . .

'Where's the costume room again?' I ask a woman scurrying by with a clipboard.

'Wardrobe? Just down on the left.'

'Great!' I say, holding up the pie as if I'm on a delivery mission.

I try the same thing with the security guard but he tells me that the room is closed for a private fitting.

My shoulders slump. 'Do you know how long they're going to be?'

'They're not here yet.' He looks at his watch. 'Should be here in ten.'

'Great! So I can drop this off?'

He looks dubious.

'Half the pie for them, half for Melvin,' I say, reading his name badge. 'Those were my instructions.'

Now I'm talking his language. I divvy it up and tell him I'll wait inside till they get here – just to check they don't need anything else from the kitchen.

He nods, his tastebuds too busy to think straight.

Right! Ten minutes to pick an outfit, I can do that.

You would think I would be spoiled for choice, rummaging through hundreds of outfits from a movie set, but of course the film is set in the twenties and I'm going on a date in the fifties. There is one frock from the section for Sweet Sue and her Society Syncopators I quite like – a black V-neck with long sleeves, a little shapeless but an improvement on my shorts. I tuck myself out of sight and slip it on. Suddenly I hear a noise. Was that the door?

As I move forward to check, I hear a voice calling, 'Is someone back there?'

I hesitate.

'Hello?'

She knows I'm here. She also sounds familiar. I stumble out from the racks and find Marilyn staring at me.

'I was just checking for moths,' I say.

Her brow furrows. 'No you weren't.'

'No I wasn't.' I sigh. I look over at the half a pie and decide that's not going to cut it either. 'Honestly? I just wanted to borrow an outfit for tonight.'

'You've got a date?' She brightens.

'Yes.'

She looks me up and down. 'With a priest?'

'No, no, it's a double date. I'm just going along to fix up a friend of mine.'

'But you don't want either of the men to find you attractive?'

'Well, it's complicated . . .'

'It can't be this complicated,' she says, waving her hand over the dress. 'Let's see if we can find something better.'

She leads me back down the aisle of dresses.

'How about this one?'

She holds out the infamous nude beaded dress from her kissing scene with Tony Curtis and I notice for the first time that, in amid the slashes of silver sequins, there's a heart-shaped cut-out on the back that would hit her right on the bottom.

'I'm just kidding,' she giggles. 'It's made to measure.'

I smile. 'Even if it weren't, you're the only woman in the world who could carry that off.'

She's already resumed her search. 'There's some outfits for the extras in the nightclub scene that might work – they're not so dated. Here!' She pulls out a simple, scoop-neck cocktail dress. 'We can jazz it up with some jewellery. Put it on inside out.'

'Inside out?'

'In case we need to pin it.'

'Okay . . .'

As I slip out of the Syncopator dress and return it to the rail, I call out, 'I hear you're quite the reader . . .'

'Oh, I love it,' she calls back. 'I love how I feel when my mind is discovering something new.'

'I know just what you mean!' I say as I unzip the dress. 'New ideas, new worlds, new ways of thinking . . .'

I hear her step closer. 'I think it's good for your character. Like Walt Whitman says, "Be curious, not judgemental."'

'Such wise words,' I agree as I emerge.

'Now that's more like it.' She has me turn and makes little tugs and adjustments. 'We just need to pin it at the waist.' She reaches for some safety pins.

'So who are you reading at the moment?'

She namechecks a mixture of classics and heavyweights: D. H. Lawrence, Hemingway, Freud . . . It's amazing how many of her favourite titles are still so current in my present day – *The Prophet* by Kahlil Gibran, *On the Road* by Jack Kerouac, *The Great Gatsby* by F. Scott Fitzgerald . . .

'That's quite a range,' I marvel.

'It depends how I'm feeling – you know, who I want to spend time with. Or what period in time I want to visit.'

My eyes widen.

'You can put the dress on the right way now,' she says, straightening up and then turning her attention to the accessories. The milky jade jewellery is perfect but the peep-toe shoes are a little higher than I would choose.

'Try walking more like this—'

Suddenly there's a knock at the door.

'Marilyn, darling?'

'Orry-Kelly!' She identifies the voice as her Oscar-winning costume designer. Motioning to me to keep quiet, she leans out to speak to him. 'I just need a few minutes with my friend then I'm all yours.'

'No worries.' I can now hear an Australian burr to his voice. 'I'll take a stroll.'

'Thank you!' She blows him a kiss. 'He's a genius,' she says, turning back to me. 'His clothes wrap around a woman like smoke.'

I sigh at the concept. The closest I've got to that was taking my Monsoon dress to the alternations guy on the corner. And then it shrank in the wash and I had to unpick all his hard work.

I watch as Marilyn rummages in a straw bag embroidered with flowers and pulls out a make-up bag. 'I only have a few things with me but at least we can add a little pizazz.'

As she strokes liner along my eyelids I feel her breath on me and inhale her perfume – I wonder if it really is Chanel N°5.

'I always cut my false lashes in half,' she tells me. 'It looks more natural if you place them on the edge. Hold still.'

As I look down I notice the print on her loose shirt dress for the first time – a selection of birds. It's not at all a look I'd expect her to go for but then again, she is just here for a fitting and it wouldn't take a lot of wiggling in and out of.

'And now for the cherry on top.' She then takes out a lipstick with gold casing. 'This is my favourite shade – Ruby Red!'

Marilyn Monroe's red lipstick on me. I have to look away so I don't lose it completely. If only James were here for this!

'Press your lips together,' she tells me, before applying another layer. 'And again.'

She finishes with a slick of Vaseline then invites me to take a look in the full-length mirror.

I blink back at my reflection. And then peer a little closer, my hand following the pronounced curve from waist to hip.

'What do you think?' She bites her lip.

'I think this is the most like a woman that I've ever felt.'

'Of course, none of this matters compared to what's in here.' She taps her head. 'But a girl still wants a guy to look her way.'

I smile. It's been a while since I hung out with my female friends, I'd forgotten how good it feels.

Before I leave, I voice my concern about returning the dress after the date.

She leads me over to the door and cracks it open.

'Melvin, can you do me a favour?'

'Of course, Miss Monroe.'

'I want you to remember this face when you see it later.'

He looks at me. 'Yes, ma'am.'

'And then once you've let her inside to change her outfit, I want you to forget it.'

He nods vigorously. 'Anything for you, Miss Monroe.'

'There, you're all set.'

I'm desperate to hug her, to try and infuse her with all the decades of love that I'm bringing back from the future, but I imagine she's had enough of hands reaching for her all day long. Instead, I say, 'You know if this acting thing doesn't work out for you, you'd make a great stylist. Or librarian . . .'

She gives a little giggle as she waves me off.

And my life is complete.

17

As I stand in the refurbished lobby, I wonder what the tipping point is for deciding it's time for a whole new look. This incarnation certainly feels brighter than the present day with large floral sofas and windows opening out onto a sunny porch. Instead of the vast chandelier centrepiece, there's an ornate, crown-shaped light. I'm considering heading up to the gallery to get a closer look when I see Jack.

If I thought he looked good as a surfy blond, he's ten times more attractive with his naturally dark, super-shiny hair. And, now he's standing up, I see he's considerably taller than I expected, lending him a distinctly Rock Hudson vibe as he makes his approach.

'Hi!' is all I manage as I look up at him.

'Wow,' he says, taking in my dress and then letting his gaze linger on my face. 'You look stunning!'

'Well, I had a little help from a friend.'

'Lucky me,' he says, offering me his arm.

'You're about to get a whole lot luckier...'

'Really?'

I roll my eyes. 'I don't mean with me.'

He tuts. 'I have to say, it's a little disconcerting having a stranger so eager to fix me up.'

'Well, technically I'm no longer a stranger – in fact, I told her we were old friends.'

'Oh really?'

'Yes, and that I just happened to have a couple of spare tickets to the movie.'

'That's probably a better line than the one you gave me about Cupid.'

'And yet yours is closer to the truth.'

He gives me a quizzical look and then says, 'You know, if you and I are supposed to be old friends, I think you should tell me all about us – help me get into character.'

'Well, let me see...' As we approach Orange Avenue, I decide we met in England when he was an exchange student and that we stayed in touch as pen pals over the years, so when I came to town we thought we'd meet up. 'Would you look at that beauty?'

Jack smiles as I'm distracted by a passing baby-blue Thunderbird with its immaculate white roof and signature circular window on the side.

'You like cars?'

'I like these kind of cars – the ones with pointy fins and

pastel-coloured paint jobs!' I stop myself short of saying, *They don't make them like they used to.* 'What about you?'

'It's kind of my main hobby. My uncle runs the El Cordova Garage around the corner. I used to spend my summers there, helping the mechanics. He has this great Chevy Bel Air – I wish I could take you for a spin.'

If only.

'So tell me . . .' he says.

'Yes?' I look up at him.

'What's your favourite fruit?'

I give a little snuffle, glad we're back on a neutral tack. 'Pineapple,' I tell him.

'Favourite TV show?'

'*I Love Lucy*?' I venture, hoping I'm getting the year right.

'Favourite movie star?'

'Jack Montague.'

He smiles. 'I've got a long way to go yet.'

'You'll do it,' I tell him. 'What made you want to be an actor anyway?'

'My dad,' he says simply. 'He used to do these magic tricks at parties and I'd see people looking at him with such wonder and I thought, *I want to do that – I want to entertain people!* You know, make them forget their worries and just get lost in the moment.'

I sigh, nodding my head, because he's caught me in that exact state – for a while I completely forgot that this wasn't my date.

*

'There she is!' I feel a curious sense of pride as I spy Jennifer beside the ticket booth. Earlier today her hair was tucked under a starched cap for kitchen hygiene reasons but now it falls in golden waves around her face. The absence of her chef's jacket reveals an athletic figure, the kind that would look especially good in tennis whites. Despite her cool demeanour, she flushes a pretty pink at the sight of Jack.

'There's no need to look quite so smug,' Jack mumbles as we approach her.

'Admit it, you're pleasantly surprised.'

'She's not you.'

'Well, nobody's perfect,' I shrug.

He grins back at me.

'Don't you look lovely!' I greet Jennifer with a kiss on the cheek, complimenting her on her rose-print dress, then taking in her male companion who's making quite the style statement in a colour-block cardigan and two-tone brogues.

'This is Teddy,' she introduces us.

'I like your outfit,' I tell him.

'I like yours.' He seems to be taking in every detail, like a fashion designer giving his model the once-over before she steps onto the catwalk.

'You'll never guess who styled me . . .' I lean in and whisper her name and the resulting shriek tells me we're going to be fast friends.

'Tell me everything!' he demands, linking arms with me as we head for the concession stand.

This really is a gorgeous cinema – art deco in style with sculpted mouldings, etched glass and low-hung lamps. As we huddle over the sweet display Teddy points out his favourites. I recognise two of the boxes from James's last work trip to New York – Hot Tamales with their cinnamon sting, and the pink and white Good & Plenty licorice pellets that look like pills from *Valley of the Dolls*. Behind us I hear Jack and Jennifer making small talk, chatting about their respective roles on set.

'And how do you know Chloe?' I hear her ask.

I turn back, checking he's going to stick to the script.

'Oh, we go way back,' he tells her. 'She's like a sister to me.'

I smile to myself. Nicely done.

Teddy ultimately decides he's going to get a large popcorn for us all to share, while Jack gets the drinks. We make it to the screen just as the overture begins, with Teddy first to step into the row, then me, then Jack, then Jennifer. As we settle into our seats and the luxuriously ruched curtain rises, I feel a sense of deep satisfaction. For the next couple of hours I don't have to engineer anything – I can just sit back and enjoy the film, letting Jack and Jennifer's pheromones do their thing. I just wish so many of his weren't pinging in my direction. I don't know that I've ever felt so aware of another human being. It's as if there's some super-charged forcefield running down his left side, warming my right arm and leg. Every now and again our elbows touch or his knee catches mine and I get way too much of a thrill. Way. Too. Much.

I sneak a look at Teddy as the screen fills with dozens of

all-singing, all-dancing Seabees (aka Navy construction workers) – with their cutesy white sailor hats, bronzed biceps, silver dog tags and faded denim, it's basically one big Jean Paul Gaultier fantasy. And then they break into 'There is Nothing like a Dame' and it seems as if every face in the audience is beaming back at them. Come the rousing conclusion, I want to stand and cheer and I rather suspect Teddy would like beefcake Stew Pot's number, not to mention his trouser tailor.

We're half an hour in when we see pewter-haired Emile de Becque for the first time. I smile to myself, imagining Ross wooing 'Arkansas' answer to Florence Nightingale'. Mitzi Gaynor as nurse Nellie is a doll, and it's so endearing to be privy to the couple's inner thoughts during their duet, especially since we hear his doubts, as well as hers. It makes me wonder what is going on in Jennifer and Jack's heads right now . . . Suddenly I'm actually glad I'm not in the running. If it was me on this date, then all I'd be thinking about is the possibility of Jack reaching for my hand. It's bad enough resisting making little comments to him. I miss talking to him. Perhaps one little quip couldn't hurt . . . I make the mistake of turning towards him just as he's reaching over me to get to Teddy's popcorn and our faces clash.

'Oops, sorry!' he says as he drops a few pieces of popcorn in my skirt.

As he goes to swipe them away I'm so sensitive to his touch that my whole body jolts and I splurge my lemonade down my skirt.

'Was that me?' He looks aghast.

'Not at all, totally my fault,' I fluster, getting to my feet. 'I'll just go mop it up.'

'Here, take this . . .' He offers his handkerchief.

'Thank you, I won't be a sec!' I scoot along the mercifully broad aisle, running straight into the ladies'.

Oh gosh, what a commotion! And then I think of the stain potential on my borrowed dress. Thank goodness I didn't get Coke. I douse the skirt with water and then dab at it with paper towels rather than use Jack's nice handkerchief. It even has his initials on it. JM. Perhaps a timely reminder that he's just one in a line of JMs, not my JM.

I have one wistful moment running my finger over the embroidery and then snap out of it. All I have to do is sit through the rest of the movie then get everyone to the diner. I'm confident the pie will do the rest. In the meantime I just need to stay out of trouble.

When I emerge, I find Jack leaning nonchalantly against the wall by the water fountain.

'What are you doing here?' I gasp.

'Just checking you're okay,' he shrugs.

'It was just lemonade.'

'It was just an excuse.'

My heart flips.

'Come on, we don't want to miss the film.'

He walks backwards ahead of me. 'I know you said you'll be gone by daybreak but we could still have the rest of the night together, just the two of us. We could leave right now . . .'

The look in his eye causes me to falter but I keep walking towards the screen.

'You thought about it for a second, didn't you?'

'For two seconds,' I concede. 'But it's still a no.'

'Are you absolutely sure?'

'It's for the best, I promise.'

He sighs and then pushes open the doors, only for us to be met with the opening bars to 'Some Enchanted Evening'.

'They'll stone us if we ruin this song.' Jack winces. 'Let's watch from here.'

He hustles me into a shadowy nook where even the light from the screen can't find us.

It feels utterly thrilling to be in the darkness with him. Add the bass of Emile's voice and the high-soaring strings, how could anyone resist the whispered invitation to dance?

As he draws me to him, I feel the warmth and muscular curves of his body through his shirt and his hand, placed so tenderly on my back. Surrendering to the sway, I lean my head on his shoulder, feeling a mixture of floating and tingling and rapture . . .

I'm both willing him to kiss me and praying that he won't, suspended in the limbo of longing. This man is not for me and yet I feel like I'm dancing with my destiny.

As the song culminates with a rousing call to *'never let her go'* he holds me so tight I can feel his heartbeat pounding alongside my own.

And then he releases me.

I step back in a daze.

'Okay,' he puffs, collecting himself.

'You missed the best bit!' Teddy hisses as we return to our seats.

'We were watching from the back, didn't want to disturb anyone.'

'Isn't Rossano a frowny dream?' Teddy enthuses.

I chuckle, huddling closer to him, trying to anchor myself away from Jack.

It feels all too apt when Mitzi Gaynor breaks into 'I'm Gonna Wash That Man Right Outta My Hair'. I hear you, Mitzi! I've got to let this attraction go. I feel guilty enough for having that one dance. That was not aiding Jennifer's cause. But it was just a minor blip. I've got her this far, I'll see her right from now on.

Oh! There's an intermission. I can't help but hoot as the screen shows the animation for the *'Let's all go to the lobby to get ourselves a treat'* ditty Ross serenaded me with on my first day. Then, as with everyone around us, the conversation turns to the cliffhanger we've been left with: Nellie finding out that Emile is the father of two children he had with a Polynesian woman – utterly shocking to her Southern sensibilities.

'He really should've mentioned it before he proposed,' Teddy decides.

'I agree, but isn't that an interesting way to approach the topic of racism?' I venture. 'Taking the nicest, most innocent character in the film and looking at why she would have such prejudices . . .'

'There have been a few clues about her mother's narrow-mindedness,' Jennifer notes. 'I just feel so lucky that my mother was the opposite – growing up in New York, visiting different neighbourhoods: Chinatown, Little Italy, Little Odessa ... She would even take me into the kitchens so I could see the chefs working with all these different spices and techniques ...'

Jack looks admiringly at her then mentions that his mother is of Mexican heritage, with innumerable recipes passed down through the generations.

'That's actually one of the reasons I wanted to come to California,' she laughs. 'To learn more about Mexican cuisine!'

'Well, if you ever want to talk chillies with my mother, it's her favourite topic.'

I smile, picturing Lilia in a violet silk apron, the world's most glamorous chef.

'What are your thoughts on chilli and chocolate?' I posture, thinking I'm giving them a shocking flash from the future, but Jack reveals that it's been a combination since Mayan times.

'Really?'

It seems Jack and Jennifer both love spicy food whereas Teddy and I prefer milder options. We really are a good match in so many ways ...

Oh, here we go – the film is starting again.

There's a moment after the 'Happy Talk' song where the young lieutenant gives his Polynesian girlfriend his grandfather's pocket watch and I get chills – I am sitting next to a man whose grandfather gave me *his* pocket watch. Could this be a sign that my matchmaking is back on track?

The mood lightens with a show for the troops and the mouthiest Seabee dressed in a coconut bra with a grass skirt doubling as long blonde hair. Jack gives a wolf whistle and Teddy claps delightedly. But then we're back to the American leads, still struggling with their love for someone from a different culture.

Mitzi's character says it is something born in her, she can't help it. But the young lieutenant disagrees – he says you've got to be carefully taught to hate and fear people whose skin is a different shade. I feel so proud of the medium of musicals, tackling the issue with such insight. It's just a little disheartening to realise that a film set in the early forties that came out in the late fifties is still so relevant in the twenty-first century. I know Marilyn would prefer everyone to be more curious than judgemental . . .

The film ends romantically, not with a big, dramatic kiss but with a subtle, symbolic gesture over a tureen of soup. I like to think this bodes well for foodie Jennifer.

She leans across us as the credits begin to roll. 'If we want to get a booth at Clayton's, we really should run there now.'

'Why don't you and Jack go on ahead?' I suggest. 'I think you're more built for speed than us.'

'Thank the Lord for that.' Teddy fans himself. 'I don't do sweat and fluster.'

'And I can barely walk in these shoes,' I confess.

So we take our sweet time, checking out the sailors that seem to have stepped straight off the screen. One young fella holds Teddy's gaze a little longer than entirely necessary as we pass.

'Do you feel you're living a kind of fantasy here?' I ask.

'Pretty much.' He grins.

He tells me he's originally from Midwest farm country and always felt like a misfit growing up. 'California suits me so much better. It feels freer here – even though there's still a lot of secrecy, at least there are people to have secrets with!'

I give a little chuckle.

'What about you – do you think you'll visit again?'

'If I had my way, I'd never leave.' I sigh – all the more emphatically as we enter the diner . . .

18

For every fan of *Grease*, Clayton's is peachy-keen jellybean.

The first thing that greets us is a 'Select-O-Matic' jukebox with speaker panels that look like metal grills from the classic cars purring by outside. The U-shaped countertop is lined with swivelly red leatherette chairs showcasing an array of perky ponytails, while the centre island is a-buzz with milkshake blending and a till that pings as it opens. Waitresses and bus boys weave around each other clearing empty plates, offering menus and balancing cherries on top of towering ice-cream sundaes.

Sandy and Danny – aka Jack and Jennifer – wave to us from a booth near the back and as Teddy slides in beside his bestie, I take the remaining place beside Jack. It's probably better than looking at him face on because I don't think I could stop my pupils dilating at his loveliness. Mind you, the fixtures and fittings are giving him a run for his money – I'm swooning at everything from the chrome napkin dispensers to the corner phone booth with its concertina folding door.

'This place is so great!' I enthuse. 'How long's it been here?'

'About seven years as Clayton's,' Jennifer tells me. 'But it was actually opened in 1939 by one of the first women to own a coffee shop.'

Jennifer then introduces us to our waitress, Ginger, who puts the pin-up in pinny as she sashays over to take our drinks order.

While the others get sodas I opt for coffee – I can't resist the chunky diner mugs and the opportunity to accept a tableside refill, just like they do in the movies. (A pretty lowly ambition considering what I've been up to today. Still...)

'Do you know what you want to eat?'

We all nod.

Again, I'm the odd one out – three burgers and fries to my one grilled cheese sandwich.

'I want to save room for pie!' I wink at Jennifer, only to give in and try Teddy's chocolate maltshake. With just one icy-gloopy slurp I already feel like I've eaten dessert.

'Does anyone have change for the jukebox?' Jack pulls a dollar from his pocket.

'*Yes!*' I reply with a little too much zeal, remembering my stash of coins from the envelope. 'Here.' I hand them out. 'Everyone pick a song.'

Each booth has its own tabletop jukebox with little metal tabs at the top so you can flip through the cards displaying the song options.

Teddy jumps in first with Bobby Darin's playful 'Splish Splash', then Jennifer chooses a surprisingly foxy 'Fever' by Peggy Lee. I half expect the lights to dim and for her to switch to a beatnik black outfit and slink along the counter, bewitching everyone with her staccato moves. She's a cool cat for sure, now excusing herself and taking Teddy with her, saying she wants to introduce him to the new waiter. Personally I think they just want the chance to discuss how the night is progressing.

'Having trouble deciding?' Jack asks me as I consider each track title, including the B-sides.

You'd think I would be at a disadvantage, this not being my era, but I know nearly all of the songs. (I also know that 1958 was the year that Madonna and Prince were born, but I keep that little nugget to myself.)

'Well, it feels such a loaded decision.' I bite my lip.

'Like this one song is going to represent your entire personality?'

'Exactly,' I laugh.

'How about I pick one for you, and you pick one for me?'

'Deal!' I brighten.

'I have the perfect one in mind.' He gets a mischievous look, covering his hand so I can't see the buttons he's pressing.

I look around at the other diners making their choices.

'How will I know which one you picked?'

'Oh, you'll know,' he smiles.

I feel a little thrill and then smirk to myself as I find the ideal one for him.

'Look away!'

I take great pleasure in leaning on him as I reach across to press B4.

And then our food arrives, Jennifer and Teddy return and we chomp and chat away, all the while shoulder-twitching to 'King Creole'.

'Not my choice,' I say.

'Me either,' Jack confirms. 'But it's a good one.'

I listen as the three of them marvel at how twenty-eight-year-old Elvis Presley is currently serving in the army and discuss how devastated he must be over the death of his beloved mother Gladys just last month. I ask after Priscilla but they say the name doesn't ring a bell.

And then a little number called 'Stupid Cupid' strikes up.

I dart a look at Jack. He gives me the nod but I say nothing as I don't want to make Jennifer feel self-conscious, not that I think she would be on home turf. She seems in her element with regular customers stopping to say hello and waitresses filling her in on gossip as they pass. Apparently one of the camera guys from *Some Like It Hot* just asked waitress Ginger on a date – next stop: screen test.

Just when I think it can't get any better, my song choice loads.

I picked 'That Old Black Magic' as a nod to Jack's family magic tricks but I hadn't quite thought through the lyrics. They are way more frisky than I anticipated, speaking of inner tingles and icy fingers running up and down your spine. The fact that the words are ping-ponging between a man (Louis Prima) and a woman (Keely Smith) just seems to amp up the sexual tension. Suddenly I feel Jack's hand make contact with my thigh.

'Pie for everyone?' I blurt, jolting forward and hastily beckoning to Ginger.

'Too full!' Jack holds up his hands. 'Can't do it.'

'Nonsense!' I rally, trying to quell my jumping bean nerves.

'I might be tempted,' Teddy concedes.

'How about we get a couple of slices for the table?' Jennifer suggests.

'Good call,' I agree.

Pie will get us back on track. I just have to hold it together for a few more minutes . . .

'One banana cream, one peach,' Jennifer tells her waitress pal, who mercifully turns the order around on a dime.

'That does look good,' Jack concedes as he eyes the wavy golden crust and inhales the buttery sweet scent.

'Just a taste?' I woo on Jennifer's behalf.

'No, really.' He holds his stomach.

'Jack!' I must look especially stern because he takes the fork from me, muttering, 'All right, one tiny bite!'

Jennifer pretends not to be on tenterhooks. Suddenly I'm nervous. How am I going to reconcile this pairing if he doesn't like her cooking?

'Now that is delicious,' he enthuses, taking another forkful.

'Try the peach!' I entice, sliding the plate towards him.

I can tell by his expression that his taste buds are in raptures. 'Wow.'

'Guess who made it?' I can barely contain myself.

He looks over to the heads bobbing around the kitchen area.

'Closer than that.'

'Hmmm . . .' He squints at the waitresses.

'It's someone at the table,' I cry, exasperated.

'You made this?' He turns to me.

I despair. *'Jennifer!'*

He grins cheekily. 'I'm just teasing.' And then he addresses her. 'These are really exceptional. I will now be coming to Clayton's every day. Maybe twice a day.'

'You know, I do have them at the craft services table every afternoon.'

'You do? I wish I'd known sooner.'

'Well, there's still a few days to go . . .' She holds his gaze, conveying the promise of so much more than pie.

He doesn't look away.

Judging from the pancake flip in my stomach, I'd say a connection has been made. Which is satisfying, but also heartbreaking. It's time for me to go. They need to be free to flirt and, honestly, I don't want to watch that.

I'm just preparing to get to my feet when Jack beats me to the punch, saying he is going to check out the larger selection of discs on the main jukebox.

I give him a head start and then tell Teddy and Jennifer it's time for me to tootle off.

'I need to get this outfit back to wardrobe!' I explain. 'I don't want to get anyone in trouble.'

'I still can't believe you got to play dress-up with Marilyn!' Teddy swoons.

'It has been a dream-come-true day,' I concede.

'For me too.' Jennifer gives me an acknowledging nod.

'Well, I'm glad,' I tell her. 'Here's to many more dreams fulfilled.'

We chink our respective beverages and then they kindly offer to cover my portion of the bill in return for the movie tickets, which is just as well because I now only have one dime to my name.

I take it with me as I make my way over to the handsome fella at the jukebox, giving him a nudge with my hip.

For a moment we sway in sync then I say, 'I just wanted to say goodbye and good luck.'

His face falls. 'You're leaving?'

I nod. 'It's time.'

He looks at me in such a way that I want to hook my fingers in his belt loops and pull him into a never-ending kiss. But I don't.

Instead, I go to hand him back his handkerchief.

'Why don't you keep hold of it, until next time?'

'Next time?' I feel a flair of hope.

'I like to think we'll meet again.'

'Me too,' I sigh, with maybe a little more intensity than I intended.

He smiles.

I look back at Jennifer. 'You know, it's just possible that woman is going to be the best thing that ever happened to you.'

'I want to believe you . . .'

'Then do,' I say. 'And send me on my way.'

He looks serious for a moment and then opens his arms to me. Friends would hug goodbye, I reason as I fall into him, revelling in his warmth and gorgeousness and giving myself permission to release all the affection in my heart. I sense him reciprocating and for a second the bliss is intoxicating. But all too soon the pleasure twists to pain as it hits home that I have to let go and walk away.

'Here,' I say, pressing the last dime into his palm. 'Make it count.'

He looks down at the coin and then leans his arm along the top of the jukebox, dutifully studying the options, as if he doesn't want to see me exit.

I'm gone before I hear his song choice.

My emotions are so strained I can't go straight back to the hotel. I need to pace this out. But every street I walk down seems to lead me back to Clayton's, testing me over and over again.

I stare wistfully at the entrance, fighting the urge to rush back in and steal him away. But I'd only be cheating myself. As I finally set my course for the Del, the tears begin to stream. I know I'm doing the right thing, it just feels quite the opposite to my heart.

I return the dress without any issues then take a last meander around the foliage of the central courtyard. As I trace my hand over the waxy leaves and velvety petals, I hear the faintest sound of someone singing. Just a haunting line or two then silence. When it starts again I move towards it – a lone female voice, infused with the kind of emotion you experience with your whole body.

It's coming from the Luau Room – closed for the night, but the door appears to be unlocked. I prise it open a little more . . . All is dark except for a pool of moonlight illuminating a living legend, reclining beside a mock waterfall.

Marilyn gasps as she catches sight of me, jumping up and ushering me in.

'How'd it go? Did they like your dress?'

I check for onlookers amid the bamboo screens but we are quite alone.

'Well,' I begin, 'the guy I can't like liked it too much and the one I could like was more interested in my accessories . . .'

She jolts her forehead with the heel of her palm. 'Wouldn't you know it?' And then she begins to circle me, tilting my face to the light. 'Now this is what I'm looking for!' she enthuses.

'What do you mean?'

'Your eyes . . .' she breathes.

What – tear-stained, confused, lovelorn? Is that what she's looking for? Apparently so . . .

'This is what I'm trying to convey with the song. I've been so happy this past week, I'd almost forgotten what this kind of heartache felt like.' She motions to a chair. 'Will you be my mirror?'

I hesitate, not quite believing the privilege of this intimate moment.

'Paula has gone to bed or I'd ask her . . .'

'No, no, of course I don't mind. It would be an honour.'

'Okay.' She shuffles, getting into position. 'I just want you to close your eyes for a minute . . .' She draws her hand across my face as if draping a chiffon veil. 'Think about him,' she begins. 'Think of how it felt to walk away from him, to know that you'll never find someone as special as him again . . . Yes, there we go . . .'

I go to wipe away my tear.

'Just let it fall,' she husks.

And so I do.

It feels such a release to let emotions stream out of me – all the sadness for all the relationship disappointments, all the times I've had to walk away from something bad, and now to walk away from something good . . . As my head falls forward, she begins to sing 'I'm Through With Love' . . .

I catch my breath. I remember this scene, it's near the end of the film. After all the laughs and the slapstick, the cross-dressing and the capers, there's this poignant moment with Marilyn perched on a piano, singing her broken heart out. She must have him or no one . . . Meanwhile Tony Curtis looks on from the sidelines, realising the pain he's caused and the love he feels.

I hadn't realised the full range of Marilyn's vocals until this moment – listening with my eyes closed, I take in the breathy, soulful sweetness. Even her voice is the embodiment of femininity, and I get goosebumps as her emotions entwine with my own . . .

All too soon it's over.

For a moment there's silence.

'I should get some sleep.' She hops up.

Still in a daze, I tell her I'm going to linger a moment.

She nods, gathering her cardigan then turning back as she gets to the door. 'You know what else Walt Whitman says?'

'Tell me.'

'Keep your face always toward the sunshine and the shadows will fall behind you.' She gives a little shrug. 'It's not always easy but I think he's right, it's important to know how to be happy, even when you're sad.'

It takes me a second to process the concept, as contradictory as the icon stood before me. Here she is with all her deep-rooted emotional pain, still so sweet and radiant. My heart may be hurting but there's still so much to be grateful for. I mean, look who I'm talking to . . .

'Thank you,' I croak. 'For everything. And I hope you know how utterly adored you are, not just now but for all eternity.'

She smiles and blows me a kiss. 'Sweet dreams!'

'Goodnight, Sugar,' I whisper as she disappears into the darkness.

*

When I do head upstairs to my room, I realise I am smiling. Instead of feeling drained and forlorn I am now brimming over with gratitude. Because the fact is, I'm not through with love. I said I was prior to this trip, it really didn't seem worth the risk or the effort, but even just a few hours with Jack has challenged that notion. And just because I can't have him, it doesn't mean I can't feel that way again. I may not even have to wait that long – if Jack and Jennifer do get together, that only leaves me one more trip back in time. Besides, they say that character traits skip a generation which would mean, in a roundabout way, that Jack would be coming back to me. And that's the heart-swirling thought I take to bed.

Present day

19

'That's a very particular look you have on your face, Ms Sinclair.' Ross gives me an assessing glance as we prepare to step into the midday sun.

'What's that?' I blink innocently before slotting my sunglasses over my still-misty eyes.

'People will say you're in love,' he sing-songs.

'I . . .' I go to protest but I can't find a single word to deny it.

'You met someone!' He darts in front of me. 'What happened? Spill, spill!'

'Don't get too excited.' I keep walking. 'It was just a brief flirtation and it can't go anywhere because he's with someone else.'

'Oh phooey.'

'Phooey?' I laugh as he catches me up.

'No idea where that word came from! Either way, I want to hear every morsel over our picnic. We just need to swing by Clayton's to pick up the pie.'

'Clayton's!' I exclaim, stopping suddenly.

His eyes narrow. 'Is that where you guys . . .?'

I nod.

'You think he'll still be there?' Ross gasps. 'Does he work there?'

'No, no. I'm just curious to see how it's changed.'

Ross frowns at me. 'Since last night?'

'What? Oh. Yes – well, it was dark. I'm sure it'll look completely different in the daylight.'

'You're still a little giddy, aren't you?'

'Little bit. Mostly just hungry!'

'Just as well,' he says, raising the picnic basket on his arm and then raving about the amazing home-baked pies. Like I don't already know . . .

He's still chatting away as we step inside. Aside from the customers in their modern-day clothing very little has changed. The big jukebox is still in pride of place by the door.

'Here, why don't you pick a song while we wait?' Ross hands me a couple of quarters then heads to the till.

I'm glad to see there are still songs I recognise from 1958, though I'm slightly bemused to also find little typed cards for Pat Benatar and Elton John.

I'm about to reprise Elvis's 'King Creole' when a vinyl disk separates from the line-up and flips into place beneath the needle. Someone's beaten me to it.

My stomach registers the stirring strings before the lyrics even begin.

'*Some Enchanted Evening . . .*'

No! I look around, scanning the customers perched up at the bar. Is Jack here? I mean, he could be. Clayton's would always have a special place in their hearts . . . But there's no match.

'You okay?'

I look up at Ross's concerned face. 'I've got to talk to you about something.'

'I knew there was more to it!' he cheers. 'The park is five minutes from here. If we're lucky, we'll have it to ourselves and you can tell me *everything*.'

'You're not going to believe half of it,' I warn him as he takes my arm.

'Oh, come now, today is our *Wizard of Oz* day. It can't be any stranger than an L. Frank Baum plot. Can it?'

Ross insists we do the 'We're Off to See the Wizard' step-skip walk and for a moment I believe my sundress is pale blue gingham and I have a scarecrow on my arm.

'And this, my darling Dorothy, is Star Park.'

It's a neat little spot – half park, half roundabout with five roads fanning off, like the points of a star. One leads to the Coronado Historical Association, one to the Del, one to the beach, one deeper into the neighbourhood and one back to Clayton's. Though all roads are leading there in my mind.

'So, here's a little guessing game for you.' Ross draws my attention to the homes forming a circle around us. 'Which one of these do you think L. Frank Baum lived in?'

I scan the options. Two are tucked behind a high redbrick wall so I can't really assess them, the sprawling Spanish hacienda looks better suited to a movie star, the pale lemon clapboard lacks the vibrancy of the Yellow Brick Road but the blooms bursting out around the gate of the storybook cottage are positively Technicolour.

'That one!' I make my call.

Ross nods. 'I would have chosen it too. It's actually the pale yellow one.'

'No!' I twist back for a closer look, only now spotting the mock street sign saying *Wizard of Oz Avenue*. 'Well, what do you know!'

Ross tells me that the Baums were regular guests at the Del before they lived here, and still dined at the Crown Room restaurant after they became residents.

'Frank even designed the first crown-shaped lights that inspired the ones hanging there today.'

'I just saw those yesterday!' I gasp as I settle onto the blanket he has laid out. 'So did he write *The Wizard of Oz* here?'

'Not the first one, but the next four in the series. And then there was this short story called *Nelebel's Fairyland* . . .' He leans in, conspiratorially. 'Nelebel gathers together this motley crew of woodland sprites, giants and immortals to create a paradise beside the Pacific, and guess what they called it?'

'What?'

'Coronado!'

'Noooo!' I lean back contentedly. 'This is so great.'

'You ready?' Ross has been busily arranging our goodies under cover of the red check cloth and is now gearing up for the big reveal. 'It's really more of a *Wizard of Oz*-themed puzzle than a picnic,' he advises. 'Let's see if you can make the connections.' He whips back the cloth with a 'Ta-daaaa!' cheer.

I reach for the Lion Bar. 'Really?'

He laughs. 'Not too much of a mystery with that one. James brought the first one over from the UK but I can even get them on Orange Avenue now.' He hands me a tub of yellow gloop. 'This is related.'

I take a sniff. 'Cowardly custard?'

'Yes!' he cheers. 'It justifies the pie.'

'Good thinking! Is that a ruby grapefruit for ruby slippers?' I point to the boule-size citrus.

'You got it!'

'If we were in England, you could have had a Ruby Murray!'

'What's that?' He frowns.

'A curry.'

He grimaces slightly then helps me out with a clue for the Tin Man. 'Think of the song – *If I only had . . .?*'

'An artichoke heart!' I exclaim, as he prises open a Tupperware lid. 'Please tell me you don't have brains for the Scarecrow?'

'No, just wheat.' He points to the bread. 'Of course it's has to be a *tin* loaf!'

I chuckle. 'I'm guessing the pink meringue is Glinda the Good Witch but you've got me at the guacamole . . .'

'Okay, this was James's idea – it's the Wicked Witch of the West after she's melted!'

I laugh out loud. 'That's so him.'

I take in the Auntie Em and Ems then ask, 'Is that a flask of Doro-tea?'

Ross claps his hands together. 'I never thought of that, it will be from now on! So, is there anything you actually want to eat?'

I point to the pie.

'Wise woman.'

He cuts me a generous slice. I take a bite.

'Good?'

I happily smack my lips. Unless I'm very much mistaken Jennifer's spiced peach recipe is still going strong . . .

The time has come for our little ceremony. We take our precious James pebbles and gently press them into the earth at the base of the tree overlooking the Baum house. Kneeling side by side, Ross treats me to a gentle, lilting a-capella version of 'Somewhere Over the Rainbow'.

I close my eyes and let the sun shine through my eyelids. It all seems so dreamy, so other-worldly, that I feel sufficiently emboldened to ask him, 'Given the chance, would you follow the Yellow Brick Road?'

'You bet!' he enthuses.

'Even if there were a few dramatic twists and turns along the way?'

'That's life, isn't it? It's never a straight road, not for anyone.'

I turn to face him. 'Ross, do you trust me? I mean, I know we've only known each other a few days . . .'

He holds my gaze. 'James trusted you – with his life *and* his afterlife – so, yes, I trust you.'

'I want to tell you something but I think it might be easier to show you – because it might not work and then I've made a big deal out of nothing.'

'Does this have to do with the guy from last night?'

'In a way but it's a bit more involved than that.'

He gives an easy shrug. 'I have no clue what you're talking about but, whatever it is, I'm game.'

I smile appreciatively, glad he's not the cynical type. 'The thing is, if we do this, there's quite a big risk that the life you would come back to would not be the same one you're living now.'

I can see he's trying to process what I'm saying, trying to find some sense to it. 'You're saying that this thing we may or may not do could change everything?'

'Yes.'

'I'm okay with that.'

'But you have a good life. Do you really want to mess with that?'

'I do have a good life,' he concurs. 'And I'm so grateful for it. But I also have an unfulfilled craving within me. I've had it ever since James left. So I'm open to change.'

I study him, feeling a sense of responsibility for this human being who has been nothing but wonderful to me since we met. Then again, who better to share this utterly unique experience with?

'Right.' I nod, busily packing up our things. 'We need to head back to the hotel and when we get to my room I'm going to tell you a date, a particular year actually, and you're going to tell me if you want to go back to that year.'

'And do what?' he frowns.

'Well,' – I take a breath – 'if my estimation is correct, there's a very real chance you could have frosted, flipped hair again.'

His eyes widen and he hurriedly throws the last items in the basket. 'What are we waiting for?'

1985

Jason & Brooke

20

On the way back to the room I tell him everything, from the Oracle on the plane to Jasper in the Victorian era, Jesse in the twenties, Jack last night. I ask him to listen to me as if I'm describing a film script he's going to star in, so he can suspend his disbelief.

'Love it!' he cheers as we approach my room. 'Are you sure we shouldn't pop back to mine to get the outfits?'

'No, they have hair and make-up covered. That part actually happens really fast.'

'Well, that would be a blessing, I've never been good at sitting for hours at a time getting prosthetics fitted.'

'Ross.'

'Yes?'

'You seem to be taking this all really well.'

'I think I've got a handle on it. I mean, it's not so far off from an escape room or murder mystery event but with matchmaking instead of murder. I wonder if I'll know any of the actors?'

Of course he doesn't believe me.

'I just don't want you to be freaked out – it's very authentic.'

'Come on, who are you talking to here? This is what I do for a living. And don't worry, I'm not going to spoil it by pointing out all the modern-day giveaways.'

I give him a sideways look: 'How would you feel about betting a Hotel Del breakfast that you can't find a single trace of present day?'

'You're on!' he cheers.

I can't deny it, I do like a wager.

'So what now?' Ross rubs his hands together as we reach my door.

'I scan the card and we find out the date.'

I hold my breath as I wait for the four red numbers to appear...
1-9-8-5.

'It's happening!' I turn to Ross, heart pounding. 'We're going back to the year that you met James! Of course, there's no guarantee it will be that night but you're going to get your eighties tunes for sure!'

'Is there going to be dancing? Did he arrange this?'

'You know, that would explain a lot,' I concede, picturing my friend in the grand control room in the sky.

And then Ross gets a strange look on his face. 'Is he really dead?'

'I'm afraid he is now. But beyond this door, who knows?'

'Come on, open up!'

'We have to go in together,' – I reach for his hand – 'as soon as I press in the code.'

'How about I carry you over the threshold?'

'That's not necess—*Ross!*' I squeal as he scoops me up, kindly making sure my dress fabric is covering my modesty. Why are all my most romantic moments happening with ineligible men?

'Press the code!' he urges.

I do.

There's a surge, a rushing-whooshing sensation as we cross over and then . . .

'What the . . .?' He takes one look at the baggy trousers now filling his arms and drops me.

'I knew that was a bad idea,' I sigh, retrieving the angular black sunglasses that have fallen from my head.

'How did you . . .? What the actual . . .? Look at your hair!'

'I can wait,' I tell him. 'Look at yours.'

'Oh my god!' he squeals as he reaches the mirror. 'I mean, *oh my god!* This is exactly how I used to have it! Did you give them pictures?'

'Give it a tug.'

'I don't want to mess it up, they've got it so . . .' He trails off as he leans closer to the mirror. His hand goes to the corner of his eyes, where his laughter lines used to be. 'I've been airbrushed.'

Now this is new. Whereas I have been thirtysomething

Chloe every era, Ross has gone all the way back to his twenty-something self from the eighties.

'I told you they were good.'

'I'm never leaving. They could make a fortune with this service! It doesn't even feel taut!' He peers closer, as if looking for tape or glue. 'Am I wearing soft-focus lenses? It's like looking through an Instagram filter.'

I get to my feet, sending a strand of pearls swinging out alongside black rosary beads. Still he's going . . .

'You know, I thought for a minute this was my actual *Choose Life* T-shirt but it doesn't have the hole in it.' He tugs at the side then looks down at his white boxer boots. 'A-ha! That's why you were in my closet – sussing out my shoe size!'

I'm in no rush to set him straight. This is too much fun. Especially now he's checking me out. Even before I reach the mirror I've got a pretty good idea of how I might look – black lacy basque, white crochet gloves, wrists full of bangles. We've got to be talking Madonna à la *Desperately Seeking Susan*.

'Get into the groove, why don't you?' Ross hoots. 'The detailing on the back of your jacket is so spot on.' He turns me so I can see the embroidered pyramid in the mirror. 'And your hair is so crispy!'

I touch it – yup, scrunchy-crunchy with a backcombed fringe and big black bow knotted on top. I love the make-up – extra black lashes, matt red lips and a single beauty spot.

'Is there going to be karaoke?' Ross asks. 'We should do the

Madonna and George Michael duet that never was. Could you carry off the Aretha vocals from 'I Knew You Were Waiting'?'

I wonder if he has any idea, any at all, about how apt that song would be? The notion that something deep in you knew that your special person was waiting to meet you and you never lost faith in finding them. Except, of course, I've never felt that. I have doubted and regretted and faltered every step of the way. I think it would be wonderful to experience that casual laughter as I recall my prior romantic disappointments. Can you imagine being able to shake off bad relationships just like that, refusing to carry them forth and let them define your future? I want that. If only such a thing were possible *without* first having to meet the love of your life who makes it all right.

'Boombox!' Ross suddenly exclaims and starts clattering through the cassettes. 'Tears for Fears, Thompson Twins, Depeche Mode! Oh, this is all too fabulous!'

While he is occupied I sidle over to the envelope by the door and take a surreptitious look at the photos within.

Jason Montague and Brooke Miller. My first impression is that he's a little distant and she's a little different. He has a slim face with pronounced cheekbones and a pretty-boy pout but not a lot going on in his eyes. She looks more edgy with a tufty, asymmetrical cut, bright paint-spatter make-up and a street-smart sass.

'Chloe!'

'Yes?' I say, quickly tucking them away.

'You ready?'

'For what?'

He presses play.

'Jitterbug!'

It takes precisely one second to identify the song as 'Wake Me Up Before You Go-Go'.

Ross's enthusiasm is contagious. As our finger clicks become hand claps and our arms swing and hips jive, he well and truly puts the boom-boom into my heart. I'm so glad he's here with me. So, so glad!

'I think you're the most fun person I've ever met!' I call over the music.

And suddenly, as I think of all my disappointments – all the men who didn't want to dance with me and all the ones who led me a merry dance – I just laugh. *I just laugh* . . .

As we collapse on the bed to catch our breath, Ross turns to me and asks, 'So what was in that envelope you were looking at?'

It's time to brief him on the mission.

Sitting up, I retrieve the photos and hand them to him. 'These are the two people we have to matchmake tonight.'

'No way!' he hoots. 'You can't put these two together.'

This is not the reaction I was expecting.

'What do you mean?'

'Well, poor Brooke, it's hard to forget – she did this terrible, desperate rendition of "Like a Virgin", obviously worse for wear, spilling out of her dress. I heard later she was trying to woo Jason but it had the opposite effect.' He grimaces. 'She was actually, er, *unwell* right on him.'

'No!' I blanche.

'I don't suppose she ever lived it down. I mean, one minute you're president of the debate team, everyone thinks you're the smartest girl in town and the next . . .'

I grimace. 'So this one night ruined her reputation and her chances?'

He nods.

'What about Jason?'

'Well, he always seemed such a decent guy, stellar at sports but too sensitive to be a jock. Him and Brooke used to be close, they were neighbours growing up. But then his actor dad got this hit series and all of a sudden he's mixing with all these super-rich celebrity kids and I guess it turned his head. I didn't see much of him after the karaoke night. I heard he ended up in rehab but I don't know if it was true.'

I flump back onto the bed. This is bad news all round.

'His dad was so lovely . . .' I sigh.

'Jack Montague? Yeah, everyone in the business speaks highly of him. I think he took a couple of years out and moved the family to Colorado to try and get Jason back on track. Perhaps he stayed out there?'

'Jason?'

'It's possible,' Ross shrugs. 'I never did see him here again.'

'Have you ever seen Jack?' I ask, a little too invested in his response.

He nods. 'I've seen him around Coronado. He's usually here for Comicon because of that sci-fi series, I always forget the name, but he has a loyal fan base, still gets plenty of character roles.'

I have a million more questions, not least whether Jack is still married to Jennifer, but Ross is on his feet now, reaching for the hairspray and carefully pinching and placing the front pieces of his hair.

'Honestly, I'm amazed they agreed to a reprise of that night, unless their therapist recommended a do-over so they could move on with their lives. It's going to be weird to see them in their fifties. I doubt I'll even recognise them.'

'Oh, I think you will,' I mutter, joining him at the dressing table and toying with a lip gloss with a rollerball applicator. 'So, hypothetically, if we were looking at this as a complete do-over, going back to their twenties . . .'

'Yes?'

'Do you think things could have gone better between Jason and Brooke if they'd made different choices that night?'

'Well, for starters, if she hadn't mixed her drinks or even chosen a different song. Or no song.' He winces.

'Not a good singer?'

'Terrible.'

'And him?'

'Well, that's trickier. He'd have to be ready to step away from his new clique to stand a chance of having independent thoughts and feelings. He's more of an introvert. I never really knew what he was thinking.'

I nod, deciding I'm going to have more luck targeting Brooke. And then, just as I'm giving myself a delicate spritz of Charlie perfume, it hits me with all the intensity of my Victorian smelling salts, shocking my brain. Why hadn't I thought of this sooner?

'The night that Brooke sang "Like a Virgin" . . .'

'Yes?' Ross looks up.

'This wasn't just any party, was it?'

'No.' He smiles. 'It was the night I met James.'

21

'I've never seen you move so fast!' Ross scurries down the corridor after me. 'What's the sudden rush?'

'Sorry, folks, not this way!' Two men in sharp suits with plastic coils snaking from their ears step in front of us, palms up.

'Oh, I'd forgotten!' Ross laughs. 'Now this is great attention to detail. Good work, guys!'

'What is it?' I ask as Ross leads us back up the stairs to take a different route.

'President Reagan was here with Nancy the night of the party. She was giving one of her *Just Say No* speeches – you know, her anti-drug campaign?'

'Those guys looked pretty serious.' I shudder.

'Well, it was only a few years after the assassination attempt.'

'Gosh.' I gulp. 'I'm surprised by how blasé people are to have a president in town.'

'Ronnie was an old friend of the hotel - he was actually the first man to cross the Coronado Bridge!'

'Seriously?'

'Yes, he was governor of California at the time.'

'You are a mine of information.'

'I am,' he agrees, then claps his hands together. 'So, you ready to have some fun?'

I stop him before he opens the door to the party. 'Just in case we get separated . . .'

'Yes?'

'Could you just give me a quick lay of the land?'

He steps back, taking a moment to collect his thoughts. 'Well, there was a small stage for the karaoke, a dance floor in front of that, two bars, one each side, a backstage area with an amazing selection of costumes and a couple of dressing rooms in case you need to change – you are going to do a number, aren't you?'

'I'm not sure I'd have time . . .'

'Too busy matchmaking?'

'Exactly,' I confirm. 'Speaking of which, you don't happen to recall at what point Brooke mangled "Like A Virgin"?'

'Let's see . . . I was second to last and I'd say she was a couple before me.'

The door opens a crack, giving us a blast of 'You Spin Me Right Round' by – of all people – Dead or Alive.

'Ha!' Ross cheers. 'This was the song that was playing when I first saw James.'

There's no time to waste!

'Ross?'

'Yes?'

What can I possibly say that can really prepare him? The only thing now is for him to see for himself.

I don't know which of us has wider eyes as we step inside. It's as if every eighties icon is parading before us – an artfully made-up Boy George, a joyful Whitney wannabe, a flame-haired Cyndi Lauper ... The guests have gone to so much trouble to style themselves after their idols we can barely move for all the androgynous layering and unisex backcombing.

'There's Jason!' Ross points across a sea of ruffles and bandanas to a complete five-piece set of Duran Duran. He's clearly come as John Taylor, taller and leaner than the rest, all floppy hair, high cheekbones and rolled-up suit sleeves.

I'm guessing the Simon Le Bon lookalike is the ringleader of the clique – he has that cocky air about him and whereas everyone else in the room seems quite chatty and upbeat, he's doing a lot of sneering and pointing.

'Coming through!'

As a curl-lipped Billy Idol squeezes past holding a drink aloft in each hand he inadvertently snags his studded belt on Ross's T-shirt. Not realising what is holding him back, he gives a tug and ...

'The hole! The hole in my T-shirt!' Ross exclaims. 'That's just how I got it.'

'Dude, I'm so sorry!' Mock Billy apologises.

'Don't worry, don't worry at all.' He waves him on his way and then turns to me and confesses, 'That's not quite how I reacted the first time.'

Ross weaves through the crowd in a daze, acknowledging friends including host Makoto in a blond wig and white shirt, dressed ironically as David Sylvian from Japan. 'This is exactly how I remember it. Exactly.'

Suddenly he stops, incredulous.

I follow his gaze and then gasp as if my heart has been tugged clean out of my chest. It's James, appearing before us as a young man, the version of him I've only ever mooned over in photos. I stand mesmerised, watching as he takes a sip of drink, his dark hair falling over his left eye, partly covering his glass. He's dressed head-to-toe in black, a chain earring dangling down to his shirt collar, dark eyes lined with kohl. He looks so smouldering and enigmatic I have butterflies on Ross's behalf.

'Is he real?' Ross's voice cracks.

I can only nod, my eyes filling with tears. I've been to such pains to convince my heart that I'll never again be able to fulfil the craving to see him, and yet here he is. Just a few feet away.

'So everything you were saying about travelling back in time . . .?'

'Don't ask me how, but yes, it's all true.'

'Will he be able to see me?' He takes a step forward. 'Can I speak to him?'

'There's only one way to find out!' I egg him on. 'Just stick to how you were that first night and you should get the same results.'

'I can't believe we're doing this!' He reaches for my hand.

'Not me.' I dig in my heels. 'I can't go.'

'What?' He turns back in confusion.

'He doesn't know me,' I say, forcing down the lump in my throat. 'This is decades before we met.'

'But I can introduce you!'

'You need to introduce yourself first,' I remind him. 'Go on! I can't do anything to mess up this night for him – this is his best memory, meeting you and all that followed . . .'

Ross hesitates, conflicted.

'Don't miss your slot,' I urge.

I am on tenterhooks until Ross reaches him, afraid someone else will step in and throw off their timing, but as their eyes meet, I breathe again. The showman and the smartypants – Ross loving James's English accent, James amazed that someone so manly and athletic would be so clearly into him.

It's only right I hold back. Even at the best of times James wouldn't want me throwing my arms around him or making a scene. I take a breath and then move towards the bar, figuring I'll be less conspicuous sipping on a drink as opposed to standing gawping in the middle of the room.

'Vodka cranberry, please.'

I'm about to take my first sip when the glass gets chinked away from my lips . . .

'Madonna! Ma-double!'

I look round and see my mirror image – scrunchy blonde hair, whisked-up brows, red lips. I can't place her outfit for a second as the top half is sheathed in a denim jacket, but the abundance of white net spewing from waist to mid-calf tells me she's 'Like A Virgin' Madonna.

Aka Brooke.

Aka my potential future mother-in-law.

'I'll have the same as my twinnie!' she instructs the barman as she drains the last of her drink.

'Did you just drop an earring?' I ask, pointing to the floor.

'Did I?'

As she bends down to check the carpet I hiss, 'No alcohol in hers.'

'Good call,' the barman confirms.

When she returns to an upright position – well, more of a tilting, swaying angle – she asks which song I'm doing.

'Oh no, I'm just an observer,' I tell her.

'Nooooo! You have to!' she insists, gripping my black bangled wrist with her pearl-draped one. 'I mean, I can't sing either but I figured if I'm wearing this . . .' She gives me a flash of her amply filled white lace bustier.

Oh jeez. I tug her jacket closed, swiftly buttoning it at the collar. 'You know, I heard they've taken "Like A Virgin" off the playlist.'

'What?' She sloshes half her new drink down me, which is fine – black trousers . . .

'I know, bummer, right? Something about the lyrics being in bad taste.'

'Nooooo! I have to do that song!' she wails. 'I've been practising all week.'

'I'm sure they've got other Madonna songs – how about "Crazy for You"?'

'And look like a complete sap?' Her nose scrunches in disapproval. She then turns and looks despairingly at Jason. 'I don't know what I was thinking anyway! It's all hopeless.' With that she tugs off her blonde-streaked wig, revealing her now-flattened crop.

'You'd make a great Annie Lennox,' I venture, fluffing her hair back to life. 'Just add a suit and tie?'

She gives me a withering look. 'That woman has the voice of an angel. Besides, subtle has got me nowhere. The idea was to shock.' And with that she flumps on the floor, all but engulfed in her white net meringue. 'Where's my gum?' She starts frantically rooting through her bag. 'I need my gum!'

I sit down beside her, collecting the items she discards – make-up bag, Walkman, 'Like a Virgin' cassette case. I give it a shake. The tape is inside, so what's in the Walkman? I crack it open and find Grandmaster Flash & Melle Mel's 'White Lines'.

'You like rap music?'

'I listen to this all day long on repeat. But there isn't one rap song in the karaoke book. I checked.'

I glance over to the stage, where a pint-sized Prince is

currently adding his own flourishes to 'Let's Go Crazy'. And then I get an idea. 'What if you created your own rap?'

She squints at me. 'With no music?'

'You could use any song – it's just a backing track. Just ignore the lyrics that come up on the screen. Or go back and forth, mix it up. That way you'll be speaking more than singing.'

I can tell the idea appeals. I'm dying to reference Jay-Z and Alicia Keys' 'Empire State of Mind' but of course that's way too far in the future.

'You were on the debate team, right?' I continue my campaign. 'How about you pick a song where you can argue a point of view, like a battle?'

'Wouldn't I need someone to argue with?' she asks before blowing a big pink bubble.

'There must be a song with a message you oppose,' I say as I haul her back to her feet. 'Let's go have a look.'

We take a copy of the song book and head into the wardrobe room where the music is muffled by all the racks of fabric.

'You could take issue with Whitney Houston saving all her love for a married man,' I suggest, only to decide that it's probably the wrong crowd for that – bit young. 'Or maybe there's a Madonna one we could toy with?' I ask as I head over to the M rail of clothing, keen to get her into a top she can't spill out of. 'How long have we got anyway?'

She flips to the front of the book for the performance list, running her finger down the page. 'Sade's "Smooth Operator" is up next, then it's The Power Station, "Some Like it Hot"–'

'What did you say?' My head jerks around.

She looks up at me. 'You know the band with Robert Palmer and two of the guys from Duran Duran?'

'Oh my god . . .' I rifle along the rail – is it possible? 'Yes!' I cheer as my hand meets a sheath of pink satin. 'I've got it! This is so perfect you won't even believe it!'

'What?'

I return to her side, switching out the cassette in her Walkman and rewinding to the first track. 'Listen to this!'

Her frown eases as she hears the lyrics. 'I have a lot to say on this subject!'

'I thought you might!' I smile back at her.

'Of course, you would have to do this with me – if we're going to switch back and forth, like alter egos.'

My heart pounds with adrenalin. No one is in a better position than me to do this, I know that. I might just need one more drink. And Brooke one less.

'Okay. I'll do it. I'm just going to get us some water and tell them you've changed your song. You concentrate on jotting down some lines, okay?' I quickly pull together what will be my outfit and bundle it into a 'reserved' bag. 'And keep an eye on this.'

'Will do. Just one more thing . . .'

'Yes?'

'Who are you?'

'Me?' I stall.

'I mean, you seem to know me, know my life. But I don't know you at all.'

I'm too old to pass myself off as a school friend of the birthday boy, too young to be friends with his parents.

'I'm with the hotel,' I tell her. 'It's my job to make sure the party is a success.'

She holds my gaze a little too long and then shrugs. 'Okay!'

22

I'm only gone a matter of minutes, first finding the woman with the clipboard of performances and updating Brooke's listing, then grabbing some water. I do have a quick look around for Ross and James but I can't see them so I head straight back to Brooke, only to discover she is not alone.

'What the . . .' I lunge at the man crouched beside her offering her a swig from a glass bottle. 'What's going on?'

'It's just tequila!' he protests as I snatch the bottle from his hand.

No wonder her stomach was in turmoil!

I look a little closer at the wearer of the tasselled leather jacket and snow-washed jeans. Ah. So this is what Alfred slash Freddy slash Alfie looks like as a twentysomething.

'Brooke, do you want to pick out your new outfit? I just need a private word with . . .'

'Alan,' he responds. 'You can call me Al.'

'What are you up to?' I hiss, as she disappears into the rails of clothes.

'What do you mean? It's just a bit of Dutch courage.'

'Is that all?'

I mean, is that all he has in mind, but he seems to think I'm enquiring about something else.

'Well, I do have a little something extra for my special friends . . .' He reaches into his inside pocket and pulls out a little packet of white powder. 'One sniff and you'll feel like a million bucks.'

My heart judders in my chest. Is this the man responsible for Jason's trip to rehab?

'First line is free,' he entices, stepping closer.

'Not here,' I tell him, grabbing his elbow. 'There's too many people around. Come to my room?'

'Sure!' His eyes bulge expectantly.

'We don't have much time,' I say, hustling him roughly towards the door.

'Aren't the rooms this way?' He looks confused as I divert him towards the lobby.

'First I want to introduce you to my friend Nancy.'

'Nancy?'

Right on cue, two Secret Service agents step out in front of us. 'Sorry, ma'am, this area is off limits.'

'Oh, but my friend so wanted to hear Nancy's speech.'

'It's a private function.'

'But they have a common interest,' I say, opening his jacket.

'What are you doing?' He panics, swatting my hand away.

As he tries to make a run for it, two other security officers apprehend him, patting him down and pulling out three more bags of white powder.

'We'll take it from here, ma'am,' they tell me.

I heave a sigh of relief as they bundle him away. Sometimes you have to enlist the professionals.

'Oh my gosh, I thought you weren't coming back!' Brooke scrambles to my side as I enter the costume area. 'Are we really doing this?'

'Of course,' I tell her. 'You couldn't look any cuter!'

She's switched to tightly belted ripped jeans and a white vest and sprayed her hair to match her bubblegum, putting me in mind of a young P!nk.

'You don't think the contrast between us is going to be too great?'

'Well, that's just the point!' I say as I begin my transformation.

On goes the tight stocking cap. I quickly tuck any stray hairs under the elastic trim then reach for the perfectly coiffured peroxide blonde curls. Brooke helps me get the hairline aligned, then takes a diamanté clip from her own hair to make sure it holds in place.

'Wow,' she coos. 'It's basically the most glamorous hairstyle that ever was.'

I have to agree. Suddenly a floor-length pink satin gown

seems like the obvious choice. I step into it, breathing in and raising my ribs as Brooke struggles with the zip.

It's as tight as my Victorian dress around the waist, with a big bow where my bustle used to be, but I'm not exactly filling it out around the bust. 'I could do with your figure,' I sigh.

'Here!' She hands me a pair of rolled-up headbands. 'Tuck these underneath.'

I assess my enhanced curves in the mirror. 'We're getting there.'

'Gloves.'

I wriggle my fingers into the stretchy satin, pulling them up over my elbows and smoothing out the wrinkles.

'Diamanté is a girl's best friend,' Brooke notes as she secures a pair of sparkling cuffs onto my wrists, then reaches for a super-chunky necklace.

I pat it into place on my collarbone. 'Okay.' I lead her in a synchronised deep breath. 'I go on first, then you come out, all guns blazing.'

She pulls me into a fervent hug. 'I don't even care if this works now, I just feel so much more like me!'

I smile back at her. I know just what she means, even though I am now about to channel someone else entirely . . .

In the seconds before the song begins, I take myself back to 1958, picturing Marilyn in all her sensual, bewitching glory. Then I wind back further to her iconic performance in *Gentlemen Prefer Blondes*. Add a little of Madonna's teasing strut and the springy start of 'Material Girl' finds me half pouting, half singing about how the boy with the cold hard cash is always my Mr Right.

As I sashay across the stage, I'm aware of a lot of whistling and whooping, the loudest of which is coming from Ross. I give him a wink and then get chills as I see James joining in the chant of the chorus. I'm getting so into the self-adoring parading I'm almost as surprised as the audience when Brooke bounds out to challenge my mercenary perspective.

'*You want a gold digger to match your gold AmEx?*
Ten supermodels tanning on your yacht deck?
A fast car to drive you to a dead end?
A Rolex watch to see how much time you spend
Wasting your life with your fake friends.'

Ooh, that's a little harsher than I was expecting. Jason does seem to be bearing the brunt of her vocal smackdown. I can't tell which way this is going to go with him, he seems to be in shock, but it's clear the guy dressed as Simon Le Bon is getting riled up. Still, anything is better than her crawling on her hands and knees. And since she avoided the tequila she's not even slurring. Quite the opposite.

I take my turn and when she strikes up again – '*Money talks but it don't listen, All the truth that you be missing*' – the Le Bon lookalike begins a jeering heckling, possibly trying to drown out the rhyme about *sniffing*, but then Jason gives him an emphatic jolt.

'Shut up, man, let her sing!'

'That's not singing!' he taunts.

'It's cool!' Jason asserts, clearly transfixed.

Le Bon sneers back at him. 'What, you got the hots for that freak?'

'Maybe I do,' he replies, his eyes never leaving Brooke. 'Maybe I always did.'

Yes!

Jason steps closer to the stage, distancing himself from the group as we work up to our finale. In fairness to Madonna who, in the video, opts for daisies over diamonds and a pick-up truck over a red convertible, we join forces for the last bars, linking arms and wagging our fingers at the audience as we chant, '*Not material, not material!*' until the whistles and applause drown us out.

'Yessss!' Brooke feels charged with joy as she hugs me. 'We did it!'

Over her shoulder I see Jason beckoning from the edge of the stage. 'Well, what about that – I think someone is trying to get your attention now!'

Her face brightens. She thanks me and then sidles over to him, tilting her head as she approaches. 'You look different without your friends.'

'I feel different.' His gaze is steady, focussed. 'I know what I want now.'

'And what's that?' she asks, biting her lip as she looks down at him.

He responds by taking a step back and then opening out his arms.

She laughs. 'You want me to jump?'

He nods.

'And you're going to catch me?'

'You know I can.'

And so she steps off the stage, landing in his arms with a swinging flourish. He doesn't set her down, just carries on walking, past his ex-band mates, past James and Ross (who is giving me a thumbs up) and out the double doors...

I smile contentedly. When done right, love is a pretty amazing thing.

'May I have this dance?'

It's not every day you get an offer from Prince Charming – aka Adam Ant aka Ken from Kentucky. Seeing as I'm dressed like some kind of Barbie princess, it would seem churlish to resist a man resplendent in gold-buttoned frock coat and silver leather trousers.

He gives a low bow before taking me in his arms – up close I can see he has taken care with every detail from the lilac eyeshadow to the braids in his hair. I am slightly thrown by his Southern drawl but when a fella with a wavy mullet starts singing Phil Collins' eerily apt 'One More Night', we settle into a dreamy slow-dance sway.

I can't help but let my gaze drift over to James and I'm glad to be held as I feel quite weak with longing, wishing I could be the one sitting chatting with him, perhaps pondering what is to become of all the saxophones once the eighties pass...

As the song fades out, Ross steps away from James, jumps up on stage, reaches for something in the wings and then makes his way to the microphone tracked by a single beam of light.

'I was going to sing "Careless Whisper",' he tells the audience. 'But suddenly I'm in too good of a mood to do that so...'

He nods to the audio guy who instantly thrums our eardrums with a pulsing, high-energy beat. As Ross begins bouncing a tambourine between the heel of his palm and his dynamic hips, the place erupts and we begin pogo-ing in unison.

'I'm Your Man!' we join in on the chorus.

The sense of celebration in Ross's voice is contagious and he commands the stage like no other – so energised and flirty, directing significant lyrics at James. Why waste time with other guys indeed! When he catches my eye I scream like a teenage fan. This proves all too much for Prince Charming, who bows out, leaving me free to dance with utter abandon – so much so that at one point I fling my arm wide and the biggest diamanté bracelet goes flying off my arm, clipping Simon Le Bon on the back of the head. Sorry not sorry.

I'm so thrilled to be getting to see Ross perform and as he is such an embodiment of George Michael I feel like I'm in his presence too. It seems incomprehensible that such a powerful purveyor of happiness could die so tragically. How many people would like to see him have a second chance at life? My gaze then returns to James – it means so much to see his face lit up like this, to be able to replace my last ghostly image of him with this vibrant, lovestruck youth.

'Thank you, thank you!' I squeak under my breath to whoever it is that has arranged this.

By the time Ross crescendos to a promise of taking us halfway round the world, I'm on a total Nancy-approved high.

'Water, please!' I rasp at the barman, still humming the tune.

Of all the times I've thought, *I never want this evening to end!* I mean it most tonight. I scan the room, trying to commit every detail to memory, and then squeal out loud as Ross appears by my side. 'That was incredible! You're so gorgeous I can't stand it!'

I can feel the heat emanating from his body, the buzz of the performance still reverberating around the room.

'Listen, I have to tell you,' he pants. 'I'm staying. Whatever happens, whatever price I have to pay. This is where I want to be. With James. Feeling like I do now . . .'

I open my mouth to speak but what can I say? I would make exactly the same choice.

'I promise I'll take such good care of him,' he continues, reaching for my hand. 'Imagine if I can get him an early diagnosis!'

My eyes widen. 'Yes!'

'And then we can come find you. I don't know how any of this works, how much will be in my control, but I'll never forget what you did for me.'

I sigh, hoping that is true - that there's a chance he could save James and that the two of them could make up for lost time.

'And now it's your turn for love,' he insists. 'You've got Jason and Brooke together so when you wake up in the present day, you'll meet your guy, right?'

'In theory,' I say.

'You gotta have faith,' Ross urges.

'All right, George Michael!'

He laughs. 'I'm doing it without even realising.' Then he heaves a breath. 'Thank you, Chloe, for bringing me back to James.'

My eyes blink tears. I've had quite a few thank yous this week but this may be my finest piece of matchmaking of all.

'Ready to go?' Suddenly James is by his side.

For a second I stand open-mouthed. The next thing I know, he's complimenting me, telling me that I was 'completely channelling Marilyn' on stage.

'Thank you.' I bite my lip. 'I did my homework.'

'Funny you should say that – I just worked Marilyn into my college thesis!'

'Seriously? What was the topic?' I ask, realising this is one aspect of James's life I know nothing about.

'The civil rights movement in 1950s America. I don't know if you know but Marilyn was close friends with, and a huge fan of, Ella Fitzgerald.'

'Ella Fitzgerald, really?' I smile.

For a few precious minutes we three huddle up and James tells us how a certain LA club initially turned down Ella as a performer. Marilyn called up the management and told them if they booked her, she would be in the front row every night of the run. Knowing it would boost the club's profile, they agreed, Marilyn kept her word and the shows were a sellout.

'Suddenly Ella is upgraded from the jazz club circuit but she's still being asked to use the back entrance in some states – until Marilyn rocks up and insists she gets the full star treatment. And that's how it was from then on!'

'Wow,' I beam. 'The more I learn about that woman, the more remarkable she becomes.'

'I know! And it's such a testament to the life-changing power of friendship.'

His words take my breath away. 'Isn't it?' is all I can say.

And then I realise Ross is addressing me. 'We were just going into town for a drink – would you like to join us?'

Would I like to? Of course. I'd like to stay up talking till sunrise. But instead I politely decline.

'I have a big day tomorrow – I really should be hitting the hay.'

'Well, it was nice to meet you.' James smiles. 'Hope to see you again.'

My heart pangs at his words. Not trusting myself to speak, I settle for an enthusiastic nod.

I reach for the bar to steady myself as they walk away, expecting to become consumed with loss, but instead I feel a sudden upswing of joy – I got to see James one more time and he got to see me. And the best part? I feel like no matter where or when we met, we were always destined to be friends.

Present day

23

I slide my hand across the bed, half expecting to find Ross lying beside me.

'Are you here?' I call out his name as I begin checking every possible hiding place – the bathroom, the balcony, even the wardrobe. Nothing. Perhaps he's woken up back in his own bed? Perhaps he's lived thirty plus years while I was sleeping and now resides in England? Perhaps he's trapped in some time travel limbo . . . I feel a sudden jab of nerves for his well-being and reach for my phone.

I scroll and scroll some more but it is as I feared – there's no trace of his number.

I switch to WhatsApp – no record of any conversation between us.

I'm breathing more heavily now. His life must have taken a radically different turn as a result of the choice he made last night. Though I suppose even a slight diversion could have resulted in a new phone number.

I try calling his apartment complex but, of course, it's not like a hotel, they can't put me through to his unit, or even confirm whether or not he actually lives there – 'We have to respect the privacy of our guests, I'm sure you understand.'

It's probably too early for anyone to be in the theatre box office but I could swing by to see if there's any kind of clue. My first instinct is to grab my sunglasses and head straight out, but of all the days to skimp on the beautification process, today is not the day. I don't want my beloved's 'first encounter' anecdote to be: 'So there was this wild woman running down the street with bed hair and pyjama bottoms asking every passerby if they'd seen a man in a *Choose Life* T-shirt.'

And so I go all out, taking the time to coat every last lash with mascara, holding the curling tongs a little longer and telling myself that this actually could be a positive scenario for Ross. He said he was ready for a change and he's obviously got one. And now it's my turn. The second I step outside my door I'm fair game for meeting Him.

What to wear, what to wear? It's been quite a blessing not to have to worry about being appropriately attired as I went back in time. I wish I knew what I was dressing for today. I want to look my best but not overdone. I scrape the hangers along the rail, folding the nos directly into my suitcase until I'm left with a blush sundress – pretty but still beachy casual. Plus, I have a shimmer lip gloss that's the perfect match.

Just keep putting one foot in front of the other, I tell myself as I strap on my rose gold sandals. They always make me feel better. I squeeze my other shoes along the side of my case. I may as well take it down to the bell desk on my way out. That way, if I run into the main man or get held up, I don't have to worry about rushing back to clear the room.

After the theatre I'll enjoy a leisurely ocean-view breakfast, possibly meeting the love of my life over the bacon and bircher muesli. Then, before I leave for the airport, I'll place James's last pebble with a view of the hotel, content in the knowledge that I not only kept my promise to be open to love, but went one better and found some. Maybe.

Well, the impossible has happened every day since I got here, surely it's time I started to believe?

Part of the reason I wanted to come to Ross's theatre was to feel connected to him but in actuality it makes me feel worse – his face is no longer on the poster for *South Pacific*.

'Excuse me!' I approach the girl setting a jar of dog biscuits at the entrance of the café next door. 'Do you know if this poster changed recently?'

'I don't think so.' She frowns.

'It's just, there seems to be a new guy playing Emile . . .'

'Oh no, it's been Cal the whole run. He's really good. You should check it out if you get the chance.'

I can't believe I never got to see Ross perform. I stand winded for a moment. I wish I knew where, or at least how, Ross is. I give him a quick google but draw a blank. As the café girl finishes clearing the plates on the outside tables, I follow her back inside, feeling the need for something reviving. I make a rather bold order of an iced blue spirulina latte and then stand to the side.

Over at the back, a group of Navy SEALS are demolishing shakshuka and waffle breakfasts, mocking one guy for ordering an acai bowl sprinkled with dainty flowers and another for his dance moves, as witnessed at last week's barbecue. I think for a moment about asking if they know Robbie but Ross did tell me there are over two thousand of them and, besides, any information about how his mission is going would surely be classified.

'Blue Mint Magic Latte for Chloe!'

'That's me, thank you!'

As I turn to head out I collide with two of the SEALS, now on their feet.

'Excuse us, ma'am!'

'No, no, totally my fault!' I say as I shake the splurge of blue milk off my hand. And then I gasp. 'Robbie! You're back!'

'I am indeed!' He smiles politely though he clearly has absolutely no idea who I am. If Ross wasn't around to introduce us, why would he?

'I'm a friend of your brother's,' I offer as a hurried explanation. 'Actually . . . I was hoping to see him while I'm in town but I think I've got his old number . . .'

'Are you calling the UK cellphone or the US one?'

'US . . .'

'That would explain it. He's back in England right now. They'll be back for their anniversary, though – they never miss that. How long are you here?'

'I'm really not sure. Sorry, when you say anniversary . . .'

'Yeah, it's their tenth so that's tin – you just know he's going to dress up as the Tin Man. He's nothing if not a cliché.'

I blink back at him.

'Are you okay?' He looks concerned.

My heart is thumping wildly as I ask: 'Can you just remind me of his husband's name? I want to get a card and I'm drawing a total blank.'

'James.'

My jaw drops. So it's true. He pulled it off.

'And he's quite well now, after the health scare?'

'He's doing great,' he beams. 'Thank god Ross got him involved with that programme with the dogs detecting illnesses, right?'

'Right!' I mirror.

'I think it might have even saved his life.'

'I'm pretty sure it did.'

I want to ask a dozen follow-up questions but Robbie's friends are now in the jeep, honking for him to join them.

'I'm sorry, I have to go – they're dropping me at the doc's.' He winces as he moves his shoulder.

'Did you get injured?'

'It's just muscular.' He dismisses my concern, though I can't help but wonder if there's a bullet lodged in there or some other fallout from his mission.

'I just wanted to say . . .' I trail off.

'Yes?'

I want to tell him how much his empowering words and self-defence training impacted my whole trip, and probably the rest of my life in terms of speaking up and taking a bolder stance. But instead, I revert to the default line I've heard around town when people want to show their appreciation for the military:

'Thank you for your service.'

I walk back to the Del in a delirious daze. I was hoping to get some reassurance that Ross was okay but this is so far beyond what I was hoping for I can barely wrap my head around it.

James is alive.

And married! I guess a near-death experience will shake up your perspective.

Suddenly I think of the pebbles – I still have the last one I was due to place today. I scrabble in my bag and unzip the special pouch I assigned. Empty. My heart feels like a helium balloon in my chest, one I'm finally ready to set free.

'Welcome to Sheerwater!' the hostess greets me.

There really couldn't be a better scenario for bumping into a fellow guest – every table in the restaurant is clearly visible and there's unlimited opportunity for parading around with plates of food like a gameshow hostess. I request a spot on the patio near the entrance. That way I can see everyone who comes and goes, as well as the glistening vista – handy if he arrives by yacht or emerges from the sea like James Bond.

I sigh contentedly as I smooth my hand over my white linen napkin. The day couldn't be any more heavenly – the bluest sky, the softest breeze. Ordinarily I might feel self-conscious about how I look – fussing with my hair or readjusting my dress – but today I am experiencing a sense of surrender: I've given it my best shot and if he's really my guy, then he'd choose me over Margot Robbie anyway. (I say Margot Robbie because the girl on the next table is dressed as Harley Quinn.)

Still unable to contain my smile, I say good morning to everyone I pass en route to loading up my first plate. My intention was to take my time over a series of elegant platters – a fruit course, an egg dish, a trio of mini muffins – but already I've gone rogue with slices of icy watermelon, waffles with whipped maple butter and roasted potatoes with sizzled peppers and courgette. I might just try one of these chia seed puddings as well.

As I start to mix and match mouthfuls, I study my options so far – he's certainly not that fault-finder on the table ahead of me, angrily swiping at the birdies hoping for a crumb. If this scenario makes him huff and puff, I can't imagine what he'd be like when life really gets tough. Oh, here comes his wife now, slamming down a plate of crispy bacon and adopting an equally surly pose – I have to concede they do at least seem well-suited.

Same goes for the cute'n'crinkly couple to my left. Despite the abundance of food options he has opted for a bowl of raisin bran and a banana, while she's limiting herself to toast and black coffee with sweetener. Behind them, some guy loudly announces his drinks order – overly assertive and overbearing. I don't want to look his way but I'm glad that I do when he requests 'one ice with water, one ice without'. And then realises his mistake. It's funny how Americans are notorious for projecting their vocals while we Brits mumble meekly as if we're only comfortable with a fifty-fifty chance of being heard.

Back and forth I go, moving on to the sliced cheeses and a spoonful of cinnamon-dusted bread and butter pudding. I'm still discreetly checking out every guest, but each time I think I've spied a possibility he ruins the fantasy by returning to sit with his family. Take the J. Crew trio to my right. Their darling baby is sporting a nautical romper and seems so chirpy and appreciative of both the giant strawberries and exceptional view. Less so the bellyaching child at the far table being forkfed sausage by his mum even though he's at least eight. I worry he'll grow up to be the kind of man who can't open his own umbrella but who am I to judge?

'More coffee?'

Sensing I'm here for the long haul, the waitress now leaves me with the entire silver flask. I reach for the cream and top off my third cup.

My initial sense of bliss and anticipation has morphed into reflection, now lightly tinged with anxiety. Now James and Ross are a pair, will they have time for me? This version of James only knows me from a brief encounter at the karaoke party, we're not even friends. Gosh, that's such a weird thought. All the times we spent together, now he'll have no memory of them? I push away my plate of pastries. I don't need to be going down that rabbit hole. Of course, we can make lots of great new memories. I'm only tilting towards negativity because I'm getting the creeping feeling that my guy is going to be a no-show.

It occurs to me now that there was no envelope by the door today – no picture of me and my mystery match. Maybe Jason and Brooke didn't make it as a couple. Or maybe they decided not to have children. But even if they did and he does show up, there's so little time left. What will we be able to do except exchange numbers and begin a long-distance relationship, like Ross and James the first time round?

Unless ... What if Coronado is The One? What if I have an ongoing affair with this place, returning every summer to have my heart filled up?

I could live with that.

I'm starting to feel better, excited even. I mean, seeing as I'm already here, what if I extended my stay, just by a day or two? I'm not due back at work until next week. It would certainly ease the ticking clock sensation – I could relax, let things happen at their own pace instead of constantly chivvying them along. I may have packed my case but I have yet to officially check out.

I look beyond the restaurant to the tiki bar by the beach. I could go there tonight, have a Mai Tai and watch the sun set. And I wanted to get a closer look at Wallis Simpson's Windsor Cottage, now located right here on the hotel grounds. Tomorrow morning I could even do that Mermaid Fitness class Ross told me about. No matchmaking, no longing for love, just being...

I take one last sip of coffee. Right, that's it. I'm staying.

The lobby is thronging, the busiest I've seen it in decades.

'Checking out?' the receptionist, Renata, chirps as my turn comes to approach the desk.

'Actually I was hoping to extend my stay for a night or two? Ideally keeping the same room...'

I give her my most winning smile but she responds with a shoulder slump.

'I'm so sorry, we're fully booked for Comicon.'

What? It's begun already? My face falls. 'Completely? Not even one room? Honestly a glorified broom closet would do!'

She turns to her screen, taps and clicks and taps some more. 'Every last room is taken. I can give you the website address for the Coronado Visitor Center, it has all the other accommodations—'

'Do you have a wait list?' I cut in, desperation gripping me. 'In case there's a last-minute cancellation?'

'It is rather unlikely at this point but of course I can take your details. Oh!' She suddenly throws herself halfway across the desk. 'Mr Montague! Jordan Montague!' She calls beyond me then grimaces. 'Sorry about this – we've been looking all over for this gentleman.'

You and me both, I think to myself, wondering if I'm going to get to look at him before I faint . . .

24

He's here. Actually here in the same room as me.

My heart feels bigger than my whole body, engulfing me with its demanding, rhythmic palpitations.

So this is where we meet – the hotel lobby.

He's right beside me as I turn, giving me a close-up of a face that feels both familiar and brand new... His hair is the same shiny conker brown as Jasper's but styled into a tufty sweep; his eyes are a rare amber, a shade more golden than Jesse's. He has his father's cheekbones but a more shapely mouth. I can't help but hope he has Jack's soul and sense of humour. He certainly cuts a similar dash, looking broad yet lean in a black shirt with the sleeves rolled up, dark denim jeans and a cobalt-blue lanyard. Though I don't catch his accreditation details, I do get a faint waft of ocean spray cologne – or maybe he's a Coronado beach baby and that's his natural scent.

'I'm so glad I caught you,' Renata cheers. 'We have your phone!'

His hand smacks onto his chest in relief. 'I've been looking everywhere for it! Where did you find it?'

'Sheerwater Restaurant,' she replies.

'Sheerwater?' I accidentally repeat. How did I miss him?

'I was just there five minutes, didn't even sit down – must have dropped it in the rush.'

Was that when I was dithering over the toppings for my oatmeal?

'They're holding it for you at the hostess desk,' Renata continues. 'Would you like me to send someone to collect it?'

'No, no, I'll go myself. And sorry to interrupt.' He acknowledges me for the first time, fleetingly, before turning back to the desk. 'I was actually coming to let you know that Regé-Jean Page has had a last-minute change of plan so you can free up his suite.'

'Is that definite, sir?' Renata's eyes flit to me.

'Well, I guess I should check my phone one more time but I'm ninety per cent certain.'

'If I end up sharing with Regé-Jean Page, I'm fine with that!' I chime.

Why? Why would I say that to the man who is supposed to be my future beau?

'This young lady was just hoping for a cancellation,' the receptionist explains. 'Your timing is perfect!'

He looks back at me. 'If you want to come with me to Sheerwater, I can let you know for definite?'

And so it begins – our first date!

Speed-walking was never part of the fantasy but that's okay, we'll have time for romance later, he clearly has other things on his mind right now. And really, what human being can compete with a phone these days?

'Oops!' I collide with a young mum as he takes a sharp left and begins descending a staircase without so much as a 'This way!' pointer.

'Sorry.' He grimaces, backtracking. 'I'm a bit frazzled – this is my busiest week of the year.'

'Comicon-related?'

He nods. 'I'm a publicist, with way too many clients on the roster. Every year I say it's my last time and every year . . .' He trails off, looking mildly irritated with himself.

Perhaps something in my face says, 'But look where you are!' because he asks me if this is my first time at the Hotel Del. I tell him this is actually the fifth year I've visited. I could probably even add that I mean five different years all in one week because he's not really listening.

'Do you have a brother?' I ask as we stride past a collection of boutiques.

'Sorry?' This throws him for a second. So much so he actually looks at me. For a microsecond I see something that could pass as attraction though I think it's actually just common or garden curiosity.

'Do you?' I persist.

Because I think there might have been a mix-up and I might have better chemistry with his sibling, if he has one . . .

'No, just a sister. This way.' He directs me through the Babcock & Story Bar, where I met his great-grandfather.

If only he knew how much there is for us to talk about. We could sit at the same window table where Jesse was doing his sums and order every cocktail on the menu to celebrate the passing of Prohibition. I'd love to find out how the lives of his forefathers panned out. But I don't think I'm going to get the chance to ask. Any second now he's going to disappear into a twister of messages and demands and even if I'm here all night, he won't be. Contrary to what the receptionist said, the timing doesn't seem right at all.

'I believe you have my phone – Jordan Montague.'

We're at the hostess stand now. I only have him for a minute or so more.

'Let me check, sir. I've just taken over from Marlene.'

He sighs impatiently, scanning the restaurant as if the phone might spot him and make its own way over.

I have to say something compelling to give us a chance –

'Jordan! Over here!'

Before I can speak, a dashing, silver-haired gentleman reminiscent of Jeff Bridges beckons enthusiastically to him.

'This will just take a minute.' Jordan indicates I should follow.

The chap has such wonderfully spiffy whiskers, I presume he must be an acting client. But then Jordan calls him 'Pops' and I see his eyes – such a particular green I'd recognise them any era. It's Jack, Jordan's grandfather. Last seen at Clayton's diner in 1958.

I feel a rushing in my skull and a jellification in my legs. Over sixty years have passed for him but for me it's not even sixty hours. It takes all my control not to throw my arms around him. It's such an unbelievable pleasure to see him again – he's wearing his facial creases well (in that way only actors seem to pull off), his eyes are as lively as ever and if he asked me to dance right now, I'd happily lean into him one more time. You've still got it, buddy!

'What are you doing here?' Jordan asks as he stoops to kiss him on the cheek.

'Waiting to have lunch with my zombie son,' he twinkles.

'He played a zombie's father in a movie,' Jordan clarifies. 'It's not his actual son.'

'Or an actual zombie,' I joke.

Jack chuckles, Jordan does not.

'Jack Montague.' He reaches across the table to shake my hand.

'Sorry, I didn't catch your name,' Jordan says, looking sheepish.

'Chloe,' Jack murmurs, still holding my hand.

I can't even speak. I've fallen under his spell. I never thought I'd hear him say my name again, at least not that way.

'You know each other?'

'It's the darnedest thing.' Jack snaps out of his reverie. 'You look just like a woman I used to know. We only knew each other for one day but—'

'Pops!' Jordan tuts.

'No, she was the reason I got together with your grandmother . . .' He turns back to me. 'What did you say your name was?'

I think about lying but even in my altered state I can see how quickly that would backfire.

'Well, it really *is* the darnedest thing.' I give a brazen smile. 'I am Chloe.'

Too. I should've said, 'I'm Chloe too.'

'No!' Jack hoots. 'Well, you have to be related to her. I mean, the hair is a little different in style but everything else . . .'

As his eyes gaze appreciatively, mine glaze with tears. Not only did he notice me back then but he's never forgotten me. Why couldn't it be this way with Jordan? All he can do is look between us in a confused fashion. But then his face changes.

'Praise be!' he whoops as the hostess hands him his phone. 'Let me just quickly check that Regé-Jean is still a no.'

I watch him as he scans his messages. How different this could have been if he'd just been interested in me. And perhaps had a slightly more appealing personality. He's lovely looking but his indifference is such a passion-killer.

'It's all yours,' he concludes, glancing up at me. 'I'll confirm with Renata on the way out.'

'Th – thank you,' I begin, but he's already in motion.

'Gotta run.'

'Right.'

As I watch him go, I feel a rhinoceros-sized weight of disappointment bear down on me. So much has been leading up to this moment. But in all my myriad ponderings about how it might be between us, I never thought it would feel like this.

'I'm sorry to say he's a lost cause romantically.' Jack grimaces.

'Oh no!' I fluster, embarrassed. Did I look that keen?

'I'd love nothing better than to see him with a good woman but he's still entirely shut down after the bad one.'

'Really?' I raise a brow. 'Just how bad are we talking?'

'Why don't you take a seat?' He smiles kindly. 'Keep me company until my lunch date arrives?'

Already he's pouring out a jangly glass of iced water for me. I take a grateful sip. For a second I think of how we chatted under our beach parasol the first day we met and how surreal it is to be welcomed again. Surreal but comfortable. He was always so easy to talk to . . .

'If only you knew what a joy he used to be to have around.' Jack strokes his whiskers, looking wistful. 'He was always a shy kid but he came into his own when he started writing for the local paper. All that time spent observing the world paid off!'

Jack tells me his writing career was progressing nicely when one day a talent scout for a national TV network noticed just how skilled he was at drawing people out with his interviews.

'I think it was because they instinctively knew they could trust him. Because he is trustworthy. Even as a kid he could never tell a lie,' Jack notes. 'Anyway, they came to him with this incredible offer of an on-location interview series with a book deal attached. There was a lot of travel involved and as he and Shannon had only been together six months she really didn't want him to go. What she wanted was for him to move to her hometown in Utah but that really wasn't practical since all his work revolved around Los Angeles. He tried to reason that he would only ever be a flight away and any weekend she could join him in Paris or Petra or wherever. But that held no appeal to her – too many variables, she wanted the locked-down certainty. So she told him she was pregnant, said she couldn't possibly go through it alone. If he was going to be any kind of father to their child, he would have to move to Utah.'

'And he believed her?'

'I think that's often the trouble with honest people, they don't have suspicious minds. And, of course, he wanted to do the right thing by her.'

'Did anyone question whether she really was pregnant?'

'Most of the talk was about the timing. We didn't think she'd actually invented a baby, just maybe engineered it.'

'God.' I shake my head. 'Either way.'

'I know,' he sighs. 'It put him in an impossible situation. Of course, he turned down the job and moved to Utah. When he struggled to find work I tried to help out, hooking him up with a PR buddy of mine, and that's how he ended up writing press releases and actor bios. Which, of course, he's really good at, but his heart was never in it.'

'What happened when he realised she wasn't pregnant?'

He rolls his eyes. 'She told him she'd lost the baby due to all the stress, but they'd try again. Thank god that didn't happen. By this point he knew he wanted out but how can you leave a woman who's just lost your child?'

'I'm not liking this Shannon,' I say, suddenly feeling quite vengeful.

'You and me both.'

'Did she ever get her comeuppance?'

'Other than seeing his face when he found out the truth – from her best friend by the way – no. At least not as far as I know. Sometimes karma takes its sweet time.'

I nod. 'It will get her in the end. As John Lennon once said, "Time wounds all heels."'

He chuckles. 'That's a good one, I'll have to remember that!' And then his jollity subsides. 'The thing is, it's actually irrelevant what happens to her. It's him I'm worried about. When I think of the toll it's taken, not just on his career but on his joie de vivre, his trust in human beings . . .'

'There's really too high a price to pay for choosing the wrong person, isn't there?'

'Is this something you can relate to?' Jack's voice softens.

'All too well,' I confirm.

'Now if only two wronged people could make a right . . .' He raises a brow.

I smile. 'When did you say all this happened?'

'Gosh, it's a few years ago now.' He frowns. 'They met right here' – he points to what is currently a grassy lawn – 'on the Christmas ice rink.'

'They have an ice rink by the beach?'

'They do indeed. Just for the festive season.' Then he sighs. 'I remember she spent Christmas Eve with us that year and she kept saying they met at seven p.m. on the seventh of December so it was obviously meant to be!' He rolls his eyes. 'If only we could turn back time!'

'If only . . .' I concur then try to sound casual: 'Can you remember the actual year?'

'Well, let me see, it was around the time my third great-grandchild was born so . . . it must have been 2016!'

I get a chill. That was the year I was supposed to come to Coronado with James. Would I have met him first if I'd come that year?

But no, that can't be it. The Oracle clearly said he didn't exist. My mind is starting to race, imagining what I might do if I could go back one more time and switch Jordan's train tracks in my direction . . . I still have the key to my room in my pocket – I could try programming in the date myself . . . It has to be worth a try!

'Oh!' Jack suddenly gets to his feet, waving over to the hostess stand. 'Here's Chris now!'

'Chris?' I say absently.

'My lunch date – you might recognise him, he looks so like his father.'

I turn and experience my second near-fainting of the day. It's Jack Lemmon's son Chris, now in his sixties but I can still see the little kid in him, the one I just met on the set of *Some Like It Hot*.

The two men hug and then Jack introduces me.

'Chloe?' Chris startles at my name.

He surely can't recognise me, it's not possible.

But then he looks up at the sky and tuts. 'Oh Pop, you always like to send me a little message when I'm back here.' Then he turns to Jack. 'You remember Chloe, don't you?'

Jack takes a moment and then chuckles. 'I can picture her now – sat up front in your father's Aston Martin . . .'

'Flying first class alongside him, only Evian and ice cubes in her water bowl.' He then turns to me. 'She was a standard Poodle, in case you're wondering.'

'I was rather!' I give a little puff of relief.

The two men are quick to fall into their bantersome memories, and it soon becomes clear that Chris has quite a specific sense of humour, liking to tease his audience. He's been touring with his one-man show – *A Twist of Lemmon* – sat at the piano and switching between his and his father's memories. Watching him 'become' Jack Lemmon is quite uncanny, a little short of channelling.

'Do you have that great picture of the two of you?' Jack prompts.

Chris shows me a photo of him seated by his father at the piano, the very child I met just a couple of days ago. As reluctant as I am to leave, it seems a suitably full circle moment to exit on.

As I get to my feet, I reach to shake Chris's hand but when I turn to Jack he envelops me in a big Hollywood hug, taking me right back to our embrace when he was a young man.

'It was such a pleasure chatting with you Chloe.' He beams into my eyes. 'I hope we meet again.'

I smile to myself, thinking, *We already did . . .*

25

I walk away in something of a daze. It's been years since I felt this riled up emotionally. I don't want to lose this feeling, as disorientating as it is. I just have to keep up the momentum a little longer. I wouldn't even need that long in 2016 – all I have to do is beat Shannon to Jordan. I can do a decent clip on an ice rink so I think I'd be in with a chance. I would just swish on up to him, our eyes would meet, our hearts would do a triple Salchow, Shannon ceases to be a factor and we're good to go!

I experience a little thrill picturing him reacting to me in a whole different way – warm and interested, as opposed to a fleeting distraction from his work.

Of course, I say all this like I have a choice in the matter – when did I get to decide any of the aspects of my time travel? Nevertheless, it has to be worth a try. I've got nothing to lose and just four buttons to press. Suddenly I'm moving with more urgency than Jordan en route to his phone.

Please, please, just one more time! I'm not even asking to go back so far – just let me pick the date this time!

I hold the key under the scanner.

Nothing.

'Come on!'

It flickers as if trying to read the card but no numbers register.

I try the door, punching in 2-0-1-6.

No bleeping, no whirring, no receding bolt. I try again and again. No response.

Suddenly I feel a dragging sense of defeat creeping over me. It's over. The magic is gone. Seeing Jack again seemed like such a sign that everything was going to work out – to think I could've been part of his family! My heart hurts to even consider what a near miss it has all been. Love really is all in the timing. Perhaps Jack was just a little parting gift before I head home.

I mean, as lovely as it would be to stay on, what would I really achieve, beyond depleting my already limited finances? I could try and track down Jordan again but then what – see if I can convince him to find me attractive? I get a resounding no from my heart. It's one thing championing someone else's romance, quite another trying to make someone love you.

I can't even hope for a classic romcom airport scene because he doesn't know anything about my travel plans. He doesn't really know anything about me at all. Yet I know so much about him, especially his family history. I'm actually a part of his history. But, as of right now, I doubt he'd even be able to pick me out in a line-up.

I sigh, desperately trying to find some hope to cling to. And then it dawns on me – this whole adventure began on the plane, that could be where I find my happy ending. Or at the very least, another message from the Oracle that makes sense of it all.

I look at my watch. I could still make my flight. Suddenly it seems unbearable to linger, wallowing in all the memories, sitting alone at dinner or alone at the bar. England could be the best antidote after all – back in my flat this will feel like nothing more than a glorious dream, just like Dorothy's. After all, I have no proof that any of this happened. The only witness would be Ross and, now I know he's in England, that could be my next mission – finding him and James. Perhaps going back to the UK is the wisest move.

I take out my phone to check my flight details and see that I've missed two calls. The area code is 619, same as Ross. My hand is shaking as I press play on voicemail.

But it's a woman's voice. Renata from reception. Apparently I left some items in the safe. She says I can pick them up from the concierge desk.

Oh my god! My passport! I didn't even give it a thought this morning!

Well, that's a sign if ever there was one – fly away little bird!

*

I feel the adrenalin kicking in as I scurry down to the lobby – I can still leave on schedule. I'll grab my passport, then my case, then a cab.

'Renata is on a roll today with her lost and found,' I note as the concierge looks for my package.

'Ah, here we go – Sinclair: one passport.'

'Thank you so much.' I'm about to ask if he can cancel my new reservation when he slides a gift box across the counter.

'And here are your other items from the safe.'

'This isn't mine.' I touch the box.

'It's just something we used to keep everything together. It's yours to take away.'

'But . . .' I prise open the lid, ready to explain there's been some mistake, but instead nearly pass out. The first thing I see is Jasper's watch. Then Jesse's money clip, Jack's handkerchief and Brooke's diamanté hairclip.

'Is everything there?' he enquires.

I blink at him in disbelief.

'Ms Sinclair?'

'Yes, yes, everything – it's all here, it's all *real*!'

I'm in an elated daze, trying to move away so he can help the next guest but not sure which direction to go in, when suddenly I'm roughly clipped and the whole lot goes flying.

'*Noooo!*' I fall to the floor, grabbing at my treasures, desperate to get them back into the box and away from trampling feet. 'Sorry, sorry! *Careful!*' I go to reach for Jack's handkerchief but a man's hand beats me to it, gripping tight and refusing to release it.

I look up in confusion and come face to face with my nemesis.

Alfred. Freddy. Alfie. Al. What now – A-Foe?

I don't use any of these aliases as I address him. All I say, as my eyes darken is: '*You!*'

His hand remains locked on the handkerchief as he looks back at me.

'What do you want?' My voice is steady. I feel ready for anything now.

'I think the more apt question is, what do you want?'

My brow furrows. 'What does it matter to you what *I* want?'

'Because I can help you get it.' That should sound sinister but there's a new tone to his voice that confuses me.

'Get what exactly?' I falter. 'What do you mean?'

'Another chance with Jordan.'

My jaw drops. How does he know about him? I search his face for clues. Physically he's just another version of the man I met each trip but there's something very different about his energy.

'Can I please have my handkerchief?'

He releases it.

I look around me. Too many listening ears in the lobby. 'I think we should find somewhere quieter to talk.'

I wait for him to suggest his room but instead he proposes the bench beside the dragon tree.

'You may have noticed I've been a recurring presence.'

I nod warily. This is the first time he's acknowledged that we have history – over a hundred years of it.

'And on account of your tenacity and creativity with your matchmaking, I'd like to offer you one more trip back in time.'

What?

'It can't be you,' I hiss.

'What do you mean?'

'It can't be you that's masterminded all this.'

'I never said I did,' he shrugs.

'But you're in on it?' I'm finding this hard to process.

'I think that's fair to say.'

'But why? Why would you have been such a thorn in my side? Hounding me and sleazing and blocking me and generally making everything more stressful?'

'There were concerns that if you didn't set up proper boundaries with men, learn to push back a little stronger, it could impact your relationship even with a good man.'

'So you were testing me?'

He nods. 'I think you got it – I've certainly got the bruises to prove it. At least I had the bruises in 1929.'

I'm surprised to find a faint smile upon my lips and then I wince. 'What about 1985 with the Secret Service?'

'No comment.'

'Gosh, I can't believe this.'

'I think you understand now that it's not about putting such huge expectations on a man to change your world – you're just as much a catalyst for change as him.'

'Am I?'

'Do you really doubt that?' he asks. 'You saved a man from drowning, reunited another with his great love, steered yet another away from a ruinous clique.'

'I did, didn't I?' I puff up. Then my eyes narrow. 'So, you're seriously saying you're now on my side?'

'That's right. And if you tell me what date you'd like to go back to, I can have it arranged.'

This seems too good to be true. My wariness returns. 'And what would I have to do in return?'

'Chloe, I'm not that guy – I was just incarnations of men you needed to learn to deal with.'

'But you understand my being cautious?'

'Of course, and I commend you for it. The most important thing is to trust your instincts and do what feels right for you.'

I do a quick check in – I'm not feeling repulsed or afraid or angry in his presence this time, just a little thrown.

'So how would this work exactly?'

'The same way it always has – you will go up to your room, scan the key card, press in the four digits and in you go.'

'But I've been assigned a different room – I don't even know which one yet.'

'The room itself is irrelevant. It's all about you.'

All this new information is making my head spin. His offer seems legit but can I really trust him? Or, more importantly, my own judgement?

'Why me?' I ask. 'Why has all this happened to me?'

He smiles. 'Love is so random – some people meet a childhood sweetheart and enjoy a lifetime of support and companionship. Others have a run of toxic relationships then finally get the chance to choose kindness in their sixties; some meet the love of their life when they'd given up all hope, others on an internet date. I'm a kind of project manager for people who were never going to meet their special person. Either through bad choices and staying in the wrong relationships too long, or because the right people in history hadn't got together prior. Wrong place, wrong time, et cetera. You were actually a combination of the last two. There was a guy you could have been sufficiently happy with but you stayed too long with Andy. But at least you had James. In many ways your true soulmate. Then when he died . . . Well, I thought it would be interesting to see what would happen if you got a shot at romantic love. I had my work cut out convincing them –'

'Them?' I cut in.

He gives me a wry look. 'You know I can't tell you everything!' Then he gets to his feet and straightens his jacket, as if he wants to get down to business. 'So, tell me, what date would you like to go back to?'

'I'm sure you already know.'

'I need to hear it from you.'

Oh jeez. To say it out loud is to admit that I want to do this.

'Okay,' I say, pushing through the nerves. '2016. December the seventh. Some time before seven p.m., if you want to get really precise.'

He smiles encouragingly. 'You can do this.'

'You really want me to succeed?' I feel my eyes sheen with tears.

'I always did.'

Well, that's a turn-up for the books: the very person I've been guarding myself against has become an ally. I feel something approaching affection for this infuriating individual because without him I wouldn't have had quite so much practice standing up for myself.

My phone buzzes a text. 'My room is ready,' I tell him.

But when I look up he's gone.

I feel a sting of remorse. I didn't even get to thank him for all he has taught me, let alone offering me this bonus trip. Plus, there are all the questions I have about James and Ross . . . I get to my feet and look around but there's no trace of him. Has he gone on ahead of me? Or has he gone for good? Either way, the best way I can show my gratitude is to knock this out of the park. And Shannon off her skates.

I've taken care of Montague hearts for four generations, I'm not going to let her spoil things now.

2016

Jordan & Chloe

26

New room, new year. Actually a familiar one to me – 2016. The year James invited me to come with him to Coronado and the year I said no for fear of upsetting Andy who, if I'm honest, I never really liked that much to start with. That was not one of my best decisions. But James didn't make a big deal about it, just said his piece then let it go. I think he's the best example of unconditional love I have known. It's a wonderful thing not to be walking on eggshells around someone. You show them all your flaws and they just shrug and offer you an extra dollop of sticky toffee pudding.

I imagine him stood beside me now as I tap the numbers into the keypad, teasing, 'That's a helluva roundabout way to get here but I'm glad you made it in the end.'

And so I step through the door, embracing the rushing-warping sensation this one last time.

'My favourite jumper!' I exclaim as I open my eyes and rush

to the mirror. A silver-beaded cashmere number I managed to shrink and mangle in the wash and still think of longingly. If only there was some way to bring it back with me . . .

Focus! I tut at myself – I'm not here for the knitwear.

I check out the rest of my outfit – I would probably have teamed it with black leggings for flexibility on the ice rink but instead I'm in dark grey skinny jeans with suede lace-up boots and a silver leather cross-body bag. Let's see if there's anything extra I need to be popping in that . . .

I look around, almost surprised to see the envelope in its usual spot on the floor. I'm officially part of the club now!

The weight of it surprises me, and the fact that there's a slimline digital camera inside. For a moment I think I'm going to be responsible for supplying the headshots for myself and Jordan but our photos are right there in the envelope. They definitely caught me on a happy day. And I have to say, Jordan looks infinitely more attractive pre-Shannon, much more shiny and alert. I hold the image of his face alongside mine. We have very different features but I can see a certain similarity in our smiles, an aspect of him I've yet to see in person.

I decide to head out via the lobby – this part of the hotel has been something of a touchstone for me, helping me get into the right mindset for each new era. I don't expect too many changes, 2016 being just a few years prior, but what greets me has me gasping in wonder.

Dominating the centre and reaching as high as the wraparound gallery is a Christmas tree, bejewelled with ocean-themed baubles in hues of ice blue, turquoise and teal. Stepping closer, I spy innumerable white starfish nestling amid branches, along with sequinned anchors and glitter-encrusted shells . . . Somehow all the winking lights manage to create an atmosphere that is both frosty and cosy. I take a contented breath. If I ever get to live somewhere with a spare room, I'm going to copy this look so I can dip in and get filled up with wonder whenever the real world gets too much.

The festive vibes keep on coming at the ice rink – fire pits huddle around the perimeter offering a beguiling yellow flicker and illuminating the faces of those toasting marshmallows and cradling hot toddies. 'Winter Wonderland' is playing and seems perfectly apt, despite the fact that snow and pines have been replaced with sand and palms.

More thrilled than nervous now, I pick out a pair of skate boots. But before I join the rhythmic circuit, I reach for the camera. If I go to the far side, I should be able to get the rink and the iconic turret of the hotel in the frame. Eyes on the screen, I edge backwards, close enough to feel the warmth from a nearby fire pit. As the skaters swish and scrape by, I get a kick thinking that any second he could glide into frame. Who says you don't get a second chance at a first impression?

I snap and snap again, shuffling backwards, adjusting the angle. And then my heart leaps – there he is, crossing the rink like a knock-kneed foal, torso bent too far forward, arms flailing, almost like he's waving at me.

I turn to face him, wondering what our first words will be,

but the second he reaches me he starts swatting and smacking me around the thigh with his leather-gloved hands.

'What the . . .?'

'You were on fire!' he exclaims, pointing to the charred fabric of my jeans.

I reach down, making contact with a hot smear of white and bronzed goo.

Around the same level there's a small boy looking devastated that the marshmallow he was hoping to squish between two graham crackers has met with such a tragic end.

'Of course I'll pay for a new pair,' he says, reaching for his wallet. 'You'll never get that out.'

'No, no, it's entirely my fault,' I insist, my hand reaching to stop him and feeling a little rush as I make contact with his arm. 'I wasn't looking where I was going.'

'I set fire to her,' the small boy announces, with a trace of pride.

'I know, buddy.' Jordan sighs then gives me a rueful look. 'I'd like to say this was a freak incident but with Spike there's always something.'

'Is he your . . .?' I can't bring myself to say the word son.

'Nephew.'

My heart pogos heavenward. 'Frankly he could've put molten marshmallow in my hair and I wouldn't care, I'm just so happy to be here!'

'Please don't give him ideas.' He reaches down and dissuades Spike from using the sticky residue as styling wax, sending him back to his mother for safekeeping. 'I think it's best we put some distance between you two.' He looks around, setting his sights on the al fresco bar. 'Could I get you a hot chocolate, or maybe something stronger?'

'Flaming Sambuca?' I suggest.

He puts his hand on his heart. 'Oh don't, it was awful to watch. I hope your leg didn't get burned?'

'I can't feel anything,' I tell him, though that's not exactly true – I'm feeling *everything*.

Especially when he places his hand oh-so-lightly on my back to guide me through the crowd. It's a simple act but it has me all but levitating – as if invisible threads have now spun us together.

Not only am I amazed at how much more engaged and tactile he is in this pre-Shannon incarnation, it also makes me wonder about the kind of vibes I used to put out into the world when I was absorbed in a dud relationship . . . I've always told myself that I stayed with the men in question because I wasn't getting any better offers but the truth is, I was probably oblivious to any positive possibilities because I was always so distracted and on edge, ever fearful of crossing the man in question. It's very different with Jordan, he has an almost sensual sweetness. And, as his grandfather said, he's trustworthy. That suddenly seems like an irresistible combination. He also has great taste in festive beverages, recommending the hot apple cider served with honey whiskey and a cinnamon stick.

I sigh as I inhale the fragrant swirls of steam then raise my glass to his, smiling in a way I would never normally have the confidence to with a total stranger. His once pinched brow is smooth and those beautiful amber eyes now have a glow to them . . . He holds my gaze then shakes his head as if remembering that we've only just met, a little shyness returning.

'So, is this your first time here?'

'First time at Christmas,' I tell him.

'It's extra magical, isn't it?'

'Total bliss,' I sigh, turning towards the rink. 'If they'd just play "Ice Ice Baby", my life would be complete.'

He bursts out laughing. 'I love that song!'

'What about you?' I ask. 'Are you a regular here?'

He nods. 'My family have been coming here for generations, but technically I'm here to work – just doing some last-minute research for a newspaper article.'

'What's the angle?'

'Hotel Del romances throughout history.'

'Really?' I smile. 'I might be able to help you with that . . .'

'The history part or the romance part?'

I falter.

Instantly he's a-fluster. 'Sorry, that didn't come out right. Are you some kind of historian?' He tuts at himself. 'Even that sounds weird.'

'Because I don't have a pipe and hair sticking out of my ears?'

He nods.

'I like to think of myself more as a time traveller,' I tell him. 'You know when you really immerse yourself in a place and feel like you're experiencing another world?'

'Totally!' His eyes light up. 'Whenever I'm on assignment I like to go out exploring in the middle of the night when no one else is around and everything is still – that way I can really imagine walking in Casanova's shoes in Venice or Gauguin's sandy footprints in Tahiti.'

I heave a sigh. 'That sounds amazing. This is actually the furthest I've ever been from London. But soon I'll be free to do my work wherever I want; maybe I'll get to travel more then.'

'Geographically or through time?' he asks with a twinkle.

'Maybe both.'

And then he checks his watch. 'Speaking of time, I'm supposed to be having a skating lesson now . . .'

He glances over to the booth.

Something tells me the petite blonde checking the board is Shannon. My heart constricts. How am I supposed to compete with that? Poured into skintight white jeans and a boob-accentuating red top, all that's missing is her Miss Utah sash.

Jordan grimaces. 'It's an early Christmas present from my sister, who I suspect is trying to fix me up, which never ends well.'

My heart is pounding. It's all come down to this moment. The choice he makes now . . .

'Unless . . .' he begins.

'Yes?' My eyes are hopeful.

'Are you a skater?'

'I've got one or two moves . . .'

'Is that so?' He raises a brow.

I feel a flush of attraction. Was that him flirting? It felt like flirting. My toes twiddle excitedly in my boots.

'I could let Spike take my spot if you'd like to show me?'

There it is – the twirling heart-leap I have been wishing for! I feel my smile spreading over my whole face. He'd rather muddle through with me than a prom queen pro – my glee spilleth over!

'Come on then.' I set down our drinks so that we can take our first tentative steps together.

'I'm Jordan, by the way,' he says as our hands meet.

'Chloe,' I tell him.

'Chloe,' he repeats with a quiet sigh. 'I like that.'

'Holiday photo?' Just before we step onto the ice, the official photographer invites us to pose on a snow-spangled platform, with the hotel perfectly positioned behind us.

'Now this is the shot I was going for earlier!' I laugh.

'Well then, we have to do it!' Jordan enthuses, extending his arm so I can snuggle into position.

The side of his body seems to have been earmarked just for me, like memory foam. As I settle in I feel a wonderful sense of belonging mingling with desire. He feels so good, so warm! When the camera clicks stop I find it hard to step away, already longing to reconnect.

'It'll come up on the big screen in just a few seconds.' The photographer points behind us.

We turn, there's a second's pause and then the image appears – larger than life for everyone to see: me, Jordan and the hotel where we met.

So this is what it feels like to be in the right place at the right time!

My heart is brimming over with contentment, knowing I have found my own slot in the Del's romantic history, when suddenly a background detail catches my eye.

I lurch forward. 'Is it possible to zoom in?'

'Sure!' The photographer obliges.

'It can't be!' I gasp.

'What is it?' Jordan frowns in concern.

My mouth gapes. There, waving down from one of the corner balconies, are Ross and James. I spin around and scan the hotel front, afraid they're just wishful thinking apparitions, but there they are, beckoning us up!

I grab Jordan's hand. 'Come with me!'

'Where are we going?'

'There's someone you have to meet. Two people actually – they'll be perfect for your article. Wait till you hear their love story!'

'Chloe?'

'Yes?'

Our bodies collide as I turn back with undue vigour and before I can catch my breath his lips are upon mine. It's the kiss to end all kisses. I feel a little dizzy as I lose myself to the sensations – the intimacy, the knowing, the urgent bliss.

When we part he looks as surprised as me.

'I was just going to remind you that we're still wearing skates!' He laughs, looking a little dazed as his fingers trace his lips. And then his eyes meet mine and his voice lowers. 'I feel like I've been waiting a lifetime to kiss you.'

'Multiple lifetimes,' I whisper back.

He glances down to my charred trouser leg. 'And to think it all began with a marshmallow!'

I go to speak but then decide my version of the story can wait, you know, for another time . . .

Acknowledgements

Boy-oh-boy have I been lucky when it comes to the Rock Hudson figures in my life! James in the book is inspired by James Breeds – my 'ride or die!' bestie of thirty years. He wasn't thrilled about being bumped off (fictitiously) but hopefully he now considers it worthwhile!

Ross is an amalgamation of Jerry Shandrew (the force of nature who first introduced me to Coronado), Jaason Simmons, John Barrowman, Sebastian Harcombe, Nigel May and Les James en France – thank you all for bringing the big energy and big joy over the years!

I'm so thrilled that this story has found its dream publishing match with the warm-hearted team at Quercus. Prohibition cocktails all round to the marvellous Emma Capron, Stef Bierwerth, Kat Burdon, Emma Thawley and dynamic publicity duo Ana McLaughlin and Elizabeth Masters. I'm always so happy when a Quercus email pops up in my inbox and fully acknowledge how hard the whole team works to get a book out into the world!

I am also thankful for editing insights closer to home courtesy of my mum Pamela Jones – never shy of saying, 'Nooo, you've completely ruined it with that line!' This book is definitely our joint project – couldn't have done it without you! For all the yummy treats and laughter, I'm so appreciative of my Devon lovebugs Lisa, Phil and Holly. You give me fireside feels whether our toes are toasting or not.

This whole book is a love letter to Coronado and its residents but extra California Love goes to Adrienne and James Gragg, Emma-Jane and Jason Wellings, Natalia and Craig White, Jan Moran, Jen Bergren, Emma Elmes, Marco Zannoni, Hailie Voskeritchian, Tony Perri, Marilyn Klisser, Sue Gillingham, Claudia Ludlow, plus the heroic Dean Eckenroth Jr and sublime Rena Clancy. (R&B forever!)

Devoted thanks to book champions Susan McBeth of Adventures by the Book, Angelica Muller of Bay Books and all at Coronado Public Library, Warwicks La Jolla and San Diego Writers Ink. Special shout-out to Gina Petrone for her impressive knowledge of and enthusiasm for the Hotel Del's history. I'm so grateful this enchanting hotel danced with my imagination, making me feel as if I got to travel back in time for real.

Follow in Chloe's Footsteps

The phrase 'walk a mile in her shoes' is spot on for Chloe in Coronado! This mile-wide island is delightfully strollable, with a tempting array of sun-kissed pit-stops. Here author Belinda Jones takes you from beach to bay, sharing the settings for key scenes in The Hotel Where We Met.

(Spoiler alert – read the book first!)

Hotel Del Coronado: Of course we have to start with the jewel in Coronado's crown and the heart of the book. You too will feel like you are traveling back in time as you wander the corridors and courtyards of this legendary and historic resort.

Sun Deck: This is where Chloe shares a Hotel Del Colada cocktail with Ross, gazing out over the diamond-sprinkled sea before her time travel adventures begin.

Coronado Beach: The setting for Chloe's starlit tussle with Jasper, in full Victorian regalia!

Babcock & Story Bar: Chloe first spies Jesse here, running numbers in 1929. The fifty-foot-long mahogany bar has stood the test of time and you can now sidle up and sip the Rye Sidecar Chloe tried to order, unaware that she was in a Prohibition year!

Est. 1888: There are glimpses of Marilyn Monroe all around the Del, especially at this eclectic gift shop which plays *Some Like It Hot* on loop and has a collection of all things Marilyn, from wine to sparkling jewels.

Sheerwater: Generations collide here when Chloe meets Jordan's grandfather Jack, who she first met as a young actor in 1958. A sea breeze brunch on the terrace here is a real next level treat.

Skating By The Sea: From mid-November to the beginning of January the hotel's ice rink covers the Windsor Lawn, as Jordan and Chloe discover in 2016. (Watch out for flaming marshmallows!)

Dog Beach: Join frolicking pups at the spot where Ross and Chloe threw their first commemorative pebble into the waves.

Peer through the rope wall and you'll see the North Island Naval Base where Ross's SEAL brother Robbie was stationed – and where the cast of *Top Gun 2* filmed their famous shirtless volleyball scene!

Star Park: Here Ross recreated a *The Wizard of Oz*-themed picnic he shared with James, sitting on the grass opposite the house where author L. Frank Baum lived. Across the way you'll see one of the prettiest gardens in Coronado, tumbling with roses.

BONUS: No novel itinerary would be complete without a visit to a bookshop – check out **Bay Books** for a compelling range of titles and an in-house café with pavement seating, great for people watching.

Clayton's Coffee Shop: Offering max. step-back-in-time vibes with retro jukeboxes and a classic horseshoe shaped countertop, this is where Chloe chowed down with Teddy, Jack and Jennifer in 1958. Clayton's fruit pies are still famous today, and go great with diner coffee or strawberry shakes, all served by waitresses in floral pinnies!

Garage Buona Forchetta: Jack speaks of working summers at the El Cordova Garage in 1958 and today you can dine at this superb Italian restaurant surrounded by vintage automobile memorabilia. Tell Marco that Belinda Jones sent you!

BONUS: Directly across the street at the **Coronado Chamber of Commerce** you can pick up a free map of the island and a copy of the local newspaper, the *Coronado Eagle & Journal* – a great reminder of the week in history of your visit!

Lamb's Players Theatre: This is where Ross was appearing in the Rodgers & Hammerstein musical *South Pacific*. Chloe never did get to see him perform but you can enjoy a show in this intimate venue where no seat is more than seven rows from the stage!

Parakeet Café: The colourful café next door to Lamb's. This is where present day Chloe collided with Ross's brother Robbie, spilling her Blue Mint Magic Latte!

Coronado Historical Society Museum & Shop: This free museum is where present day Chloe discovers that Jasper had indeed had a child with Sadie – the lovely Jesse! The museum connects to the **Tent City** café, where Ross and Chloe got their smoothies.

Village Theatre: This vintage cinema is an absolute gem with its art deco foyer and Coronado scenes painted on velvet walls. In 1958, Chloe takes Jack, Jennifer and Teddy to see the movie version of *South Pacific* and then shares a special, secret dance with Jack to 'Some Enchanted Evening'.

Night & Day Café: In 1929, the bus bound for the racetrack stops at the D&D café and Chloe helps Freddy to carry the hot dogs and burgers on board. In the present day, she visits the Night & Day café (which took over the D&D flattop grill in 1954) and indulges in pancakes the size of hubcaps!

Flagship Ferry: Like Ross and Chloe, you can take a roundtrip ride from the Coronado Ferry Landing to the USS Midway on the Flagship Ferry. The trip offers a stunning view of the San Diego skyline, and keep an eye out for Shovelnose Guitarfish!

BONUS: In the summer you can hop on the **free shuttle** that will take you from the Ferry Landing back to the Hotel Del and you can take this trip time after time after time . . .

If Coronado Island is now on your bucket list, you can transport yourself there via a multitude of pics and videos on IG **@belindajoneswriter** and with the dreamy website **discovercoronado.com**!

Enjoy!

Belinda xx

Escape again with Belinda Jones, writing as Molly James

One Day to Fall in Love

The clock is ticking, don't let love run out . . .

When the love of her life falls for someone else, Rena finds herself desperately scrolling for a solution. That's when an ad for a new dating app pops up:

24 hours to fall in love ❤ A guaranteed love match by the end of the day or your money back.

Fueled by heartbreak and tequila, Rena signs up and prepares for her life to change. What she doesn't know is that she is bound to repeat her day over and over again, until she finds her perfect match.

One day they said, but there was no mention of how many times that day would play out . . .

Available now in paperback, eBook and audio

QUERCUS

Skip to the End

If you knew how the love story finished, would you turn the first page?

Amy has been keeping a secret most of her adult life . . . The women in her family have a gift, or is it a curse?

Since her first kiss, Amy has had visions of how her relationships will end. A date fleeing through the bathroom window. At the altar – runaway-bride style. There seems to be no end to the unhappy endings.

Then she drunkenly kisses three men at her best friend's wedding, only to wake up with no memory of who she kissed. She knows she's found 'the one', but now she must find out which one . . .

Roping in her friends, Amy sets off on a mission to find her true love.

Available now in paperback, eBook and audio

QUERCUS

Discover more from Belinda Jones

Winter Wonderland

Imagine waking up in a snow globe . . .

That's how travel journalist Krista feels when she arrives in magical Quebec to report on Canada's glittering Winter Carnival.

Over ten sub-zero days, Krista's formerly frozen heart begins to melt as she discovers an enchanting world of ice palaces, husky dog-sledding and maple syrup treats galore. And then she meets Jacques, a man as handsome and rugged as he is mysterious . . .

The two share a secret that could bond them forever, but can they find a way to break through the protective layers around their hearts to warm up this winter wonderland?

. . . let the snow-spangled adventure begin!

Available now in paperback and eBook

QUERCUS

The Travelling Tea Shop

A delectable tale of love, friendship and cake . . .

Laurie loves a challenge. Especially if it involves teatime and travel. So when British baking treasure Pamela Lambert-Leigh needs a guide on a research trip for her new cookbook, she jumps at the chance.

The brief: Laurie and Pamela – along with Pamela's sassy mother and stroppy daughter – will board a vintage London bus for a deliciously unusual tour of the USA's East Coast, cruising from New York to Vermont.

Their mission: To trade recipes for home-grown classics like Victoria Sponge and Battenburg for American favourites like Red Velvet Cake and Whoopie Pie.

All the women have their secrets and heartaches to heal. As well as cupcakes galore, there's also the chance for romance . . .

But will making Whoopie lead to love?

Available now in paperback and eBook

QUERCUS

California Dreamers

Ever wished you could makeover your life?

Make-up artist Stella is an expert at helping other people change their images, but when it comes to transforming herself, she doesn't even know where to start.

So when her new friend, glamorous Hollywood actress Marina Ray, summons her to a movie set in California, Stella can't resist the chance to start afresh – it is the land of sunshine and opportunity after all!

But are they really friends or does Marina have an ulterior motive? What is the secret that both women are hiding about the nautical (but nice) men in their lives? And what will it take to really make both of their California dreams come true?

In a Pacific Coast journey that takes in Los Angeles, the world's most romantic ranch and California's very own castle in the sky, this story of friendship, long-distance love, kissing (and making up) is the perfect escapist read!

Available now in paperback and eBook

QUERCUS

Living la Vida Loca

Carmen has been feeling the need to break free for Too Darn Long!

So when her equally frustrated friend Beth suggests the ultimate escape – dancing their way through a series of scorchingly hot countries – she can't resist!

There's just one catch . . . they can only go on this adventure if they participate in a reality TV show, one intent on teaching them the mournful tango in Argentina, the feisty flamenco in Spain and the sassy, celebratory salsa in Cuba!

As they travel from Buenos Aires to Seville and ultimately steamy Havana, each dance has a profound effect on the girls – and indeed the sexy gauchos, matadors and dirty dancers who partner them . . .

But, when the sun goes down, do they have what it takes to go beyond the steps and free their hearts for love?

Available now in paperback and eBook

QUERCUS